OCT 1 3

BOB MAYER

AREA 51

THE NIGHTSTALKERS BOOK 2

THE BOOK OF TRUTHS

47N○RTH

Text copyright © 2013 by Bob Mayer

Published by 47North
P.O. Box 400818
Las Vegas, NV 89140

ISBN-13: 9781477807293
ISBN-10: 1477807292
Library of Congress Catalog Number: 2013936765

AREA 51

THE NIGHTSTALKERS BOOK 2

CHAPTER 1

Roland stood near the closed ramp of the Snake, rigged with parachute, M249 squad automatic weapon strapped tight to one side and dressed in a Level A hazmat suit. His fellow Nightstalkers made an over/under bet whether there actually was a nuke in the site he would be jumping down toward, and then whether it would go off when Roland landed on top of it.

Roland had big feet.

In the cargo bay, between the cockpit and the ramp where he waited, the other five members made their next bets . . . well, four, since Moms rarely joined any betting pool. She considered it unprofessional of a team leader to engage in pecuniary entanglements with team members. At least that's the way Eagle, the pilot, explained it. On the other hand, maybe she had more important things on her mind, like the possibility of a nuke going off.

The ones taking the over on the detonation didn't contemplate that none of them would be around to collect if they won.

"Fifteen minutes," Eagle warned over the team net from the cockpit. "Depressurizing in two."

"Check oxygen," Nada ordered. All five in the cargo bay made sure their rigs were pumping oxygen into their hazmat suits from the internal bottles, then gave Nada the thumbs-up. "Ready back here," he informed Eagle.

Moms held up a finger, cutting the betting chatter on the team net. Her head was cocked slightly to the side, which indicated she was listening in on the secure frequency back to the Ranch outside of Area 51. Which meant she was being briefed by their boss, Ms. Jones.

After thirty seconds, she nodded and spoke on the team net. "Doc, are you getting the alert message Ms. Jones forwarded?"

Doc was seated toward the front of the cargo bay, a laptop open. He'd pulled off his hazmat gloves so he could work the mouse pad and keyboard. "Yes. I have it," he said in his clipped Indian accent. "It is most strange. I have never seen this alert code before. Rather archaic."

"Figure it out," Moms said. "ASAP."

"Where did the alert show up?" Doc asked as he typed. "Are we certain it's nuclear related?"

"The indicator came on in the old command and control bunker at the Strategic Air and Space Museum at Offutt Air Force Base," Moms said.

"That explains the archaic," Eagle said from the cockpit.

"It's a nuke," Nada said glumly, which was his version of happy.

CHAPTER 2

How it had started appeared to be the way many Nightstalker missions began: by accident, after stupidity, following just plain government incompetence. If one had asked Moms, she would have quoted, and often did, the exact time and date it *all* started—both the nuclear problems and the concept of the Nightstalkers—at 05:29:21 on the sixteenth of July, 1945, at the Trinity Test Site in New Mexico—when and where the first atomic weapon was detonated.

She was more correct than she realized.

The scientists who'd labored through the dark days of World War II and put the first bomb together also had a betting pool as the countdown to the test began on that warm July morning in the desert. The low was that it would be a dud, the high being a chain reaction ignition of the atmosphere with the resulting incineration of the entire surface of the planet. They didn't think the latter likely but a few still took the high. Someone always takes the high. The fact there was even the slightest possibility that the world would be destroyed did not stop them, just as the dire warnings that firing up the Large Hadron Collider sixty-three years later in Switzerland might possibly open a black hole and consume the planet were ignored. The scientists in New Mexico can be cut some slack because there was a World War raging, but Switzerland?

The ultimate winner at Trinity, after all the readings were tallied and the world was not incinerated, was a physicist who picked 18 kilotons as the yield.

But that's much too far to go back and too vague to explain why the Snake was flying over Nebraska, about to jettison its team of highly trained covert operatives over an abandoned ballistic missile launch control complex. Closer in time and space, only six hours earlier, in the part of Nebraska that was the middle of nowhere—which, unfortunately, most of Nebraska is—was a woman named Peggy Sue. (Really, her mom had loved that movie.) She was innocently hanging clothes she'd just finished hand-washing to dry over an old rubber-coated pipe.

But when that pipe is in a supposedly defunct launch control center (LCC) that had been auctioned off (only one bidder, so not much of an auction), the odds of such an event went from impossible to ridiculous. And the US government often ran on ridiculous, so that meant it was quite possible.

Ignorant of what she'd just initiated, Peggy Sue JoHansen was thinking she didn't like the underground facility much to start with. She was beginning to feel the same way about her husband of four months, six days, and, checking her watch, a few too many hours. They'd gotten married in the passion of pending annihilation, just before the last "end of the world" deadline. She was beginning to forget which one exactly as there'd been three since, and when the world had not ended, well, here they were.

It was one of the conundrums of being a doomsdayer to actually not have doom.

As she draped another pair of his tattered jeans over the pipe, she heard him thudding down the eight-story stairwell, one heavy footfall after another as he hauled two more cases of bottled water. He bought a Blazer full of water with each trip to Sam's over in Omaha, and she knew from weary experience it took him thirty-two trips to bring it all inside.

They had plenty of bottled water and she no longer offered to help.

That their new home, the LCC, had come without running water was just one of Peggy Sue's many gripes.

Another was that the only warmth came from several electric heaters scattered about, which barely put out enough heat to keep the pants on the pipe from freezing.

She was soon going to have more.

At the same time that Peggy Sue was laying cold, soaking clothes over a rubber-coated pipe, not too far away (in Nebraska terms, far in Manhattan terms) on Offutt Air Force Base outside of Omaha, Horace Egan combed his hair, running the brush lightly across his scalp twenty times. No more. No less.

Every action was done to exacting standards, the way he'd lived his life for the past seventy-two years.

In most areas.

He slid the brush with depressingly little resistance through the few white wisps of what had once been his best feature: a gloriously thick head of hair that had earned him the call sign Samson back in the day when he was still allowed in the cockpit. When on active duty, he'd had his hair trimmed every other day so that it was always just on the edge of regulations. As he was part of the air force, that meant its length exceeded what the army or marines would have allowed, but probably would have passed muster in the navy.

Then he brushed his teeth. He had his mouth mentally cordoned off into sectors, each the width of the brush, and he took the sectors with the same number of strokes, moving right to left, top to bottom, left to right, and then done. Flossing. Then mouthwash.

His teeth looked good in the mirror. The hair was a different story because the current scarcity revealed scars and divots from decades of ducking not-quite-enough under too many things, usually wings festooned with bombs and fuel tanks or the edges of hatches leading into all sorts of airplanes.

He left the washroom only after carefully drying the sink and faucet ("Ready for inspection, SIR!"—old habits died hard), and walked out into the dim lights of the closing museum, the dim being the signal for all to leave. All being the four who'd wandered in, probably after taking the wrong turn on the interstate: a family led by an overweight father and a bored mother dragging two kids who'd spent the entire time trying to get on their smart phones, bitching about the lack of reception. Egan thought the term "smart" apt, since the phones were most likely smarter than their two slack-jawed users. He had little hope for the future of the country if those two were any indication. It was the only solace he took out of being old: He wouldn't be around to see what the next generation screwed up. The Greatest Generation was about done, the next greatest was teetering like Egan, and God help America after that.

He paused to take in the collection of planes positioned around the cavernous hangar floor. He could fly pretty much everything in the place and sometimes he didn't know if it was irony that he and the machines were both too old to fly or just plain depression. But it was an honor to have done so much, because in the end, they'd been successful. There'd been no nuclear exchange during the Cold War because of men like Colonel Horace Egan, USAF Retired, and planes like these. The Greatest Generation had won World War II, but Egan's generation had won the Cold War, and they'd gotten little recognition for it.

That was their story and they were sticking to it.

This was the museum for the Strategic Air Command, although the name had recently been changed to the Strategic Air and Space Museum, trying to posture a little less ominously to the public. Not that the museum drew any more action. The air force had even done away with SAC, merging it with TAC, Tactical Air Command, into the ACC, Air Combat Command. All those letters meant nothing to civilians, but to lose their cherished organizational designation was a deep blow to those who had served for years and lost comrades-in-arms.

Egan not only knew the numerical nomenclature of every craft, but could also rattle off the nickname and story behind each, knowing many of their secrets.

The most dominating plane in the hangar was the B-36 "Peacemaker" (the military has an odd way of naming tools of death with opposite-sounding names), the largest mass-produced propeller aircraft ever built. It was also obsolete before its first flight in 1946 as jet fighters took over the air after World War II. It is a maxim of military thinking that armies (and air forces) are always preparing to fight the last war. The B-36 faced the future as an attempt to give the United States a plane that could fly to the Soviet Union, drop the oversized atomic bomb of its time, and make it back.

It was damn nice of high command to factor in the *making it back* part. Actually a rarity in military planning at the strategic level.

Egan walked over to the plane and gazed up at the nose looming above him while he unconsciously rubbed one of the scars on his head. He'd gotten that one as a seventeen-year-old crewman bailing out of a B-36 en route from Eielson Air Force Base, Alaska, to Carswell Air Force Base near Fort Worth, Texas. They'd lost three of the six engines over British Columbia in a storm. Combined with severe weather and icing, they'd been forced to bail out.

After, of course, dumping their heavy load, a nuclear warhead.

The official after-action report, classified Top Secret and only recently declassified, stated that the warhead was a dummy with conventional explosives.

That was the lie from the beginning and still was to this day if one checked Wikipedia. What is true is that it was the first nuclear "incident" where a weapon was reported lost.

The report also stated that the warhead had been dumped over the ocean, with the conventional explosives detonating on impact.

That was a double lie. They'd dropped the bomb over land. And it had not exploded on impact. It had drifted down underneath its large main parachute.

The updated report still claimed that the weapon was never recovered.

That was the final lie.

Egan knew it had been recovered and he'd seen who had recovered it and to the day he died he would never speak of it to anyone because even now, so many years later, he knew if he did, someone would come, and his retirement would shift from "still breathing and telling silly war stories" to "deceased: no check need be issued anymore."

Shaking himself out of memories, where he seemed to get lost more and more each day, he spotted the wife of the VIP standing by a B-52, the workhorse that replaced the B-36 and was *still* flying. Most of the B-52 bombers in the air were older than their crews.

Egan ignored that he easily could be her grandfather because getting some action wasn't what he sought. At least that's what he consciously told himself. But he was still a man, and he was still breathing, and hot blood still coursed through his veins, so of course it was what he sought on some level. On a deeper, visceral level, he was looking for something more mundane, which is why he volunteered at the museum (besides having no family, hating daytime TV, and having a right shoulder too damaged to play golf anymore). He wanted admiration, and that took some work at his age. He got the ritual respect given to elders, but admiration was a tougher objective. He didn't know why her husband, the VIP, wasn't here yet, but a pilot always took to the attack during a window of opportunity.

He'd have to tell her stories (but not about British Columbia and the nuke). Still he had plenty of others, most true, told in so many variations even he wasn't certain anymore what the facts were. But what did it matter? The goal was to get her to understand how special he'd once been. Old pilots never die, they just have to work harder for the ego boost that used to be there for him every day, issued with the leather jacket and the crumpled cap and the silver wings, rewards for facing death every time the wheels left the ground.

He left the B-36 and headed toward the B-52 and the young woman, preparing his attack approach. He reflected that it was strange how he'd forgotten most of the missions, especially the combat bombing ones dealing death from high in the sky, but not one piece of tail that he'd ever gotten. When he was young his mind had been full of flying, but now it was full of memories of blondes and brunettes and Asians and African Americans. They had full breasts or just enough. Bodies ranging from skinny to voluptuous; blue-eyed, green-eyed, black-eyed, brown-eyed. He'd done them all. They'd been glorious, every single damn one of them, and he missed them more with each passing day.

It never occurred to him to wonder why none had ever stayed at his side.

Maybe because the next, not yet discovered one had always been potentially more glorious?

As he got closer he realized, okay, so she wasn't so young, but definitely a trophy wife, a second one for the old businessman who made something the government liked having and thus rated the after-hours personal tour. Still, she was holding on well to her twenties in her midthirties with the dyed hair, tight body, and expensive clothing. And Botox, surgery, and whatever else women did to hold on.

Egan had his pills to hold on, in case the occasion should arise.

Lately not much had risen, but he was always hopeful and she was alone. A gentleman would not send his wife unescorted, so that was one strike against the husband. Egan had learned, from decades of experience in seducing other men's wives, that if you could get them to three strikes, one could most likely get to first base. He paused as that twisted metaphor confused him for a few moments, then shrugged it off as he shrugged off a lot of thoughts lately.

As he came up beside her, he allowed himself to put his hand on the small of her back, one of the few perks of being old. Her very small and lovely back.

She had her hand on the ladder that led up into the belly of the beast.

"Colonel Egan." She nodded at him.

"Mrs. Floyd."

"I never imagined these planes were so big."

"Size isn't everything, Mrs. Floyd."

She glanced at him, a single, perfectly maintained eyebrow, arched.

"Where would you like to start?" Egan asked, gesturing with a flourish at the sprawling facility.

"Why don't you wait ten minutes?" Mrs. Floyd responded.

"Why?"

"For my husband. The tour is really for him, isn't it?"

"I suppose, but I'm sort of getting over the idea, if you know what I mean."

A spark lit in his mind when she responded to the obscure reference.

"There's a speed limit in this town, Colonel. Forty-five miles an hour."

Egan grinned as he made the run toward first base, which in his case was more like a shuffle. "How fast was I going?"

"I'd say around ninety."

So she wasn't just a pretty face and tight body. "Suppose you get down off your motorcycle and give me a ticket."

Mrs. Floyd smiled and stepped away from the hand on her back. "Suppose I let you off with a warning this time?"

First base seemed a little farther away. "Suppose it doesn't take?"

"Suppose I have to whack you over the knuckles?"

"Suppose I burst out crying and put my head on your shoulder."

"Suppose you try putting it on my husband's shoulder." And then she went off script. "Really, Colonel. He'll be here shortly."

"But he's not here now." But Egan stopped, about two-thirds to first, called out, but keeping it in mind.

"Remember what happened to Fred MacMurray by the end of that movie." She turned from him and looked about the museum. "Only planes?"

"There are some missiles in here." Egan stepped next to her and pointed. "Over there."

"Ah yes. Missiles. Men love their missiles."

He put his hand once more on her back. She didn't step away. He let his fingers spread a bit so he could feel the slight arch of her spine as it curved outward from her tight bottom. He assumed it was tight, not being that forward yet, because women these days all worked out more than any physical drill the air force had ever pressed upon him. Sometimes he missed the softer, rounder girls of his youth. He often reflected that Marilyn Monroe would never have lasted long with today's standards. He'd seen her in a USO show once in Korea. Or was it Alaska?

He couldn't quite remember.

"Planes and missiles," Mrs. Floyd said. "That's it?" And once more she stepped away from his touch.

"No, that's not it," Egan said. "This hangar was built on top of the war room for SAC—the Strategic Air Command."

"*Dr. Strangelove or: How I Learned to Stop Worrying and Love the Bomb*," she said, and Egan tensed. He hated that movie.

"We kept the peace," Egan said. He strode toward a concrete bunker in the middle of the hangar, not caring if she kept pace.

She did, looking at her cell phone. "I'm not getting a signal. I can't check on when my husband will get here."

"The entire building is Tempest-proof," Egan said. "Shielded. Everything in and out goes via landline." He reached the bunker. "When nuclear weapons go off they release an electromagnetic pulse, which fries most electronics. So, naturally, we shielded our command post."

"*Battlestar Galactica* stuff," Mrs. Floyd said. Egan was getting tired of the media references as they weren't heading toward first base anymore but rather the fog covering the outfield. He opened a heavy steel door. Metal steps beckoned on one side, descending into dark depths. Large elevator doors were directly ahead.

"This isn't part of the normal museum tour," Egan said as he walked up to the elevator and pressed a button. The two doors rumbled open, exposing a freight elevator. The paint was gray and peeling. The museum wasn't high on the air force's budget priority list, although most military personnel knew how that worked. The longstanding joke was that when the air force opened a new base, they built the officers' club first, then the golf course, then asked Congress for more money to build the airstrip and hangars.

Those in the other armed services had a lot of respect for the air force's base priorities—as long as they were officers and played golf.

Mrs. Floyd hesitated at the hatch. "Perhaps we should wait for my husband?"

"I don't need his shoulder," Egan said. He looked back at her. "Do you?"

Mrs. Floyd got into the elevator. Egan hit a button and the doors shut with a solid thud. The elevator lurched and then descended, faster and faster.

"How deep are we going?" Mrs. Floyd asked.

"Five hundred feet, and passing through forty feet of reinforced concrete. This place could take a direct nuke strike and continue functioning."

"What about the people in the hangar above?"

Egan didn't answer because one simply did not think of the people above. The elevator came to a jolting halt. The doors slid open, revealing a yawning darkness. A musty smell wafted over them. One could almost smell the cigarette and cigar smoke from generations of men watching screens, on edge for entire tours of duty, the fate of the world in their hands.

"Maybe we should go back up?"

Egan took two steps forward, turned left, took one and a half paces, reached out, and pressed an unseen button.

Banks of fluorescent lights flickered on. They revealed descending rows of consoles facing a stage on which there were several large Plexiglas boards. The tables were wood, and even the consoles had wood framing. There were numerous empty holes where monitors and other gear had been ripped out. Phones were scattered about, some rotary dial. All had red warning stickers on them. There were toggles and buttons and there was almost nothing digital about the place at all except some boxy clocks, their red numbers long dead, along the top edge of the walls.

It was a war room from an age when the United States could put a man on the moon using a computer less powerful than the average "smart" phone and bring them back when things went wrong using slide rulers and ingenuity.

"It's old," was Mrs. Floyd's only comment from the safety of the elevator.

"My dear, it worked," Egan snapped. He waved a hand. "The men in here controlled the fate of the world. They controlled power beyond what you can imagine."

Mrs. Floyd shook her head. "Men and power."

"It kept you safe."

"From other men and their power."

Egan snorted. "I've got a theory. You want to know how I think the first war started?"

She sighed, knowing she shouldn't respond, but playing along. "You're going to tell me anyway."

And he did. "Back when we were in caves, armed with clubs and spears, some woman from a tribe saw a woman from another tribe and she had this here bowl. And the first woman wanted that there bowl. And, by God, she was gonna have it. So she harassed and henpecked her husband until he got his buddies together and they went over to that tribe in the next valley and they got that bowl for her. And that was the first war."

"Women start wars?" Mrs. Floyd was incredulous. "Over a bowl?"

Egan shrugged, but didn't reply. He gestured. "Over there is where the launch control—"

"Should that thing be blinking?" Mrs. Floyd asked, her hand pointing to the right with a large, expensive diamond reflecting the cheap lighting.

Egan followed the flow of the elegant finger. An orange light was flickering on a large panel full of dead lights.

He was finally speechless as his aging neural network tried to process what was happening. Everything he was seeing was important and he struggled with the logic flow.

Orange.

On that panel.

In that location.

Flickering. Not steady.

He'd been briefed verbally on this when he took the job, but he'd thought the old fart he was replacing had been a bit touched in the head to believe anything down here still worked. And word of mouth, from one generation to the next, was like playing telephone as a kid—the message eventually got garbled down the line. "Emily farts in class" became "The homily darts in the ass."

He had to call someone. Of that he was certain. He went to the console right below the flickering light. There was a red phone. No buttons, no rotary. Just a phone with the word PINNACLE written on a piece of tape on the handle.

He'd heard whispers of Pinnacle and his hand hesitated for a moment, hovering over the receiver.

As he picked up the phone, his heart thrilled for a moment until the pacemaker slowed it down for him. Funny, he thought, catching a glimpse of Mrs. Floyd out of the corner of his eye as he put the handset to his ear. Now that he had a mission, and an important one, because saving the world or at least a chunk of it was important, he'd almost forgotten all about the woman.

Almost.

The phone was dead.

"What's wrong?" Mrs. Floyd asked.

He didn't hear her as he closed his eyes and focused his mind. He'd had another briefing years ago. A way to report an incident.

Egan ran, shuffled fast, to the elevator. Mrs. Floyd, being no fool, was right next to him as he shut the doors and the elevator accelerated upward.

"Something's wrong, isn't it?" Mrs. Floyd asked.

Egan smiled his confident smile, the one copilots had seen on his face as they flew through horrendous weather or dodged surface-to-air missiles or landed with a shot-up plane. Trust me, the smile said.

The doors opened and Egan made a beeline for the admin office on the side of the hangar, Mrs. Floyd still at his side. He entered and went to the landline. He picked it up and dialed: 666.

The earpiece crackled as circuits that hadn't felt electricity in a long time made connections.

Egan was startled and almost dropped the phone when, instead of a voice answering, there was a blast of music and then a deranged man singing over and over:

"Send lawyers, guns and money!"

CHAPTER 3

And that was why the Nightstalkers were ten minutes out from drop.

Moms filled them in. "It's an old launch control center. It was bought a few months ago by a couple of civilians. Since we've been airborne, Ms. Jones had her sources run their background: a pair of doomsdayers."

"The end of the Mayan calendar must have bummed them out with no payoff," Kirk said.

"They probably hit the wrong button," Mac said. "But how can there still be a nuke there?"

"It's a launch control center," Moms repeated. "It has fourteen outlying silos. Ms. Jones just had a Key Hole satellite do a deep ground penetration and it picked up radiation from a cluster of silos. There's still a nuke in at least one of them."

"Nada wins," Mac said, which wasn't surprising since Nada always predicted the worst and Nada often won. Mac shook his head, the movement unnoticed inside his protective hood. He was a good-looking man, part young Tom Cruise, part more rugged than the actor from actually being a soldier instead of playing one. He was the best explosive ordnance man to come out of the army, which is why he was now a Nightstalker.

Partly.

Ms. Jones's means of recruiting were a mystery, although it basically entailed combing the ranks of the elite, looking for those who had the added benefit of being unique in ways she felt the team needed. Often that uniqueness was something their former units didn't really appreciate, or in fact rejected.

"No way it can go off," Mac continued. "We're talking—"

He was cut off by Doc. "I've broken apart the signal. It's two overlapping transmissions. One is a countdown."

"Fuck me to tears," Nada muttered.

"What's the count?" Moms asked.

"Twenty-two minutes, sixteen seconds, and dropping," Doc informed them.

"Except there won't be a launch," Moms said, "because all those silo covers were welded shut and had concrete poured on top when the complex was closed."

"That's not good." Roland stated the obvious, because Roland always focused on the obvious. It was irritating at times but very effective in combat.

Like Roland.

Moms ignored him and addressed Doc. "What's the other transmission?"

Doc was frustrated. "I can't make it out yet. Some old code that keeps repeating over and over."

"Ten minutes out," Eagle announced.

Ears popped in the cargo bay as pressure finished equalizing to fifteen thousand feet above ground level.

"All right," Mac said. "The pool is now open as to cause."

"Human error," Nada said. Because Nada always thought it was human error. His faith in his fellow men was never above the half-full level, and usually pretty much near empty, and often he thought the glass simply didn't even exist, but rather was a mirage, a cruel joke of an uncaring Fate.

"Of course there is some human factor involved," Doc said, blinking behind his thick glasses and peering through the protective plate in the hazmat hood, focused on his keyboard. "It is part of my rule of seven."

"Well, you gotta pick one, not seven," Mac said. "The bet is on the primary cause."

"Computer glitch," Kirk said. Kirk always wanted it to be something to do with computers, because that made it his responsibility to fix the situation as the team communications man and computer specialist.

"Hardware or software?" Mac pressed.

"Hardware," Kirk said.

Mac was using a felt-tip marker to record the bets on the arm of his suit. "I got Kirk with computer glitch, narrowed down to hardware malfunction. Nada with human error as primary. Doc?"

"I do not speculate," Doc said, ending his participation.

"Sure it's not a bug?" Mac chided him. Doc always wanted it to be a bug, the more exotic, the more interesting.

"Come on, Moms," Kirk pressed.

Moms sighed, the sound echoing inside her hood, and for the sake of teamwork allowed herself to be drawn in. What most of the team, other than Nada, didn't quite grasp was that she allowed the betting because it was an active way of getting everyone involved in "war-gaming" possibilities. The Nightstalkers often jumped into confusing and rapidly changing scenarios, and the more open their minds were to the range of problems they could face, the better they could face them.

She spoke: "Someone left an inspection plate open or an inner tube in the rocket from the engines fell apart and a rat got in and chewed through some wires. Or the doomsdayers were playing make-believe launch-the-missile, pretending they were actually ending the world not knowing they had a loaded silo."

Mac whistled. "Now that's specific. But you do remember that's what happened in South Dakota when we went there two years ago?" He wrote *R-A-T* on his sleeve.

"Of course," Moms said. "History has a way of repeating itself."

Doc got up and waddled over to Roland to do one last check of the hazmat suit as per protocol. Moms did one more check of his parachute rig, not protocol, but she was a worrier. Doc tapped Roland lightly on one shoulder and Moms tapped him on the other, a mixture of reassurance and support, and they both sat back down.

"Keep working the second freq and code," Moms said.

Doc was already back on his laptop.

"Five minutes," Eagle announced. "Opening ramp."

The Snake was a tilt-wing, jet-powered Black Ops aircraft, so experimental Eagle could have put in for test pilot wings with the air force. Except Nightstalkers never put in for badges, or awards, or wings, or any of that.

At the rear of the Snake, a crack of late daylight appeared as the back ramp lowered until it was horizontal. Very cold wind swirled in and the sound level increased accordingly.

Roland yawned and stretched his massive arms wide as he walked onto the ramp, stopping a foot short of the edge of the drop into potential oblivion. He'd been fast asleep at the Ranch when the Zevon alert came in, and he hated having his sleep cycle interrupted. Even for a nuke.

Especially for a nuke. You can't shoot nukes and Roland lived to shoot things. Roland was a large man, four inches over six feet, with the build of an athletic middle linebacker. The scar that curved along the right side of his head from temple to behind his ear hadn't been earned on a football field, though, but in combat during his first tour with the Eighty-Second Airborne in Iraq. Years ago and miles away.

"Eagle?" Mac asked.

"At the height of the Cold War, the United States had thirty-one thousand, two hundred and fifty-five nuclear weapons," Eagle said, drawing on his vast reservoir of useless information. Useless until they needed it to save their asses. "It is not improbable that our government lost track of some. This is the fifth Bent Spear we've been on this year, which is a two hundred and fifty percent increase from last year." The Bent Spear was a reference to a nuclear event that did not involve the possibility of nuclear war. "My summation," Eagle continued, "is that there was a paperwork error and the missile and warhead were simply left behind."

"Yeah, but that don't explain why it's going off now," Mac said.

"It's old," Eagle replied. "Old things malfunction."

"Like Nada," Mac said with a grin no one could see but everyone knew he had. Mac liked to push everyone's buttons. Usually for fun.

Nada was indeed old, in military terms, having passed his fortieth birthday several years ago, the oldest member of the team and the longest serving. He was of Colombian descent, although many mistook him for Mexican, with graying hair poking straight out his skull as if seeking to escape his head, and a pocked, dark-skinned face. He'd plowed through a stellar Special Ops career: Rangers, Special Forces, Delta Force, Black Ops freelancer . . . and now he was a Nightstalker. It was either the tip of the spear, or the shit depth of the ocean depending on which day of the week it was. Today it plunged toward the latter.

"Three minutes," Eagle announced and Roland shuffled another inch closer to the edge of the ramp.

"*O-L-D*," Mac spelled out as he wrote it on his sleeve. "Old what? You always say it's old with nukes and there's no way we can really pin that down. You gotta pick something specific."

"That's because pretty much our entire nuclear arsenal is old," Eagle said. "Old and falling apart."

"That's the reason," Moms said, "they're going to sign the SAD treaty at the United Nations soon." She was referring to the Strategic Arms Disarmament Treaty, in which all nuclear powers were pledging to work to zero weapons in ten years. At least those countries that acknowledged actually having nuclear weapons. It was what Reagan and Gorbachev had come within one word of achieving in Iceland in 1986.

"And pigs will fly," Nada muttered.

"They do if you toss them out of a plane," Mac observed. "It's just the landing that ain't pretty."

"I'll be glad when they get rid of all the obsolete material," Doc said. "Both hardware and software," he added.

"I'll be glad when we don't get called out on these anymore," Nada said.

"I'll be glad to get some dinner," Eagle muttered from the cockpit.

"Roland?" Mac asked, ignoring all of them.

"Something broke," Roland said simply. "And we're going to fix it."

"*B-R-O-K-E*," Mac wrote on his arm. "I think Roland, once more, in his finite yet elemental genius, will win theoretically."

"Did you just insult me?" Roland asked, a scowl crossing his ugly mug.

"It's not just the aging arsenal," Moms said, stepping into the banter because Roland and Mac sometimes went a bit too far turning banter into something darker. "Remember what's in your nuke briefing book? The '95 Black Brant scare?"

"Norwegian clusterfuck," Nada corrected. "Fucking scientists launched a weather satellite and forgot to tell the fucking Russkies. It went right into the flight corridor a missile from a silo in North Dakota would be on to hit Moscow. Yeltsin had his nuclear football open and was ready to toss the damn thing by pushing all the right buttons."

"Only time a world leader has ever activated its nuclear suitcase," Eagle threw in, because Eagle always threw in knowledge . . . and history . . . and movies. "Never even happened during the Cuban Missile Crisis."

"We were lucky Yeltsin was probably drunk," Mac said. "That's one thing you can at least count on with the Russians. Remember in Albania with the biological—"

"Eagle," Moms cut in, "inform the personnel on the ground we're coming in and they can disperse."

Mac snorted. "Run for the fucking hills more like it. They only took an outer perimeter, anyway."

"One minute," Eagle announced.

"Thirteen on the countdown," Doc added, still typing away.

"Going to jump soon, Doc," Moms said. "Secure the computer. Kirk, when we touch down, I want you working with Doc to figure out that second code."

Roland moved to the very edge and looked down. The sun was setting in the west, casting long shadows across the high plains. Snowdrifts were piled here and there, but at least they weren't at the height of winter, with Christmas not far away.

"Go!" Eagle announced as the green light flickered on above Roland in the tail section of the plane. The verbal prompt wasn't necessary as, like Pavlov's dogs, Roland was gone at the green.

Roland let gravity take charge. He spread his arms and legs to get stable. Then he pulled his arms to his sides, tucked his head into his chest, and missiled down toward the target.

"Clarence?" Peggy Sue knew exactly how to slide her husband's name under his rib cage by putting the emphasis on the second syllable.

Her mother had taught her well.

But not well enough since she was living inside a practically unheated, no-flowing-water concrete bunker in the middle of Nebraska.

Clarence dropped the last case of water, frozen solid from sitting in the bed of his pickup during the two-hour drive back. "What?" he demanded in that tone men use to indicate to their wives, significant others, and even one-night stands that they don't want to hear the real question following the question mark behind their name.

"I ain't never seen this light blinking before."

Clarence checked his irritation. "What light?"

"This here." Peggy Sue pointed to an open metal cabinet next to the pipe she'd been using as a clothesline. "I just pulled that cupboard open to see if—"

"It ain't a cupboard," Clarence said. "I told you not to touch nothing."

"What is it then?" Peggy Sue had picked up the uncertainty in his voice and twisted the dagger a little. "You don't know what it is, do you?"

It was a flashing orange light. Anyone could see that.

On a piece of crumbling masking tape underneath it, someone had scrawled PINNACLE in black marker. The container had a metal door, which Peggy Sue had opened, and was four feet high by two wide. There were a lot of lights, but only one was active. An old keyboard rested at the base of the cabinet connected to the panel by a single cord. Another piece of masking tape, which had half-peeled over the years, was above it. The same hand had simply written, ENTER CODE—GOOD LUCK OR GOOD-BYE! If they'd used emoticons back in the day, there probably would have been a :) there. Below it in pencil, someone had added: *Smoke 'em if you got 'em.*

"Oh, crap," Clarence muttered. "You sure done it now, Peggy Sue." He slammed shut the door as if doing so solved the problem.

"You don't even know what I done."

"Get ready!" Moms called out on the team net as she staggered to the edge of the ramp, loaded down with weapons and gear. She was tall, though not as tall as Roland, spotting him a little over four inches. She had wide shoulders above surprisingly narrow hips, giving her a body a beach volleyball player would envy. Her short brown hair had streaks of premature gray, more coming with each op, and it had never occurred to her to get it colored. "Eagle. Stay at altitude, just in case."

The rest of the team was startled at that last sentence.

"That's not Protocol," Eagle said, his voice carefully neutral to mask his concern. "I will descend to be on station overwatch at five hundred AGL to give you cover and provide exfiltration as needed."

"Don't hit us on the way down," Mac added, because Mac always had to add something, but also to cover Moms's gaffe.

"Follow me," Moms said, shaking it off and stepping from the ramp. Without hesitation, the others followed.

The four got stable, then pulled, getting full canopies. The quick pull was because they were conducting a high altitude–high opening drop, designed to give Roland some time with feet on the ground before they touched down. It was Protocol, the way the Nightstalkers normally ventured into an unknown and abnormal situation. One team member on the ground first for the quick recon, and the rest following right behind. Protocol was what the team lived and breathed, what kept them alive, but lately, it had started to fray at the edges.

"Time hack on the countdown?" Moms asked Eagle.

"Ten minutes, thirty seconds," Eagle responded.

Moms was focused on the mission ahead, listening to some last-second updates from Ms. Jones back at the Ranch; Mac was mentally running through nuclear warhead Protocol, cut the blue or red wire sort of thing; Kirk was monitoring Moms's radio traffic and scanning local freqs to see if word of a problem had gotten out; Doc was focused on trying to fly his parachute and dreading the inevitable impact with the ground.

It occurred to Nada as he twitched his toggles to get his position above the rest of the team that they might see a mushroom cloud race up toward them as they descended. Such thoughts filled Nada's dark mind when he was on an op.

It was why he was still alive and the longest-serving member on the Nightstalkers.

Roland could see the compound—a gray concrete blockhouse surrounded by a high fence with razor wire on the top. The gate to the compound was wide open.

He could also see the flashing lights of emergency vehicles from various government agencies racing *away* after having secured a far perimeter on Ms. Jones's alert. The *spear* was *bent*, according to the official government code, but if it went to *broken arrow* or *nucflash*, they'd better be damn far away to survive.

For a moment, Roland pondered spears and arrows as weapons, because Roland always pondered weapons when he wasn't actually using them. He decided he'd prefer the former, because while the arrow had the advantage of range, the spear gave a definite advantage close in.

These thoughts, however, did not stop Roland's mind from processing the ground racing toward him. He'd done enough jumps to have a fairly good idea of altitude. Five thousand, five hundred feet give a hundred, he experience-estimated. He took a quick glance at the nav board on top of his ruck. Five thousand, six hundred. Off slightly, not important at this height, but fatal closer to Mother Earth.

Roland pulled his rip cord and the parachute blossomed above him. The opening shock pulled him upright and he did a quick check for full canopy and grabbed the toggle on each riser, a slightly more difficult task given the hazmat gloves encasing his fingers.

He hated hazmat suits, not for the same reason as the others—because it meant an NBC op: nuclear, biological, chemical—but because it restricted his movement and meant he had to leave his body armor in the team box lashed down in the Snake's cargo bay. Roland felt naked without body armor.

He turned his attention back to the compound. He spotted a cluster of concrete-covered silos to the north. Another to the west. A few sprinkled to the east and south. "Moms, do we know which silo holds the nuke?"

"The satellite narrowed it down to area, but it could be any of four silos to the west of the facility."

"I'm getting a schematic of the compound," Eagle cut in. "All the silos were sealed and buried. You can't get in from the surface. You're going to have to use the access tunnel from the LCC to get to the right one."

"Find out which is the right one ASAP," Nada said. "Clock's ticking."

Moms and the rest of the team were passing through ten thousand feet, circling beneath their canopies. Doc was just above her, with Mac close by to make sure the team's scientific expert didn't do something stupid like "cut away" his main. Doc never liked jumping, but his desire to be on the Nightstalkers outweighed his fear of parachuting out of a perfectly good airplane.

Above Doc and Mac was Kirk, the team's communication expert. He was also the latest addition to the team, joining them just in time for the "Fun in North Carolina" that had gone down six weeks ago. He was a lean, taut-muscled man whose main claim to fame prior to joining the team was that he'd successfully changed his scorecards in Ranger School in order to pass. His right earpiece crackled with an incoming message. He quickly let go of his toggles for a moment and tapped in the code on his wrist transmitter to open the secure link to Moms.

"The silo you want is number seven," a voice with a Russian accent informed Moms over the radio. Ms. Jones was the voice from which all information flowed to the team. And all orders.

"The first responders only formed a far outer perimeter, unaware of what the incident is," Ms. Jones continued. "My data says there are only two people in the vicinity. They are not of consequence. However, we cannot rule out that there is terrorist activity."

"Roland will be down in a few seconds," Moms replied. She took a quick glance up, counting chutes.

And above the team, keeping a careful eye on all of them like a good shepherd, was Nada, the team sergeant.

Two hundred feet above the target, Roland grabbed air with his chute, slowing his descent. He touched down on top of the LCC with a slight puff of dirt. He unbuckled from his parachute harness and readied the M249, even though this most likely was not a shooting op. One could always hope though, and Roland fantasized a wave of terrorists rushing out of the LCC.

He was rarely that lucky.

He ran down the side of the bunker and around to the front door. He glanced into the beat-up pickup as he went by, but there was nothing of interest. Roland tried the handle on the heavy steel door, but it wouldn't budge.

He lifted the M249 and pounded on the door with the stock.

Eight stories down, Clarence and Peggy Sue snapped about and stared upward as the thuds on the door echoed down to them.

"This is *my* damn home," Clarence said, heading for the weapons rack.

They had no running water but they did have a dozen assorted weapons. Clarence snatched an AR-15 off the rack and slammed home a magazine, pulling back the charging handle and letting it slide forward.

"Fill your hands, woman!" he barked at Peggy Sue.

She grabbed a pump-action shotgun and resignedly ratcheted a round into the chamber.

"Nine minutes," Eagle informed them from his overwatch position, hovering five hundred feet above the LCC.

"The door's locked," Roland said. "Want me to shoot it off?"

"Negative," Moms said. "Mac will blow it. We'll be there in twenty seconds. Any sign of foul play?"

"Negative." Roland lowered the machine gun with a sigh, which echoed inside his hazmat hood, and scanned the immediate area, hoping something would pop up that he could shoot.

The team touched down right in front of the bunker, all landing lightly.

Except for Doc, who made a sack of potatoes look graceful as he crumpled onto the ground. As he scrambled to his feet and out of his harness, he checked to make sure he still had suit integrity.

"Mac, get the door," Moms ordered. "Everyone else, back up. Eagle, give us a rundown on how to get to silo seven once we're inside." With time running out, she made a command decision. "Suits off, people. We're not going to need them based on the readings."

Mac ran up to the old metal doors and opened up his rucksack, taking out a charge and placing it over the lock as the rest of the team stripped off the bulky hazmats.

"Back in the day," Nada said, "I was on one of the last backpack nuke teams."

"You mean when Eisenhower was president?" Eagle asked as he circled the Snake overhead. The chain gun mounted in a compartment in the nose of the aircraft was extended.

"SADM," Nada continued as Mac jogged back toward the rest of the team, as best as one can jog in a hazmat suit, a remote detonator in his hand. "Strategic atomic demolition munitions," Nada said. "I jumped with a live one on a training mission. That wasn't fun. Heavy as shit."

"Fire in the hole," Mac warned, and then hit the toggle.

A brief flare of light and crack of explosion meant the doorway to the bunker was now unlocked. Eagle was relaying directions to them on how to proceed once they went inside.

Moms moved to the front of the team. "I'm taking point with Nada."

Mac ripped off his hazmat suit.

Moms walked forward. "I'll lose satcom in there," she said. "Kirk, make sure you keep an open relay between me, Ms. Jones, and Eagle from here in the doorway. And use your own pad to work on that code. There's got to be a reason it's piggybacked on the countdown."

"Roger that," Kirk said.

Roland grabbed the edge of the heavy door and pulled. "Nobody's oiled this sucker in a while," he said as he grunted with effort. With a screech of protesting hinges, the door opened wide enough to invite them into its darkness.

There was an elevator directly in front crisscrossed with yellow warning tape, indicating it was nonfunctional. A set of stairs beckoned to the left. A dim glow seeped up from the depths of the LCC.

"Seven minutes," Eagle said over the net.

Moms and Nada took point, a smoothly coordinated team, starting at the top of the stairs and clearing their way down. The countdown made them move faster than Protocol.

Thus they almost ran on top of Clarence and Peggy Sue on the landing just above the LCC Control Room.

"Who the fuck are you!" Clarence screamed, gesturing with the barrel of the AR-15 at Moms, his eyes wide with fear at the armed figures looming above him on the stairs.

Protocol was Moms should double-tap him right between the eyes while Nada took out Peggy Sue.

She broke Protocol by lowering her submachine gun, raising her hands in surrender, while still taking the last two steps and moving forward toward Clarence.

"Hey! I said—"

Before he got the next word out, Moms snatched the automatic weapon from Clarence's hands, spun it around, and knocked him out with the stock. As Clarence crumpled to the steel grating, Moms turned to Peggy Sue. "Are you going to be a problem?"

Peggy Sue dropped the shotgun and the Nightstalkers shoved past her and took the last flight of stairs into the LCC.

"Six minutes," Kirk relayed from above.

Moms paused in the LCC, getting oriented to the verbal directions Eagle had given her. She pointed. "That hatch. Mac, you take point. Roland, behind him for muscle. Nada, you make sure the two idiots don't do anything and relay commo into the tunnel from Kirk. I'll be behind Roland. Doc, keep working on that second code."

They ran to the hatch and Roland grabbed the metal and tried to turn the handle. It resisted. Mac pulled a charge out of his pack, but didn't have to use it as the wheel suddenly turned with a screech. Roland's massive biceps bulged as he spun the protesting wheel, unlatching the hatch. It was slow going and Moms considered having Mac blast it, but decided against it; something was already wrong here and setting off a charge in the LCC wasn't going to help. Mac put a headlamp on, as did the rest of them.

"Five minutes," Kirk announced over the net.

The hatch began to open and Mac slithered into the three-foot diameter access tunnel for silo seven. Moms followed, then Roland.

Doc was seated at one of the consoles, typing away on his computer. Nada took up position at the open hatch. Peggy Sue timidly came down the stairs. "Who are you folk?"

"Shut up or I'll shoot you," Nada said.

Peggy Sue was used to that kind of talk, so she shut up.

In the tunnel, Mac moved as fast as one can move in a three-foot tunnel that doesn't quite require you to crawl, but doesn't allow you to run. He shuffled forward, his pack in front of him. His headlamp penetrated about thirty feet, but all he saw was more tunnel.

"How far?" he asked Moms.

"Eagle said three hundred and fifty feet."

Nada's voice crackled in their earpieces. "Four minutes." A slight pause. "I got a stupid question," he continued, "but is the countdown for a launch or for the warhead to detonate? And can that thing even initiate launch not having been serviced for so long? Eagle?"

"Wait one," Eagle replied.

Mac spotted another hatch ahead.

Mac tried the handle, but it wouldn't budge. Everyone flattened against the floor of the tunnel as Roland slithered over them, a torrent of muscle. He grabbed the wheel and grunted with exertion, but still nothing.

Behind him, Moms knew they were in a bind. There was no time to back out and have Mac blow the door. Nada's voice delivered bad news as he relayed Ms. Jones's information via Kirk: "The countdown is an Orange; a self-destruct for the warhead. In case the complex was ever compromised. The Area 51 nuke Acme tells her there's a forty-two percent chance the bomb is still viable, plus or minus fourteen points. A ninety-one percent chance the conventional explosives will go off."

"That's not very precise," Doc muttered.

"Frak me," Moms muttered as she was forced into another razor's-edge decision: Leaving the hatch shut would protect them from the conventional explosives going off and the resulting dispersal of radioactive material. But not the nuke going off. The rational odds said leave the door shut. "Roland?"

The weapons man contorted himself sideways in the tunnel, trying to get a better grip. Frustrated, he jammed his M249 into a spoke of the wheel, got leverage, and applied his entire weight.

The barrel bent as the wheel gave a shriek and moved a quarter of an inch.

"Faster please," Moms said. "Doc? Anything on the second code?"

"It's very old," Doc said. "Not yet."

"Kirk?" Moms asked.

"Negative."

"Ms. Jones?" Moms asked, the message relayed via Nada to Kirk to the Ranch.

"The Acmes are on it," Ms. Jones said, referring to the group of scientists across a wide spectrum of specialties the Nightstalkers had on call. The Acme moniker came from the company Wile E. Coyote bought all his gear from in the *Looney Tunes* cartoon. Given the gear rarely worked, like the Acmes' advice, it was appropriate.

"Three minutes," Nada announced.

In the access tunnel, the wheel creaked another quarter inch. Moms reached around Roland, barely able to get the tips of two fingers on the wheel, but it was better than nothing. They applied pressure and gained a half inch. Squeezed as tight as lovers, all Moms and Roland cared about was opening a door that was an invitation to an explosion.

"If there was an alert at the SAC museum," Kirk said from the upper doorway, "then there has to be a live circuit between the two. Some sort of signal. How did this get triggered?"

In the control room, Nada turned toward Peggy Sue. "What did you guys do to set this off?"

"I didn't do nothing," Peggy Sue said. She rushed to continue the explanation because she'd learned growing up that words spoken quickly could sometimes stop the fists. "Clarence, he was bringing water down. Me, I was doing the wash. Hanging the laundry." She pointed at the rubber tube, festooned with dripping clothes. "Swear, mister, didn't do nothing. Was just—"

"Two minutes," Kirk relayed from Eagle.

Moms paused in helping Roland. "Eagle, I want you to gain a safe altitude in case this thing goes off. Nothing you can do for us anymore. That's an order."

There were a few seconds of silence, then Eagle replied, "Roger."

Nada followed the rubber pipe from its entry point in the wall to the metal casing. He was over there in seconds, throwing open the door.

"Oh yeah," Peggy Sue continued. "That light ain't never been on before, but I swear I didn't do nothing."

"I've got an orange light on a warning board," Nada reported. "Reads PINNACLE on a piece of tape. There's a keyboard below it. Someone wrote ENTER CODE—GOOD LUCK OR GOOD-BYE! with an exclamation point at the end."

"Doc," Moms said as she shoved her arm along Roland's side to give him two fingers of extra effort. "The code?"

"It's encrypted," Doc said.

"Kirk?" Moms and Roland got another inch.

"Negative. One minute," he added.

Roland let out a surprised grunt as the wheel spun. He shoved Moms's arm out of the way and lifted the hatch open. The latch to lock it in the open position was rusted shut, so he bore the entire weight, muscles vibrating.

"Go!" Roland said.

Moms pressed to the side to let Mac into the silo holding the missile. Moms started to follow, but as Mac went by Roland, he punched the big man in the solar plexus and grabbed the inner handle of the hatch, adding his weight to it. Between the punch and the extra weight, Roland couldn't hang on and the hatch slammed shut behind Mac, locking him in and Moms and Roland outside.

"What the hell!" Moms yelled.

Mac's reply was barely audible on the radio even though they were only feet apart. "If only the conventional implosion goes off, no need all of us being in here."

In the LCC Control Room, Nada was staring at the keyboard. "Someone give me a code. Something!"

In the silo, Mac had his power drill out and was working on opening the access panel on the nose cone holding the warhead.

"Thirty seconds," Eagle relayed to Kirk, who relayed to Nada who relayed to Moms who relayed to Mac.

Who only had half the screws off. The analytical part of his brain knew he'd never have them all off in time.

He kept working.

"Twenty seconds."

"Mister Nada, is there any date in that panel or on the board?" Ms. Jones asked.

Mac was down to four screws.

"Ten seconds."

Nada picked up the keyboard attached to the panel by a single wire and looked at the bottom. A manufacturer's name and date was stamped on it. "Nineteen sixty-two."

"Five seconds."

Mac was on the last screw. It came out and he slammed the tip of a screwdriver in the edge and pried the panel open.

"Time!"

Mac had wire cutters in each hand, but the bundles of wire were so twisted and knotted and numerous in front of him that at Nada's announcement he couldn't help but hunch over and shut his eyes, waiting for the conventional explosives, at the very least, to go off and blast him into nothingness.

But nothingness was what happened.

No conventional explosion.

No nuclear explosion.

"Ortsac," Ms. Jones said. "*O-R-T-S-A-C.*"

Despite time being up, very aware that a nuke might have a hang fire as easily as a mortar, Nada typed the letters on the keyboard.

The orange light went out.

In the silo, Mac slowly opened his eyes and looked more carefully inside the nose cone.

Then he started laughing.

CHAPTER 4

As men wearing black suits and sunglasses hauled Clarence and Peggy Sue away in a black Lincoln Town Car—the infamous Men In Black, who were really support personnel for the Nightstalkers from Area 51—the team gathered in the cargo bay of the Snake, which Eagle had landed just outside the front gate of the LCC compound. Roland was mournfully cradling his M249 squad automatic weapon, the bent barrel curving around his upper body like a devoted pet. If one kept lethal, metal snakes as pets.

"Smoke 'em if you got 'em," Nada said, and he meant it, as he pulled a pack out of his combat vest, took one, and passed it around.

It was a sign of how frazzled they were that every member of the team took one, even Doc for the first time, and fired up. Doc's parents had both emigrated to the States from India and his bookish appearance was out of place among the warriors of the Nightstalkers.

"The clock ran out." Roland said the obvious, because, well, he was Roland.

"It's never run out before," Doc said, and this was his second startling thing of the day because Doc never stated the obvious.

"There's a first for everything," Nada said. "We're still here."

And that was almost a first, Nada being upbeat.

Moms exhaled, the chill Nebraska wind taking the smoke and blowing it across the plains. "All right. Let's figure out what happened. Mac. What was so funny when you got into the missile?"

"You won the pool," Mac said. He held up a handful of frayed wires. "This is the main firing component. Rats, or some other kind of vermin, chewed them all up. But we'll go with rats." He held up the sleeve of his hazmat suit where he'd written RATS and MOMS.

"So we got saved by rats?" Eagle said.

"Yep." Mac dropped the cables. "I got the access panel open just as time ran out. If these wires had still been intact, I'm pretty sure the conventional implosion would have gone off and I'd be splatted inside that silo. As far as the nuke"—he nodded his head to a bunch of Acme and support personnel at work, calling in heavy equipment to rip off the concrete cap on top of the silo to get access and remove it—"they can figure that out. There was a gap at the base of the nose cone in the gasket. Rats must have come up through the engine into the nose cone."

"How could they lose track of a nuke?" Kirk asked.

"This place is old," Moms said. "Eagle told us they had over thirty thousand nukes at the height of the Cold War. We've all worked in the real world for the government. Anyone ever had any paperwork that got lost?"

"Hell, they lost *me*," Eagle said. "When I went into Task Force 160, all my paperwork was gone, just like that."

Nada snorted. "We've all disappeared as far as our original services are concerned. We only exist in our cover IDs."

"Nukes getting lost or misplaced has happened before and it will happen again," Eagle said. "Back in '07, a B-52 took off from an air base to deliver some cruise missiles for 'retirement' to another air base. Except the maintenance crews failed to remove the nuclear warheads in six of the missiles."

"Oops," Kirk said.

"Someone didn't follow the checklist in their Protocol," Nada said.

Eagle continued, "In essence, the air force lost track of six nukes for almost two days and flew them over most of the country without the aircrew being aware they were carrying live warheads. Parked the plane on both airstrips without any guards and the nukes just hanging on the wing. Cost the secretary of the air force and the chief of staff their jobs. And it was all a paperwork error. As Nada noted, a failure of protocol."

"Speaking of failure of Protocol," Nada said. "Why didn't you shoot the civilians?" Nada was the only one who would dare raise the issue to Moms.

"It didn't cost us any time," Moms said, a weak defense at best.

"You had second shot," Roland pointed out to Nada, "and you didn't shoot the woman."

Roland's logic ended Nada's questioning. Another almost first.

Moms shook her head. "We don't shoot civilians unless we have to. We're not merks."

"That we are not," Nada echoed.

"Eagle," Moms said. "Did you gain altitude when I ordered?"

Eagle dropped his cigarette and ground it out on the metal floor of the Snake, the only one who was allowed to do that since the aircraft was his turf. He was a tall black man, a scroll of scars on the left side of his face a testament to a fiery IED incident years ago. He had not a hair on his head, making his large skull even more prominent. "No, I did not. If it were a conventional explosion there was a good chance someone would need medevac and I wanted to be close."

Mac snorted. "Those conventionals had gone off, you'd still be scraping pieces of me up."

Moms shook her head. "We're a mess. Violating Protocol, then violating orders about violating Protocol. What's next?"

"Dogs and cats living together?" Eagle ventured, earning a weak smile from the team, including Roland, as *Ghostbusters* was one of the few movies he'd seen.

"I'll be happy when they sign the arms treaty," Moms said.

"Won't change much," Kirk pointed out. He glanced at Eagle. "How many nukes do we have now?"

"Approximately five thousand, one hundred and ten," Eagle said without a pause or pulling out a cell phone and Googling it. "That's all combined: strategic, tactical, and mostly nondeployed. Ready to fire, drop, or sneak in? A little under two thousand."

"And how long," Kirk continued, "will it take to tear most of them apart?"

Eagle laughed. "We're still backed up from the last treaty, but SAD gives everyone ten years, although the inspection and enforcement part is a bit lacking."

Kirk shrugged. "So the treaty is a show, with no teeth."

Ms. Jones's voice crackled out of the speaker hanging in the cargo bay. "Oh, SAD has teeth, Mister Kirk."

As the newest member of the team and still not acclimatized to the ways of the Nightstalkers, Kirk jumped to his feet and snapped to attention at Ms. Jones's voice.

"Relax, Kirk," Nada said to him.

"Is Mister Kirk showing some respect?" Ms. Jones asked. She almost sounded pleased.

"He still thinks he's in the Ranger Batt," Nada said.

"The treaty is important," Ms. Jones continued, "because it keeps us headed in the correct direction. More importantly it sends an important message to the rest of the world about the intentions of the United States."

"I got a question," Kirk said, relaxing as best he could. "Was this nuke one of those in the numbers Eagle counted?"

"It was not," Ms. Jones said. "And that is the disturbing thing. We've run the serial number on the warhead. It was supposed to have been dismantled and destroyed after a reorganization and update back in the mid-1960s. The records say it was."

"Paperwork glitch, Ms. Jones?" Moms asked.

"I earnestly hope so," she responded.

"What else could it be?" Nada asked, catching something in her voice. He knew Ms. Jones better than anyone on the team by virtue of being the longest-serving member. "Knowing" her though was a misnomer, because no one on the team could actually claim to have seen her. They all "met" her during the in-brief to the team, a shadowy figure seated in a large chair on the other side of a large desk. Doc still claimed the figure was a hologram and Doc was not prone to much speculation. But Nada had heard her voice more than any of the others.

"I would prefer not to guess," Ms. Jones said.

"How did you get the code?" Nada asked, switching the subject since her tone indicated he should switch the subject.

Ms. Jones laughed, which sounded like a mixture of a death rattle and a desperate gasp for air. "Operation Ortsac. The year 1962 was the key since that was when it was planned and almost implemented. If someone hooked up an override in the silo and added in that comment, that meant the world was quite close to the nuclear brink. It's quite a simplistic code name if you think about it."

Eagle, as usual, was quickest to the mark. "Castro backwards."

"Indeed," Ms. Jones said. "History is not as most people believe. Ortsac was the plan to take out the missile sites and invade Cuba. Most Americans still believe the blockade turned away the Russian missiles. Not true. They were already in place in Cuba and ready to be fired at the height of the crisis. Even more astounding is that operational control of the nuclear warheads on the island had been given to the Russian officers there in the field. Any invasion would have been met with tactical nuclear weapons with tremendous loss of life, most likely precipitating World War III and a wider strategic exchange.

"I remember it quite clearly," Ms. Jones added. "We all expected our world to end. We knew Khrushchev would take West Berlin if the Americans invaded Cuba. We knew the Americans had already used nuclear weapons on Japan—only seventeen years earlier. We were quite convinced that the imperialistic Americans were going to kill all of us. It is strange how Americans rarely understand how the rest of the world perceives it as a nuclear power."

"It's amazing that Khrushchev released control of those weapons to the officers on the ground," Moms said.

"It's amazing we're still alive," Eagle muttered.

"That's very out of the norm," Nada said. "Nuclear protocol is usually written by someone who never has to actually do what the protocol says. Control is almost always kept at the highest levels. When I was on the SADM team, we were told we could set a three-minute to a three-hour delay on the nuke once we emplaced it and hit the arm. Our theory was that there was no delay. The moment we armed it, it went off. What's four guys when you consider it had to be a target worth a nuke?"

"That's pretty cynical," Kirk said.

"That's Nada," Mac said.

Nada ignored both of them. "Even if there was the delay, protocol dictated we keep sniper coverage on the nuke until detonation. It's a pretty thin line between max sniper range and even a tac nuke's blast radius, not to mention the rads. We weren't packing hazmat suits in our gear."

Ms. Jones's voice came over the net. "In my former Soviet Union, we were all issued anti-radiation pills. Soldiers were assured that if they took the pills, they would not be affected and could fight on."

"*They Were Expendable*," Eagle said.

"They were. We were," Nada said. "Still are."

"It's a movie," Eagle explained. "About PT boats in early World War II. John Wayne. You get the idea."

Nada snorted. "Ever notice how John Wayne never hooked up when he pretended to jump in *The Green Berets*? Splat."

"It's a movie," Eagle pointed out. "Suspension of disbelief."

"He couldn't hook up?" Nada said. "How hard is that to do?"

"Pinnacle," Kirk said.

Everyone turned to look at him. He had a penchant for noting what passed others by. "You said it was on the board with the warning light," he said to Nada.

The team sergeant nodded. "Written in marker on brown masking tape."

Ms. Jones spoke up. "It was also written on the warning light at the old underground bunker for SAC. In the same way."

"What is it, Ms. Jones?" Kirk asked. "You told us about Ortsac. What does Pinnacle stand for? The fact it was in both places and seems to be written rather informally is significant. I think," he added, hedging his position as the newest member of the team.

"We're checking on it," Ms. Jones said, "but an excellent observation."

Mac pursed his lips at Kirk and imitated a smooch.

"And Mister Mac," Ms. Jones said, as if she were watching them, "your effort with the hatch was noble. We had a man at Chernobyl who did the same. He died."

Mac frowned, uncertain if he were being praised or reprimanded.

Ms. Jones continued. "As Ms. Moms has noted, there have been breaches of Protocol on this mission. There were breaches on your previous mission in North Carolina and all turned out well in the end. All has turned out satisfactorily here, but not due to your efforts. I would like everyone to take some time to reflect on what it is we do."

Nada turned to Moms with a wry smile and everyone on the team knew what was coming: Why We Are Here in some version. It was to be expected after a failure and it was a mantra Ms. Jones repeated over and over to the team, not because she believed they forgot it, but because working in the black world of covert ops, it was easy to lose track of the larger picture.

"The missile you just dealt with, the entire complex, the nuclear arsenals of every country that has the technology, are part of man's insanity and also the peak of our genius. Scientists were able to split the atom, to gain power over an elemental and powerful force and at the same time give mankind the capability to annihilate itself. It seems the nature of man that we can do both at the same time. It is not just in the field of nuclear engineering, but, as we have discussed, the same is being done in genetic engineering, where scientists will develop cures for many ailments and afflictions. Yet at the same time, we know there are those in deep, dark labs who are working on genetically coded, biological weapons. They are the two edges of the same sword.

"We are here," Ms. Jones finally got to her catchphrase, "because of that and more. We are here because as mankind advances scientifically, we also teeter farther and farther over the abyss of self-extinction."

The sound of the lonely Nebraska wind filled the cargo bay for a few moments, and then they realized Ms. Jones was done.

"Let's look at the bright side," Moms said. "We have two weeks off when we get back." She paused. "Correct, Ms. Jones?"

"Yes. After debrief. That's two weeks away from the Ranch on two-hour recall," Ms. Jones clarified. The only way Nightstalkers ever really got true time "off" was when they retired, were medically or mentally disabled, or died.

"Everyone enjoy the holidays," Moms said, signaling for Eagle to get into the cockpit and power up the Snake.

"Bah, humbug," Mac said.

"You know," Kirk said. "Those carolers always sing about peace on earth, but they never say where it is."

"Nowhere we've been," Mac said.

"I celebrate Festivus," Eagle said as he banked the Snake and gained speed, racing along just above ground level.

"Ah!" Nada was animated for once. "The airing of grievances! Feats of strength!"

"Forget I brought it up," Eagle said.

"Hey!" Roland said, as if a major synapse had just fired.

Everyone in the cargo bay looked at him as he sang: *"Always look on the bright side of death. Just before you draw your terminal breath."* He began whistling and it took a few seconds, but then they caught on.

As they flew away from the site where they had almost died, the Nightstalkers all pursed their lips and whistled away: *Always look on the bright side of death.*

━━━━━━━━━━

"We were lucky," Pitr said. Ms. Jones sighed, which was difficult to do with all the tubes stuck in her body. Any movement brought discomfort; a lot of movement brought pain. She'd lived with the situation for years and she hoped, but did not pray, that she had several more years. Unfortunately, she was a realist and she knew time cared as little for her hopes as it would for her prayers. She kept the speaker on, and in the background they could hear the team whistling that part of "Always Look on the Bright Side of Life," but there was that edge to it. It was forced.

"Was it luck the warhead was activated?" Ms. Jones asked her assistant. "If we say there is luck, then isn't one as likely to have bad luck as well as good luck?"

"It was those fools who bought the silo that caused the problem," Pitr said. "More so, it was whoever left that warhead in the silo."

"Which brings up an interesting point," Ms. Jones said. Her office was dimly lit and was actually a room behind the office where she "met" each new Nightstalker and in-briefed them and held debriefings with Moms and Nada. She'd been impressed when Doc had quickly surmised that the shadowy image sitting in the dark shadow on the other side of the desk was usually just an image, not a person. Not that it mattered. She always said what she needed to and she could see and hear everything pertaining to the Nightstalkers from her hospital bed.

"And that point is?" Pitr pressed, making her realize her thoughts had drifted off, which concerned her as it was happening more and more. It was a luxury of the elderly, but a person in her position could not afford that luxury.

"What if the nuclear warhead being left there wasn't a mistake?" she asked. In the background, the whistling had petered out and there was no sound coming out of the speaker except the muted roar of the Snake's engines. Ms. Jones turned the speaker off. "Here in the Nightstalkers we are so used to ascribing incidents to mistake or oversight or scientific malfeasance, we rarely consider that often there are those who scheme and plot and act. Sometimes in ways counter to what we believe is in our country's and mankind's welfare."

Pitr frowned. He glanced over at the machines helping to keep Ms. Jones alive, scanning their various lights and indicators. He'd been doing this for so many years that anything amiss would have screamed out at him. All was within normal parameters. Pitr spoke with less of a Russian accent than Ms. Jones, but that was because he left Area 51 and interacted with other Americans. Ms. Jones had not left the Ranch in eight years. Pitr was a former Russian helicopter pilot whose life Ms. Jones had saved by stopping him from overflying Chernobyl, telling him it was a one-way mission even while she risked her life to save the man who'd started the chain reaction of that disaster back in 1986. Pitr was a tall, rugged-looking man with graying hair. He had perfect teeth that he revealed often when he smiled.

That was why Ms. Jones knew he could never replace her: the smile. The person who ran the Nightstalkers rarely had anything to smile about. He was good at his job as her assistant, but the mantle of leadership was not something she could drape around his shoulders.

That a former Soviet nuclear engineer was in charge of the Nightstalkers and had a former Soviet helicopter pilot as her aide was as improbable as an actor who had played the Gipper in *Knute Rockne, All American* becoming the fortieth president of the United States.

Probably less so.

"You suspect a plot?" Pitr asked, intrigued. Ms. Jones was not given to idle speculation.

"This weapon was listed as destroyed," Ms. Jones said. "That's not a simple oversight of forgetting it in the silo. Someone also deliberately wiped out any trace of it by recording it as having been dismantled. One event is an oversight. Two is a plan."

"If it is a plan," Pitr said, "it is a very old plan."

"When I heard the year, 1962, I knew right away what the code name was," Ms. Jones said. "Operation Ortsac is in the Nuclear Protocol binder. What is *not* in the binder is what *didn't* happen. General LeMay was the chief of staff of the air force at the time. He advocated preemptive nuclear warfare from the moment he had any voice in the matter. Even after the Cuban Missile Crisis was resolved, he pressed for an invasion of Cuba anyway. His deepest desire was to take advantage of the missile gap.

"While publicly the military and CIA were claiming our former country was far ahead in terms of nuclear warheads, the truth was the opposite. If the United States had initiated a first strike in the fifties or sixties, the result would have been devastating to Russia. Indeed, Pitr, I would have to say if the generals in our old country had had the same advantage, many would have advocated the same thing. What good is such power if it is not wielded?" She did not wait for an answer.

"The first mention ever of a so-called 'missile gap' was by JFK in 1958 when he was up for reelection to the Senate. He then ran his presidential campaign based on trying to catch up to the Russians, when he didn't know the United States was actually far ahead. That is how effective the propaganda of the CIA and the Pentagon and the military-industrial complex was. Only after he was in office and briefed by the Keep about the reality did he change his views."

"You bring up an interesting point," Pitr said. "If this warhead was kept there as part of a plot to secret away nuclear weapons in the face of mandated drawdowns due to the various treaties over the years, we are facing another critical era with RAD. You mentioned the Keep. Perhaps you should consult with Hannah? She might know something about this."

"She might," Ms. Jones conceded, but it was clear she was not warm to the idea. One did not go to Hannah with anything unless absolutely necessary.

"My thoughts," Pitr said carefully, "are that this is more than just a mistake or an oversight."

"Mister Kirk, of course, drove to the heart of the matter," Ms. Jones said. "Pinnacle. It is not a term we have run across."

Pitr glanced at his phone. "The Acmes haven't reported back on it, which means it's either completely black, completely forgotten, or worse."

"I fear worse."

"You always do."

Ms. Jones did not respond, which Pitr took to mean she was considering his recommendation. They'd been together for so long they could read all the little signs in each other.

"They're almost back," Ms. Jones said, raising a single finger off the bed toward one of the many monitors that lined the wall.

One of them displayed the image from a video cam on the top of Baldy Mountain, which was fifteen miles northeast of Area 51.

The Snake was flying fast and low, treetop level, except there were no trees to top here in Nevada.

In fact there was pretty much nothing here other than the government facility known to most as Area 51. Which is why it was out here. Founded in 1941 as an auxiliary base to Nellis Air Force Base, adjacent to massive bombing ranges, Area 51 gained its moniker by the simple fact that's what the location was labeled on a map. There was an Area 50 and an Area 52 and so on in either numeric direction, but 51 held the distinction of having a dry lake bed that was perfectly flat and hard packed. On that lake bed was built a landing strip that currently held the distinction of being the fifth longest in the world at 23,270 feet, or almost four and a half miles. Why it needed to be that long, no one knew anymore, although it had been a backup landing strip for space shuttles and the lake bed made going longer easier. It was built in the days when the US government definitely believed bigger was better.

Interestingly, the officers' club wasn't built before the runway at Area 51.

Actually, there was no o'club at Area 51.

Nor was there a golf course.

That was because it wasn't the air force that was pumping in the dollars, but rather an organization called Majestic-12 via a massive black budget.

As the years went on, more and more land in the emptiness of Nevada was gobbled up by various government agencies for various reasons. The Department of Energy grabbed over a thousand square miles to the west of Area 51 in 1951 to test nuclear weapons, and test them they did—over seven hundred. Many of those black-and-white reels of soldiers watching a mushroom cloud in the distance were filmed there.

The films still survive; the soldiers are another story.

To the north, Nellis Range is still used, and many conventional bombs are dropped there along with millions of rounds of ordnance being fired. Nothing living lasted out there long. Drone pilots, headquartered at Nellis, used the range to hone their skills so they could reach out to their worldwide network and attack with precision.

It was as if there had been a plan to even further isolate Area 51.

The Nightstalkers, under a different name, had been established at Area 51 when it became a hotbed of research and, as was inevitable, the scientists screwed up. Someone opened a Rift (scientists still don't know what they are) and Fireflies came through (ditto on the not knowing). After many casualties and much consternation and blame, in 1948 a covert unit was formed to deal with Rifts, Fireflies, and the wide range of possible scientific misadventures, screwups, and accidents. The Nightstalkers *were not* formed, though, to deal with plots and counterplots within the US government. That was another unit's responsibility, the Cellar, which Hannah ruled.

In fact, Hannah ruled an empire of Black Ops, of which the Nightstalkers were just one arm.

When Area 51 became so popular that tours were coming out on Extraterrestrial Highway—aka Route 375—to sit at the mailbox and stare at pretty much nothing other than a mailbox and a dirt road leading off toward a gate, it became time for the Nightstalkers to move to someplace less noticeable.

Still close enough to draw on the vast resources of Area 51 and have its support personnel based there, the operators moved into an underground bunker built below what appeared to be an old abandoned gas station. Actually, the bunker was built, then an "old abandoned gas station" according to specifications was built on top of it. Not far from the Ranch was the Barn, which was the hangar for the Snake.

Ms. Jones and Pitr watched another screen as the top of the Barn, which looked exactly like an old abandoned barn, split open, landing lights flashing inside as Eagle guided the Snake down. A sign on the outside boasted: SEE ALL THE POISINUS SNAKES 75CENTS. Though it was unlikely that anyone could make it this far into the Ranch, if they did dare enter the Barn, they'd run into things far more dangerous than poisinus snakes.

There were always twenty-six security personnel scattered around the Ranch, secure in bunkers that were not only invisible to the eye but had thermal shielding. They were armed beyond to the teeth, because the teeth put one back to pre-caveman days. Armament included automatic weapons, Hellfire missiles, surface-to-air missiles, and the ability to call in cruise missiles and air support from Nellis. Of more practical importance, they could exercise deadly force more easily and legally than the contract guards at nearby Area 51 because the Ranch was on "private" land.

The doors shut on the Barn and in exactly eight minutes, because that was Nada's Protocol for off-load, the team would come racing out of the Barn in a Humvee, with Roland in the gun turret, singing one of his songs.

Rumination over, decision made, Ms. Jones hit the button that killed all the screens. "Let's give the Acmes a day to research this incident and Pinnacle," she told Pitr. "If they fail to unravel this, I believe it will be time to talk to Hannah. Check on what the Acmes have discovered so far."

The Humvee tore out of the Barn, Eagle expertly handling the wheel so that they cleared the closing doors by inches. Everyone was crowded inside. (Doc had once made the mistake of suggesting they get a minivan and no one spoke to him for a week.) Roland, as always, manned the .50-caliber, spinning the roof turret, more than ready to kill something. The security personnel always made sure they were deep in their hide sites when the Humvee came flying by.

It was quiet inside, unusual for a mission return, as if Roland's attempts at high-spiritedness on the Snake had sucked their spirits dry. Moms looked over her shoulder from the passenger seat and caught Nada's eyes. She raised her eyebrows in question and then nodded up at Roland, wondering when he would start singing. It wasn't Protocol. It was tradition, and that was something every soldier valued because they often had little more than that to hold on to.

Kirk tried. As the newest member of the team, he felt he had to. *"I saw a werewolf with a Chinese menu in his hand—"* he began, singing Warren Zevon's most famous song, but when no one else joined in, he fell silent.

Apparently they saved werewolves for successful missions.

The only sound was the Humvee engine and the desert rolling under its oversize tires.

When Roland started, his choice wasn't surprising, but he didn't start with the chorus, because that indicated the beginning of a mission.

"I'm the innocent bystander," Roland more yelled than sang. *"Somehow I got stuck . . ."*

Eagle, who had more movies, books, and song lyrics stuck in his head than most Mac hard drives, joined him.

". . . between the rock and the hard place."

Moms, Nada, and Mac were on board for the next, appropriate line.

"And I'm down on my luck."

Kirk finally got it and the entire team did the next two lines:

"And I'm down on my luck.

"And I'm down on my luck."

And then they fell silent and that's the way the Nightstalkers pulled up to the Ranch, which pretty much summed up what Nada would later call "The Clusterfuck in Nebraska."

If only that was all there ever was to it.

Pitr walked back into Ms. Jones's office. She could tell by the look on his face that it was bad news. She lifted a finger, indicating for him to deliver it.

"An Acme has decoded the missile's guidance system. It had two targets preprogrammed into it, with an option switch back at SAC headquarters. And the warhead was a W59 one megaton."

"Large yield."

"Yes."

"And those targets?"

"The first, naturally, was Cuba. That was a secondary targeting overlaid on top of the missile's original, primary target."

"And the primary target was?"

"Area 51."

CHAPTER 5

Neeley had long ago learned that waiting to kill people could be boring. Technically her mission here was recovery, but she'd accepted during Isolation that it would inevitably involve killing at least a few people. Since she'd been on the ground, she'd revised that number upward, because all was not as it had seemed in Isolation.

It never was.

She used the night-vision portion of her retina, just off-center of vision, as Gant had taught her so many years ago. She was experiencing déjà vu, and for good reason. The alley running between ramshackle concrete buildings held several Dumpsters, a burned-out car, and piles of refuse, very similar to an alley in the Bronx so many years ago. Except tonight she was in Abbottabad, Pakistan, and the clock was ticking on making contact with the extraction package.

Except there was a problem, one which Neeley had raised to the dismissive CIA liaison in Isolation. This was an ambush. It was a proven tactic of terrorists to draw in rescue forces and hit them hard. Except forces in this case was "force," singular, in the person of Neeley, primary operative of the Cellar and the closest thing Hannah back at Fort Meade had to a friend.

Which meant not much of a friend at all, except they'd saved each other's lives years ago and they'd die for each other. Hannah also sent Neeley on missions like this, where she could get killed.

It was all part of being in the Cellar.

Neeley was buried inside one of the six-foot-high mounds of refuse. She'd squirmed her way in twenty-four hours ago, stayed in it without moving all day as more trash was heaped on top, including various liquids that seeped down on her. She actually appreciated the fouler-smelling and disgusting items because it made it that much less likely someone would come rooting through.

Living was worth a little, and a lot, of discomfort.

Neeley leaned her head to the right, pressing her right eye socket up against the rubber socket on the end of the thermal scope mounted on the sniper rifle. A tiny switch inside automatically turned the scope on.

With little twitches, making sure she didn't disturb the trash surrounding her hide site, she peered out the tunnel she'd poked clear with a stick just after dark to get a field of fire.

She had three positions identified from the previous night. She'd picked them up as she maneuvered into the alley. They were careless, but they could afford to be. They were in friendly territory and Neeley had picked up the distinct impression that they hadn't expected any action the previous evening.

Which was interesting.

Actually, *disturbing* was a more accurate word.

If they knew which night to expect extract, it meant the mission was compromised. Which meant she should back out and call for exfiltration and forget about extraction of the package.

Neeley wasn't a big rule follower for those other than the ones Gant had given her.

The Cellar did not have Protocols like the Nightstalkers.

It had Sanctions, which this wasn't, so that didn't factor into it.

Neeley didn't ruminate on why or how the mission was compromised. The very fact the Cellar had been called in to do this had been an indicator. Hannah would deal with it.

There were four men in a second-story apartment across the street from the package. They had two light machine guns, AK-47s, and one RPG rocket launcher. Of more danger were the half-dozen "insurgents" in a minaret towering over the mosque at the end of the street. They had a cluster of RPGs and, ominously, at least two SA-24 Grinch shoulder-to-air missiles. The Grinch was the latest variant of Russian surface-to-air missiles, technically not available for export, but what were rules to bad guys? You could buy anything in Russia these days.

Who named a missile a Grinch? Neeley wondered as she scanned the minaret. Really, not long till Christmas and she was literally going up against the Grinch? She rarely considered irony, since it was often the baseline of any operation she was on, but this time it seemed a bit over the top.

She counted six heat signatures in the minaret. All awake and alert, unlike last night.

They were waiting.

As were the last two. They'd come just after dark, like last night, and crawled into one of the Dumpsters next door to where the package was. They'd wedged the top open six inches and were peering out with night-vision goggles, the latest American version, most likely stolen by an Afghan soldier from his American counterparts and sold on the black market.

An old woman came walking down the street, the weariness in her step indicating a long day at work. She had little clue about the firepower amassed all around her and disappeared into one of the buildings on the left side of the street.

A voice crackled in Neeley's ear. "Status?"

She whispered her reply, picked up by her throat mike and encrypted and transmitted back to Hannah while being frequency hopped and relayed through several Milstar satellites. "Go. Status of Pakistani air defenses?"

That was the key question. How far up did the betrayal go and who was involved?

"Inactive. You've got a local problem."

"Roger," Neeley said. "But we kept this tight, so the only way word was leaked was via the Agency."

"Naturally. I foresee a Sanction in the future, but for now it is your call whether to proceed or not."

"I'm on mission," Neeley said.

"The missile countdown has begun and exfil is inbound," Hannah said and nothing more, because after so many years and so many missions, there was nothing they could say. It was all down to the execution now.

Neeley pulled her eye back from the rubber gasket, the ease of pressure automatically turning the scope off. She slithered one hand into a pocket and extracted a pill. She carefully put it in her mouth and, twisting her head to the left, took a sip of Gatorade from the CamelBak built into her MOLLE combat vest.

The pill would give her four hours on the edge. Since she hadn't slept since infiltration, going on fifty hours now, she would need that edge. But if she weren't out in four hours, the crash would be bad. She didn't worry about that because if she weren't out in four hours, she'd be dead.

Her pulse quickened as the speed hit her bloodstream.

She didn't need to check her hide site. She'd taken nothing out, so there was nothing to indicate she'd been here. Gant's rule number four: Always pack out what you pack in. They were Neeley's rules now, as much of her as they had been of Gant.

In fact, there was nothing on her to indicate who she was or where she was from. Well, there was DNA, but it wasn't like the Taliban or Al Qaeda or whoever was waiting to kill her was going to run that, and even if they did, she wasn't in any database. She didn't exist and hadn't for a long time.

She pressed her eye back against the rubber, the alley coming alive in heat once more. The rifle was an old one. She knew there were better models now on the market, but Gant had also impressed on her that familiar was sometimes better than newest. It was an Accuracy International L96A1. British made, it chambered the NATO standard 7.62 by 51mm round.

The rounds loaded in this rifle, though, were anything but standard.

Neeley had prepared the rounds herself, building them to be subsonic so they wouldn't produce the distinctive crack of breaking the sound barrier. A bulky suppressor on the end of the barrel would reduce the sound of the gasses propelling the bullet as they escaped the barrel. There is no such thing as a true silencer, but her rifle was pretty damn quiet.

A new voice crackled in her ear. "On station. Target Alpha locked in. Fifty seconds."

Of course the suppressor combined with the low-power bullets meant a greatly reduced range, but that was why Neeley was in the pile of rubbish, needing to be close to the package.

"Forty seconds."

Neeley placed the crosshairs right between the goggled eyes of one of the men peering out of the Dumpster.

"Thirty seconds. Missile away."

Her finger caressed the trigger. While she remained focused on target, part of her mind began to monitor her breathing and heartbeat.

"Twenty seconds. Tracking positive."

She knew that the Global Hawk that had fired the Hellfire missile was already roaring back toward Afghanistan. The "pilot" flying it was safely ensconced in a bunker on the other side of the world at Nellis Air Force Base on the edge of Las Vegas.

"Ten seconds. Tracking positive. Eight. Seven. Six."

Neeley slowly exhaled two-thirds of the air in her lungs to her natural respiratory pause and paused her breathing.

"Three. Two."

Neeley fired in between heartbeats, the round ripping through the target's NVGs and his skull, splattering the lid of the Dumpster with brain, blood, and bone matter.

The minaret blossomed in an explosive ball, and as Neeley worked the bolt, she wondered if Allah would curse her. Then she figured she'd pissed off pretty much every god on the planet if there was a higher power, so it was a little late to worry now. She fired, killing the other man in the Dumpster while he was staring to the side, trying to see what the cause of the explosion was.

She stood, garbage falling aside, and slung the sniper rifle over her shoulder. She pulled a short, stubby grenade launcher out of a sheath on the side of her pack. She'd bought it on the black market in Kabul, then spent time modifying 40mm rounds for it. She had six rounds in loops on the front of her vest and one in the chamber. The first thing she'd done to the rounds was remove the safety that only armed the round after a hundred feet. These were live as soon as they left the barrel.

As she dashed down the alley, she pressed herself against the right wall and fired the first round. Right into the window where the four men were. It exploded while she broke open the M79 and loaded another round, still moving rapidly down the alley. She put a second round into the room for good measure and a body came flying out of a window, landing on the concrete with a solid thump.

Neeley dropped the thumper on its lanyard and drew her MK23 .45-caliber pistol. As she passed the body, she put two rounds into its head, then pivoted right and kicked open the door where the package lived, weapon at the ready, the muzzle following her gaze.

The package had one arm around his wife and the other around his daughter. His eyes widened as he met Neeley's and she had no time to deal with his surprise that it was a woman coming for him. She was focused on the two men standing behind the family, scimitars in hand, raised for head-chopping strikes at the neck of the two adults.

One of them started to shout something, but the second syllable never left his mouth because the first .45-caliber round Neeley fired hit right between his eyes. She spared him the double-tap in the name of expediency and to help the wife keep her head. As blood and brain and bone still flew out of the back of the first man's head, Neeley had shifted right and fired, this time double-tapping, the bullets blowing apart the second man's head and flinging his body back, the scimitar flying away with the body.

Neeley shifted back left and fired a fourth time, hitting the first man as the body crumpled back, the bullet passing the package's side by less than an inch.

One of Gant's rules was always make sure with an extra round.

She was making sure because she'd passed up the first double-tap. She was sure Gant would have approved. Neeley strode into the shack, taking charge with action and presence, not words. She was tall, just under six feet. Her short hair was still dark; she dyed the gray because it made her stand out and she was distinctive enough as it was. Her face was all angles, no soft roundness. The lines deeply etched around her eyes told of years of stress living on the edge.

She gestured and the family ran toward her. She exited the building, glanced over her shoulder to make sure they were following, and then began to jog at a steady rate, pistol at the ready, weaving through the alleys and streets of the slum as if she'd been born there. It wasn't far, three blocks, and she counted on the explosion to keep everyone indoors for a little while. She had a good idea of response time and felt she had a sufficient window.

She reached the soccer field, sirens wailing in the near distance. Neeley shrugged off her pack as the three Pakistanis caught up, breathing hard. They were staring about fearfully, looking for the helicopter they and the ambush team had expected, Neeley supposed.

They were out of luck in that regard.

Neeley signaled for them to put their hands over their heads. They hesitated and she gestured with the .45 and they complied. She pulled harnesses out of the pack and quickly snapped them on the man, woman, and terrified child. The harnesses were already linked with twelve-foot lengths of high-strength rope. One end was still in the pack and the other end had twelve feet and an empty loop.

"Thirty seconds," a different voice whispered in her ear.

She reached in her ruck and pulled a cord. A large balloon blossomed forth from the tank that had taken up half the space in the pack, rising rapidly into the air and lifting the rope still in the ruck. Neeley went to the free end and buckled in.

"*What are you doing?*" the man demanded in Pashto.

Neeley didn't answer. Coming in from the south low and fast, its dark form barely visible, was an MC-130J Commando II. It was the Special Operations–modified version of the venerable Lockheed C-130 Hercules cargo plane, first deployed in 1956 and still the workhorse transportation vehicle of the air force. This version was capable of all-weather flight and loaded with enough navigation, communication, and countermeasure electronics to make Apple headquarters in Cupertino weep with envy. A pair of metal whiskers protruded from below the nose of the aircraft. The pilot centered on the blimp and dove down an extra fifty feet, barely missing rooftops.

The whiskers caught the rope and it immediately slid to the center where a sky anchor locked onto the rope.

The Pakistani was opening his mouth to say something else when the rope tightened and he abruptly left the ground, followed by his wife, child, and then Neeley.

The MC-130 gained altitude and speed, turning for the Afghan border as its forward momentum swung the rope along the belly of the plane. On the open ramp in the rear, several air force crew manned a crane. They expertly snagged the rope, then began hauling it in along with its passengers.

At the very end of the rope, buffeted about, Neeley spread her arms to reduce the spinning and stared down at the lights of Abbottabad as they began to recede.

Despite the air whistling around and the roar of the engines, she heard Hannah's voice in her earpiece.

"Good job."

As she was reeled into the MC-130, Neeley finally allowed her thoughts to drift, to naturally think of Gant as the freezing wind ripped into her. Of his strong arms around her, holding her tight against the Vermont winter that penetrated the stout walls of the cabin he'd built. And then how it had been her holding him, keeping him warm, as his body wasted away.

Those thoughts always led to one place, one she was visiting in her mind more and more often: the grave they'd dug together that last year, in the early fall before the ground froze. Gant always thought ahead and he'd known he would not be around for the spring thaw and this was something that had to be done now. She'd done most of the digging, as he tired easily at that point. Resting, he'd sit on the growing pile of dirt, which he'd soon be part of, drinking a beer, telling morbid jokes and mixing in his Rules, knowing she was soon going to need them more than ever before. They'd had ten years together, long enough for Neeley to learn all his Rules and be taught all his tricks and tactics of covert operations.

But not long enough for her to grow tired of his arms.

As gloved hands reached out and pulled her into the cargo bay of the Commando, she pictured his lined, aged face, peering out the window at that dark hole as winter set in. She'd kept the fireplace blazing, the red glow flickering on his skin. She'd used so much wood, she knew the pile wouldn't last the winter, but neither would he, and once he was gone, she would be too.

There had been more than the cancer and the specter of the hole eating at him though. He'd been unable, even in love and even dying, to break his oath and tell her of the organization he worked for, the Cellar, and why her life would now be in jeopardy.

As the back ramp rose up into the tail and shut, Neeley shrugged off the harness. Had he known where the journey he'd sent her on would end? Had he known she'd end up taking his place in the Cellar? Had she even had a choice? It was a question she asked herself more and more as she grew older and knew her life options were closing off with each year.

Neeley sat on the red web seating lining the side of the plane as the three Pakistanis were met by an interpreter, the parents' arms gesturing on all sides, mouths open in argument. She tuned out the voices already muted by the roar of the turboprop engines and inadequate insulation of the Special Operations plane. The front half of the Commando's cargo bay was hidden behind a curtain, covering the screen watchers and countersurveillance experts who kept the plane cloaked from electronic detection and helped the pilots navigate a spiderweb route back to safety. The pilots were flying 250 by 250: 250 feet above the ground at 250 knots, which made for interesting maneuvering as they reached the mountains between Pakistan and Afghanistan.

Neeley leaned her head back, still feeling the speed surging in her veins.

Had she ever had a choice? Maybe, but it was so many years ago, well before the Cellar. Everyone has a key point, a golden moment in their life, where there is a fork in the road and sometimes we make that choice and sometimes we're shoved onto a path.

Ten years before Gant's death, she'd been a teenager, living in Berlin. She liked to think she'd been innocent and naive, but as the years passed, her retrospect shifted also. She'd been walking through Tempelhof Airport, a large, brightly wrapped package in her hands. She could understand the lilting Berliner accent of the natives, and even then, so many years after the blockade and the airlift, there were still those who remembered and gave Americans, like Neeley, an extra smile.

The men had also noticed her because of her cut-off Levi's and tight T-shirt. Inappropriate attire for the first week of October in Berlin, but she knew now it was a diversion, set up by her boyfriend who'd given her the package to take to England. It was before 9/11 and security at airports was almost nonexistent.

Except for Gant, for whom there was no such thing as a lack of security. He'd later told her he spotted her right away. Not because of the long, lean legs or taut breasts straining against the thin shirt, but because she clutched the package to her, just below those breasts. It was a tell those who worked in counterterrorism easily recognized.

His row had been called, but he had not boarded. He always joked the plane would leave when the last person boarded, so there was no point rushing, but the reality was, he watched every single person as they entered the gangway.

He had reason to be extra vigilant that day. It was 1993 and the news was full of stories of the Battle of Mogadishu. Helicopters shot down, soldiers dead, bodies being dragged through the streets by angry mobs.

His role in that affair, he'd never been very clear on.

Neeley had paused, short of the entrance to the tunnel that would take her onto the plane. Gant had walked up to her, eyes hidden by dark aviator glasses. For such a hard man, his face lit up when he smiled.

She'd always remember that smile in Berlin, as much as she remembered the look on his face peering out at his waiting grave in Vermont.

And that was why she'd handed him the package and said: "It's a bomb."

Neeley realized she was staring at her hands. She shook her head, as if she could dislodge all those memories. The memories that she called "no do-over." Where a decision was made, an event happened, a path was taken, and you could not go back.

Death was the ultimate no do-over. She'd knelt next to Gant's grave after filling it, howling at the moon all night, shrieking and pounding the ground until her hands bled and the tears froze on her face.

"You all right?"

The crew chief was leaning over her, hanging on the straps as the plane banked hard, flying up a valley between high peaks.

Neeley blinked. She reached up and wiped her eyes and looked in confusion at the moisture on her fingers.

It was only then she accepted that she'd been crying. Just two tears but it was the most since that night.

This was not good.

The vice chairman of the Joint Chiefs of Staff, General Riggs, knew there was stuff going on that people were hiding from him. Not just here in the Pentagon, but throughout the government. The Clowns In Action over at Langley liked to act like they knew what they were doing, but really, ever since 9/11, the military had taken the lead not only in terms of covert action but also intelligence gathering.

But closer to home and heart, he'd known there was some secret around him, spreading from one person to another like a game of telephone and he wasn't in the loop. No one was going to whisper it in his ear.

But this time, it was real bad.

He'd gotten the report on the Bent Spear in Nebraska. Cleaned up by the Nightstalkers. He could care less about that and more about the inquiries going on about how that damn nuke had been left there. Simple oversight, incompetent bureaucracy—all the usual excuses were going to have a hard time holding up on this one.

The general looked like a classic Roman senator. With hooked nose, silver hair, high brow, and tall, erect carriage, he exuded, "Don't fuck with me, because you can't, and pray I don't fuck with you, because I can."

He was also like a Roman senator in that he was over-weight, his uniform jacket stretched to the limits. The upside of that was there was plenty of room for all the ribbons and badges that crowded the cloth. A smaller man would have had to leave some off.

He had a tingling in his fingers and in his toes that reminded him of that night sitting in a bunker, body armor strapped on, helmet cinched tight, waiting to die. His fingers twitched and he yearned for a weapon. His feet ached to run. It didn't matter which way. They just wanted to move.

Nothing was right. Nobody was where they should be or doing what they ought to be doing.

Pinnacle was threatened. On top of the looming treaty, that was a double blow that the country simply couldn't absorb. Those fuckers from Area 51 thought they were saving the day when ac-tually they were sitting on top of a danger to the country as bad as the Russians or the Chinese or the Iranians, and definitely worse than those fools in North Korea.

Riggs leaned back in his chair and it squeaked loudly in pro-test. He considered how fat he'd gotten in the past year.

It was the first time he'd ever accepted the reality that everyone else could clearly see.

And he even accepted the obvious reason.

He was fat because he'd quit drinking and switched over to eating.

Odd. He'd never thought about how easy that explanation was. When he'd accepted there was a higher power, he'd accepted he'd have to give up the flask he'd kept in his top right drawer, and, when outside the office, inside his dress coat pocket, covered by all those colorful ribbons. It was surprising how many hoagies it had taken to replace the bottle, but who cared about that now?

He swiveled in the chair, the springs protesting. He'd have to get his aide to oil the damn thing, and why the hell hadn't the man taken the initiative and done it the first time it started making noise? He looked at the saber in the frame on the wall, the one his parents had gotten him his Firstie year at West Point. Across the top of the blade were all the insignia of rank he'd earned over the years: butter bar of the second lieutenant, shifting to the silver of first lieutenant; captain's bars; gold oak leaf of major, when he'd turned down the job of being the aide to the commanding general of the 101st and earned his Combat Infantry Badge; silver oak leaf of lieutenant colonel, when he'd commanded the Third Airborne of the 187th Infantry in the Screaming Eagles; full bird colonel and a brigade command of the 187th, the Rakkasans. First star. Second star and so on through three with his corps command and now he wore the fourth.

You couldn't go higher, unless World War III broke out and they decided to bring back a general of army. Ulysses S. had been the first. Omar Bradley had been the last.

It had never occurred to Riggs before about attaining the fifth star.

Not consciously that is.

Riggs was rubbing his ring finger as he reflected on the saber and his career and rank, and that reminded him of what was missing on that finger.

His ring, *the* ring, was in the same drawer the flask used to rest in, next to a bag of chips. His finger had outgrown it and he'd had it cut off because he'd gotten fatter faster than he'd realized he needed to take off the ring. He'd never taken it off in thirty-plus years. Not in the shower, not in bed with his wife, not in combat. He slid the drawer open and stared at the gold ring adorned with diamond set in black hematite. The thin slice in the gold band. He'd had them press the ring back to size for now, an empty oval where his finger had once been.

He still had an indent on the finger that had once been adorned with the ring—Academy crest turned the heart, class crest out, done immediately upon graduation—and his wedding band. (He was damned if he could remember where that was.) He'd simply given up trying to put it on one day, and now that he considered it, that should have been his warning about the ring.

There was no point getting the ring resized until he finished expanding, and Riggs wasn't quite sure that would ever happen. It just seemed that there was something bigger than him making him larger.

He frowned at that thought, then smiled, because he knew it was part of his destiny. He'd sensed it on the Plain at West Point so many years ago, right hand raised, getting sworn in, head shaved, head buzzing from the screams of upper-class hazing, ill-fitting uniform hastily thrown on.

Everything was destiny.

They could fix the ring after his hand finished expanding. Everything had to expand to its largest point until it could be fixed. And the president and his treaty was all for decreasing. Making everything smaller.

His army. His nukes. His defenses against all enemies, foreign and domestic and whatever the fuck Fireflies were and whatever else was on the other side of those Rifts.

Oh yeah, the top people at the Pentagon knew about all that Area 51 hush-hush bullshit. They'd known from the start.

It had to be fixed.

Soon. In one fell swoop. He could wipe the table clean for America.

Riggs smiled. Destiny. All great men believed in it. And the greatest of the great seized it when the opportunity presented itself.

The country was lucky to have him. Really. One might consider the United States blessed that General "Lightning Bolt" Riggs was in the right place at the right time.

He lifted the report from DORKA (Department of Research & Kinesthetic Application). Opportunity was here and he was the one to seize it.

As he thought these great thoughts, his left hand automatically went into a drawer and pulled out a Snickers bar. The big one. The one that sometimes made him a little sick before he finished it.

He took a big bite while he thought long and hard and dark about the future.

Hannah Masterson sat alone, as she almost always was, contemplating betrayal.

As she almost always did.

This combination was not unusual for this room, the office of the head of the Cellar.

The occupant of this position—Hannah being only the third since it was founded—spent considerable time searching the nooks and crannies of other people's souls, often finding them lacking.

The office was devoid of all charm or comfort. It had been that way when she inherited it from her predecessor, Nero, and the only major change had been the addition of more lighting since she was not blind, like Nero. He had gone through considerable trouble to recruit the once-Mrs. Hannah Masterson to replace him, searching for a unique mixture of personality type and experiences, and then forged her in action with a form of assessment that included numerous bodies and betrayals.

Ms. Jones would have envied the exhaustiveness of Nero's search methods. Of course, Nero had also found her and placed her in charge of the Nightstalkers, so there was more than just an organizational connection. In a way, Ms. Jones and the now-Ms. Masterson might be considered covert progeny of Nero. It was why there was an engineer from the former Soviet Union in charge of the Nightstalkers. And a former suburban housewife in charge of the Cellar. The person was much more important than the nationality. Those whom Nero sought out were very, very special and very, very rare, so one could not limit oneself to arbitrary borders set up by nations.

Unlike Ms. Jones though, Hannah disdained the formality of a title and went simply by her first name. The last name had been her husband's and he was long dead. He had betrayed her, and she didn't need the name to remember that betrayal. This was her new life and "Hannah" would do just fine, thank you.

The office lacked any feminine touch, which was a bit surprising considering Hannah had been that suburban housewife when recruited over a decade ago and teamed up with Neeley as they went through their "assessment" period.

They'd survived, which Nero had considered a passing grade.

Sometimes Hannah wondered if she had been Nero's first choice or if there had been a long list of possibilities and none had passed before her.

The office was unlike the offices of most others in power as Hannah saw no need to impress and she very rarely ever met anyone here. There were no pictures with arms around persons of note, no plaques, no awards . . . nothing. Nothing but the drab gray of concrete walls.

This was a trait she shared with Ms. Jones.

But not because Hannah Masterson was ill and needed to project herself as a hologram. Indeed, now in her midforties, she would be considered attractive if she ever went out into the world and desired to present herself as such, as she once had. She had thick blonde hair, discovering the first gray just a year ago. It had not bothered her as she'd once feared it would when she had thought a normal life would be her fate. In fact, given the world she now lived in and the problems she dealt with, she thought her genetic code was working quite well in keeping the gray at bay.

The life she'd thought she'd have when she married as a very young woman—garden club, white picket fence, children, PTA, husband on golf trips while she flirted with the tennis instructor—all that had been torn asunder years ago by the secrets she had never suspected her husband held. Today, a lesser person's hair would have turned white long ago with the knowledge now locked in her brain.

She had not been shocked at what she'd learned from Nero, her faith in mankind shattered well before by betrayal at a fundamental level, a trait she shared with Neeley. To accept betrayal as an integral part of the human race was a key attribute required of the head of the Cellar.

Beyond her hair, her eyes were the color of expensive chocolate. She had worry lines etched on her face, to be expected after a decade on the job. She hit the midway mark between five and six feet and still weighed what any self-conscious suburban housewife would weigh, but it was now the result of a desire to be healthy rather than look trim and keep up with the other wives in the homeowners' association.

Like Nero, she kept her desk sparse. A wide space with just a secure phone and stacks of folders. She had added a computer, but like everyone else in the black world, preferred to deal in paper that could be shredded and contained. Since her office was three hundred feet below the "crystal palace" of the National Security Agency at Fort Meade, her distrust of electronic communication was not paranoid but an acceptance of the modern world's reality. She had no doubt those upstairs were very interested in what happened in her office. She was not of them, but separate, different, and in the world of government bureaucracy, such a thing was both dangerous and envied.

Some of the very few in the sort-of-know wondered if her organization drew its name from the location of the underground office, but of course it didn't. The Cellar had been formed (although not mandated for another six years) in December 1941, as smoke still rose above Pearl Harbor and the last, desperate taps echoed out of the USS *Oklahoma*. (Some of the men trapped inside the capsized ship lasted two weeks before finally dying.) This was long before the NSA was founded and the building above her constructed. If the Nightstalkers could trace its lineage to Trinity, the Cellar could trace its heritage to Pearl Harbor.

Like the Nightstalkers, the Cellar had initially been housed where it was most needed: at the War Department in Washington, DC, in a basement office of the building that currently held the State Department. The years had brought many changes, one of them the founding of the NSA in 1952, growing out of and separating from its predecessor, the Armed Forces Security Agency.

The CIA have its Memorial Wall with a single star representing each of those who had fallen in service. The current total was 103. Many of the names those stars represented had still not been released and some would never be. The NSA had its National Cryptologic Memorial listing the names of those who had fallen in service, underneath an inscription which read: *They Served In Silence*. That current total was 163.

There were no stars or plaques or inscriptions or museums for Nightstalkers or Cellar employees who died in service.

What only Nero had known, and Hannah now knew, was that a handful of those stars and names had been the result of a Cellar Sanction, corralling in rogue agents.

Nothing was ever exactly as it appeared in the covert world.

The NSA had recently outgrown the facility above her. Interestingly the organization's need for power had grown larger than the electrical infrastructure surrounding the facility, so an adjunct facility was being built in Utah. Hannah would remain here though. As the Nightstalkers needed to be near Area 51 because that's where the initial problems they had to solve had originated, the Cellar needed to be near Washington, DC, because most of the problems Hannah had to deal with originated there.

The Cellar, the Nightstalkers, and other small but powerful secret agencies officially began sprouting like snakes on Medusa's head in 1947 when President Harry S. Truman formed a committee named Majestic-12. That organization has long been cited by UFOlogists as having been started after the 1947 Roswell incident. Majestic-12 was accused of suppressing information of extraterrestrial visits and keeping aliens locked up in Area 51.

If only that were true.

Although it also wasn't totally false. The opening of the first Rift at Area 51 in 1948 and the "invasion" of Fireflies had caused great concern throughout the highest echelons of the government. Scientists, working on the cutting edge of physics combined with the new field of nuclear power, had opened a Rift, best speculated as a tear in our universe. Fireflies came through, beings of pure energy that took over animate and inanimate objects. Since 1948 there had been twenty-seven recorded openings of Rifts. Each had been shut, and the Fireflies annihilated (along with whatever they possessed), but it was a threat that no one knew the full scope or nature of.

Majestic-12 were the most powerful men in the United States intelligence and military communities. Truman gave them the mandate to bridge the gap between domestic and international security (and into whatever space a Rift consumed), in essence covering what the FBI and CIA couldn't quite grasp and protecting the world from threats that might be, well, not human. Like Fireflies. Overall, Majestic-12 operations were meant to transcend petty bureaucratic infighting, and even national enmity, and look to the greater good. While the Nightstalkers focused on scientific mishaps, the Cellar was on top of all Majestic-12 groups, because any elite operative or organization can be a double-edged sword.

The secret cops for the secret agencies.

The ones who tracked down and took care of transgressions by highly trained operatives that no normal police force could capture. The specialists who could never see the inside of a court-room because of the secrets they knew—thus producing stars on the wall at CIA headquarters, those who were now serving in eternal silence.

The Cellar operated outside of most laws because it had been formed directly by presidential decree, which made it legal for the operation to do the illegal.

Wrapping one's brain around that was difficult, so Hannah Masterson believed in working with a light touch.

Until a sledgehammer was needed.

She had a feeling hammer time was approaching.

Hannah's phone buzzed. She hit the speaker. "Yes?"

"Ms. Jones for you, ma'am," said Lois Smith, the ancient sec-retary who had served Nero for decades and now served Hannah. Smith was no Miss Moneypenny. She was the type of old woman with a graying bun and functional clothes you'd walk by on the street and not give a second thought to. She was efficient and, most importantly, could keep secrets.

"I'm not running a whorehouse, so don't call me ma'am."

"That would be madam," Smith corrected her. It was a game they played every so often, a very subtle way, after years of inter-action, of judging the forecast. Today it was stormy, with a chance of a tropical storm blowing in, if not a hurricane.

"Connect me, please," Hannah said. There was a click, then the secure line was open to the Ranch. "What can I do for you, Ms. Jones?"

"My people just did an operation in Nebraska. A Bent Spear."

"Summarize, please."

Ms. Jones did so in three minutes, even more succinct than Moms had been in her office upon returning to the Ranch during debrief.

"And your concerns?" Hannah asked when Ms. Jones came to an end.

"Naturally, my first priority is that a nuclear missile under the control of SAC was targeted at Area 51."

"That is troubling," Hannah murmured.

"I have not been able to ascertain what Pinnacle refers to," Ms. Jones said. "I am also concerned about the weapon being reported as destroyed. Forgotten or lost is one thing. But someone deliberately covered this up."

"Someone quite a while ago," Hannah said.

"This incident happened this week. Over the years I have had concerns about the handling of nuclear warheads. There have been too many incidents. Perhaps there are more warheads that are believed dismantled that were never taken to depot?"

Hannah leaned back in her chair and considered that as she hedged on answering. "The impending treaty has everyone on edge."

"Do you know what Pinnacle is?" Ms. Jones asked.

Hannah closed her eyes. It had just been a matter of time before the Nightstalkers crossed paths with Pinnacle.

"The Cellar has lost four agents investigating Pinnacle over the years," Hannah replied. "Mr. Nero advised me to leave it alone, but perhaps times have changed."

There was just the slight hiss of static on the phone as Ms. Jones waited for clarification.

Finally Hannah spoke again. "Pinnacle is a program the military started in the very beginning. *Our* very beginning, right after World War II. When that first Rift opened and Majestic had to deal with it, and other problems. Some of the men on that committee were military and while they were handpicked by Truman, they still owed allegiance to their services."

Ms. Jones was quick to the mark. "They didn't trust we could handle a Rift. So they targeted Area 51 with a nuke."

"No one knew what a Rift or Firefly was," Hannah said. "We still don't. And the unknown frightens people. And frightened people act in irrational ways."

"The question I have," Ms. Jones said, "is that the only nuke in Pinnacle?"

"No."

"How many are targeted at Area 51?"

"We don't know."

"And how many more are targeted elsewhere?"

"We don't know. But Pinnacle is concerned with more than just Area 51. Treaties such as SALT, START, RAD, and others always bothered many in uniform."

"That is troubling," Ms. Jones said. "How can my team help?"

"I'll contact you when needed. Until then, call off your Acmes checking on Pinnacle, please."

Hannah cut the connection and leaned back in her seat. She felt the buzz. Misanthropes might call it woman's intuition, but Nero had described it to her and it was not gender specific. It was a sixth sense of information beginning to coalesce into intelligence. The world was full of information; the Internet boiled over with more than any human could ever dream to process even in a thousand lifetimes.

Intelligence was useful information. Hannah had the ability to process large amounts of information from sources, both deliberate and random, and distill out of that quagmire threads to be pursued. Sometimes they led nowhere. But sometimes they led to great unravelings. The fact that Ms. Jones had seen fit to call about this was part of it. But there were rumblings in DC and Hannah paid attention to that.

Hannah knew from Neeley's report of the package being compromised that someone in the CIA wanted that family dead. They never planned on paying out 25 million to some Pakistani garbageman and, more importantly, they wanted to keep their Zero-Dark-Thirty glory. That was very apparent. It was why she had co-opted the extraction mission rather than let the CIA send in a merk team to be massacred with the resulting bad press. She knew she'd made more enemies over at Langley by doing so, but it was better to know one's enemies and accept there were no friends.

Hannah had already made some slight nudges, some pebbles thrown into the dark, scummy surface that covered covert operations.

It was going to be interesting to see which of the ripples brought the desired results.

CHAPTER 6

The scientist held the case containing the hypodermic needle with the same care believers would hold a chalice containing the blood of their Lord. Of course, it was all an act, setting the stage for the big "reveal." He waited with the impatience of knowledge watching ignorance in action as the contractor poured water into the towel draped over the detainee's face.

Enhanced interrogation.

The CIA contract thugs had no idea what *enhanced* was.

The scientist knew they'd been doing this to the subject for six years. What was another few minutes to them? Cavemen. That was what they were. The two doing the work were not government, because even though various judges and the Department of Justice had tacitly, and not so tacitly, approved enhanced interrogation, no one with a federal pension wanted to get their hands dirty. So much easier to pay the contract muscle to do the grunt work.

In fact, the two doing the work weren't even American. They muttered in low voices to each other as they worked, something that sounded Eastern European. They wore black balaclavas to hide their faces.

The detainee gagged and spit as the wet towel was pulled off his face, retching, nothing more than tainted water coming up as he'd long since emptied his stomach of anything of substance. He had not done the same with information. Not during the six years he'd been held in Guantanamo. And not now.

He wasn't in Cuba anymore. He was in a strip mall in Springfield, Virginia. In a room with two merks, two scientists, and one soldier. It had once been a lingerie shop, but the front glass was presently covered with sheeting that looked like plywood to the outside—another small business victim of the economy—hiding metal plating covered with thick soundproofing on the inside. All the walls were lined with the same material, except one, which had a twelve-foot-long plate of dark glass from floor to ceiling. On the other side of that glass were twenty-four chairs, stadium seating, to view the room. The viewing room had once housed an adult bookstore.

The scientist looked at Colonel Johnston and raised an eyebrow.

Colonel Sidney Albert Johnston was a distant relative by blood and the years between, but he was close in spirit to the general of the same name who took a bullet behind the knee at the Battle of Shiloh and bled to death because he'd sent his surgeon to care for some "damn Yankee" wounded prisoners. Johnston glanced at the pane of dark glass. According to the memorandum, on the other side were staffers for the congressmen and senators on the committees who voted money to who the hell knew what or wanted to know; high-level Pentagon aides who would go back and brief their bosses; and some suits from the alphabet soups: CIA, NSA, FBI, NRO, and a few that had no initials because they thought they were even cooler that way. They all wanted to be one pane of glass removed from the indictment that might come someday if the bureaucrats and politicians suddenly grew a conscience and remembered America was founded on principles that didn't include torture. Not likely in Johnston's opinion or experience with bureaucrats and politicians.

Colonel Johnston raised a hand and the two merks stopped, one with the towel hovering over the detainee's face, the other with a bucket in hand.

"It's Doctor Upton's turn."

Johnston had a rough, gravelly voice that went with his imposing stature. Every inch of him emanated warrior, and his leathery face was lined with the creases of worry a good commander bore from years of leading men into battle. He had a square jaw and his hair was gray barbed wire, trimmed short every week. With a wave of the same hand, Johnston invited the scientist and his assistant to the prisoner, as if allowing them to enter the foyer of a grand mansion.

Upton turned to the black glass. "I am the head of Project Cherry Tree. This"—he held up the syringe case—"is the result of five difficult years of research and development." His first lie, but the truth would not serve here. Upton nodded over his shoulder at the detainee. "Which is less time consumed by the other methods used on that man, and he has not once ever given up any useful information. He has been waterboarded"—Upton paused—"what is it, Colonel? One hundred and sixty or so times?"

Colonel Johnston's jaw remained square. "One hundred and eighty-seven."

"I stand corrected. One hundred and eighty-seven times. And never said a word. Truly remarkable." Upton turned from the glass and walked over to a small table. The detainee was strapped to a heavy wood chair with an adjustable back. Right now it was almost horizontal to the floor to allow the water-soaked towel to press against the man's mouth and nose to simulate drowning. Upton gestured and the two merks put down their towel and bucket and roughly pulled the chair upright, locking it in place. The detainee was blinking, eyes on Upton, waiting for the next chapter in the tragedy his life had become. His forearms were strapped to the arms of the chair, his ankles to the front legs, and a thick leather strap wound about the chair and his chest.

The scientist reached into his pocket for a pair of gloves, and his assistant, a young man named Rhodes, also put on a pair. Rhodes went to the detainee's left arm and efficiently strapped yellow tubing around it. Then he walked around and waited on the other side.

Upton opened the case. The syringe glittered against black velvet. It was the smallest gauge, 32, and the best metal, designed to have deep penetration and minimal drag force. At least that's what the ad said. Almost a work of art.

"This is the first clinical trial of Cherry Tree on a human." Another lie, but it sounded more dramatic for this to be the first.

Only an idiot would walk in here not having tested it, and Upton was many things but not an idiot.

Upton lifted the needle up, higher than needed, so that the audience could see. "We've tested it for toxicity and other side effects on rats, but rats can't tell the truth, can they?" He laughed, alone, at what he thought was a joke. There was no way to tell if those on the other side of the glass got it. He didn't realize he'd just made a serious logic flaw, underestimating his audience.

Upton lowered the needle, eye level to the suspect whose head was pivoted left, focused on the glittering spike of steel.

Thus he didn't see as Rhodes pricked him with a small needle in the right forearm, the same used for TB tests, a short 27 gauge, right under the skin.

He reacted though, body jerking away. He spit at Rhodes and glared about, his last refuge of defiance.

"My assistant," Upton said, "has just injected point-one milliliters of Cherry Tree intradermally into the subject's forearm." He waved the fancy syringe. "This was just a distraction." He put it back in the case and snapped it shut. Then he made a show of looking at his watch. "Cherry Tree is quick acting. Less than one minute." He stepped back. "All yours, Colonel."

Johnston came forward, stopping out of spitting distance. "Wahid."

The prisoner's eyelids were fluttering as if trying to pull a curtain call on the softening glare.

"Wahid," Johnston repeated.

The glare was gone. "Osama," the detainee said with the rasp of a voice that had not spoken in a long time. "He's in Pakistan. They always, always ask, so there is the answer."

Johnston straightened in surprise.

"Water," Upton said with a sharp nod at Rhodes. The assistant peeled off his gloves and went to a table in the corner of the room, grabbing a plastic bottle. He brought it over to Wahid. The prisoner arced his head back and Rhodes dribbled some into his open mouth.

Wahid swallowed. He started nodding, as if memories were flooding his brain. "Osama moved there"—he paused, at a loss for how long he'd been a prisoner—"in 2006. Abbottabad. A compound. I can show you. Pigsty." Wahid shook his head in disgust. "It's not even wired to explode. My house was wired. You were lucky to catch me away from it. Very lucky for you. Very unlucky for me. Such is Allah's will. I cannot fight the will of God. No man can. But why does he curse me so? Why is not all his will and not luck? Good or bad?" Wahid looked at Johnston as if he expected an answer to the question.

Johnston took a step back and glanced over at the glass. "Wahid. We know about Osama. Tell us—"

But Wahid wasn't listening. His eyes were blinking fast, tears forming. "Please take me back to my cell. My home cell. Not the one here. I miss him. I miss him so much."

"Miss who?" Johnston asked, but it was like a pebble thrown into a waterfall of words.

"The Jell-O. The lime Jell-O. They must stop serving it. It is disgusting. Not fit for a man or even a beast. I do like the pizza. They serve it every Thursday and that is how I know a week has passed. I should not eat it as it is food for capitalists, but I like it. Not the mushrooms though. I think that is part of the torture. But I eat them to show that you cannot break me. But I am speaking now. Why am I speaking now?" Wahid's entire body shook as if it were fighting the words pouring out of his mouth.

He shifted into Arabic, the words flowing, the tape recorders capturing every one. Johnston gave up for the moment, stepping farther back, letting the man who had never spoken, speak, with the recorders catching it all. The moment went to minutes. Three times Rhodes had to come forward and give Wahid some water, a dark twist considering the waterboarding. Minutes passed into an hour and then a second hour.

There was no doubt somewhere in that flow was information that was going to lead to a Predator drone or two, letting loose Hellfire somewhere in the world.

By now, even the ones in the interrogation room could sense the impatience of those in the viewing room. Wahid might be giving up every element of Al Qaeda, but they had places to be and things to do. Cherry Tree worked. That was obvious.

Then Wahid shifted into English once more. "He watches me."

Johnston jumped into the slight pause. "Who does?"

"The man in the next cell." Tears began to stream down Wahid's face. "He watches me all the time. I cannot stop him. I cannot stop myself. He watches me in the shower. He watches me when I please myself, late at night, between the guards coming through. I cannot stop myself."

The watching-room audience, which had first listened with rapt attention, then some impatience during the Arabic, shifted with unease.

"But I do not really mind," Wahid continued. "I watch him too. He is beautiful."

Johnston looked at Upton. The truth was good, but perhaps too much was too much? Everyone fears unadulterated truth, the cutting edge of it ripping into a man's soul, his darkness and his despair, and worse, his longings.

Wahid slipped back into Arabic, his voice rattling to a rough whisper.

Johnston definitely knew enough was enough. He turned to the glass, stepping between the muttering prisoner and the observers. Upton stood by his side.

"Gentlemen, do you have any questions for Doctor Upton?"

A disembodied voice came out of the speaker. "How long does the effect last?"

"Four hours," Upton said. "Give or take a deviance of two percent, which is very precise overall."

"Aftereffects?" a different voice asked.

Upton shrugged. "None that we've seen but we'll be monitoring the subject at a max security facility."

"Outstanding," a third voice echoed out of the speaker, startling even Johnston with its easily recognizable Boston accent.

General George "Lightning Bolt" Riggs, vice chairman of the Joint Chiefs of Staff, was the number-two ranking military officer in the country and the man who did the dirty work for the chairman. He had not been noted on the attendance list in the memorandum for the experiment.

That's the way Riggs worked. Be where no one expected him to be, keep his finger on the pulse of the darkest of secrets, looking for opportunity and also for danger.

The door next to the glass opened and Riggs stepped into the room with a man in civilian clothes next to him—the Joint Chiefs of Staff scientific adviser, Brennan. No one else who'd been behind the glass mattered now.

Colonel Johnston took an involuntary step back, perhaps some genetic memory of his ancestors facing Riggs's "damn Yankee" ancestors on battlefields during the War of Northern Aggression. Perhaps just a normal reaction to Riggs's imposing presence. Angry with himself, Johnston reclaimed the lost step.

"Good morning, General."

Riggs walked over to Wahid, who was muttering in Arabic. "Broke the son of a bitch and didn't have to touch a hair on his head. Outstanding," he repeated. "The bleeding-heart cowards who wail about rights won't have dick to say about this. A little prick of the skin to get the prick talking." His coarse language betrayed his Beacon Hill accent, a strange combination. The result was something Riggs had practiced since his upper-class years at West Point upon realizing it kept others off balance, not sure who or what they were dealing with.

Riggs snapped his attention from Wahid to Upton. "I assume you have more of this . . . what did you call it?"

"Cherry Tree, sir."

Riggs smiled. "Cute, very cute. We have more trees to chop down. Do you have to inject it?"

Upton blinked. "Well, we've, uh, always injected, but it could probably pass through the stomach lining and have an effect. Perhaps even be absorbed through the skin. It doesn't take much in the bloodstream, as long as it gets to the mind."

"Can you put it in a drink?" Riggs asked. "Drop some in a glass of water?"

Upton's eyes shifted to Rhodes and Riggs didn't miss it, turning his imperious gaze to the younger scientist. "You were the grunt on this, weren't you, son? You did all the dirty work?" He didn't wait for an answer, indicating he believed his suspicion was correct, and whether it was or not in reality, it now was in this room.

"I did the lab work, sir," Rhodes managed to get out.

"So can we?" Riggs pressed.

"I don't know, sir."

Riggs frowned. "Okay, listen to me." He glared at Upton and then Rhodes. "Don't bullshit a bullshitter. You've used this on a human before. You had to, because as you pointed out with your dipshit, not-funny joke, rats can't tell the truth. All you could tell by injecting them was whether they'd fucking die or grow a second head, right?" He didn't wait for an answer. "How many times have you tested it on humans before this and how?"

Upton swallowed. "Three times under tight lab protocol."

"On who?"

"Subjects supplied by the Agency."

"Subjects supplied by the Agency's merks from Deep Six you mean," Riggs corrected. "Which means people that were snatched somewhere and are never going to see the light of day again and we don't think hold any useful information."

"I guess, sir," Upton said.

"You didn't ask?"

"No, sir."

"Did that right at least," Riggs said. "I don't do dog and pony shows. So if you know it fucking works coming in, tell me it fucking works, then show me it fucking working, but don't fucking lie to me, understand?"

Upton nodded, but a small flicker of defiance still flared up. "We weren't ready, sir. We anticipated more trials and at least six months of analysis before field deployment."

"Then maybe you should have waited," Brennan said in a calm voice, trying to smooth the storm-tossed waters in the room.

"I was *ordered* by directive to do this," Upton argued. He belatedly added: "Sir."

"By who?" Brennan asked.

Upton spread his hands in surrender. "A directive from the head of DORKA. I tried getting clarification. I sent a memo telling him we weren't ready. I was told to do this anyway."

Riggs had already moved on, ignoring Upton's excuses. "We need to take this to the next level ASAP. Slip it to the Russian ambassador. If it doesn't go through the stomach, then we jab him with a fucking umbrella like the Russkies used to do to assassinate people.

"We need to find out if they're as full of shit as I suspect they are about the nuke treaty. Pulling a fast one on us to make up for their crappy-ass military. Couldn't beat us fair, so no doubt the sons of bitches will cheat like they've been doing ever since Truman wouldn't let George S. loose on them." He used Patton's first name, as if they had an intimate relationship, which he actually believed, given Patton had also felt he'd served in other armies at other times.

"The Cold War is over," Upton said without thinking, chagrined that Riggs had jumped from him to Rhodes so quickly with the credit and then getting his ass reamed for his stupid ploy—it was accepting that the show had been stupid he couldn't get past. On top of the fact he hadn't wanted to do this in the first place.

The room froze, even Wahid in his drug-induced state picking up the momentary arctic blast from the general and pausing in his monologue of truth.

Riggs, strangely enough, smiled. He walked up to Upton, who surrendered four steps until he bumped against the table, unable to retreat, like Custer upon his final hill.

"The Cold War was never cold," Riggs said. "Do you know what the life expectancy of a second lieutenant commanding an armored platoon in the Fulda Gap was if World War Three broke out? Eleven seconds. I was there. We didn't think it was cold at all. When a T-72 tank mirrored your every move with its main gun? When an 'accidental' round comes across all the barbed wire and tank traps and blows up a track full of your soldiers and everyone hushes it up because the Cold War is supposed to be cold?"

Behind them, Wahid lifted his hand as much as the restraints would allow and grabbed Rhodes's forearm. "Help me to be quiet. Please."

Rhodes shook off the grab, focused on his boss and the general.

Riggs's face was now within six inches of Upton's. The general hadn't raised his voice at all, but the profanity was suddenly gone. There was only the chill of Beacon Hill in December blowing down on the scientist.

Riggs spun away from Upton, just as he'd been taught to about-face as a plebe at West Point sweating through Beast Barracks, drilling on the Plain. He stopped next to the civilian who'd come in with him. "What do you think, Brennan?"

Brennan nodded. "I like it."

That was good enough for Riggs. "We're going to use this, gentlemen. I want a complete briefing for myself and Mr. Brennan on how that can be done in twenty-four hours. The treaty is being signed in seventy-two hours and you have given us a superb tool just in time. Well done. Well done."

And with that Riggs was out the door. Brennan didn't immediately follow. He went to Upton and shook his hand. "Good job." Then he turned to Rhodes and shook his hand also. "Congratulations." Brennan tried to smooth the ruffled and stormy waters left in his boss's wake, one of the many tasks he did for the general. Then he left.

Johnston just as quickly regained command. "Get him out of here," he snapped at the two merks. He stabbed a finger at Upton. "You heard the general. A report in eighteen hours."

───────

"Twelve hours," Upton told Rhodes as they walked down the sidewalk of the strip mall. "I want the report on my desk in twelve hours." He paused in front of an ice cream shop in the same strip mall, three doors down from the interrogation center. A more astute person might have sensed some irony in the contrast, but Upton had been in the world of covert research for too long to have any irony left in him.

"Let's celebrate," Upton said, swinging open the door to the shop. "We'll be getting funding out the ass with General Riggs and that brownnose shit Brennan on our side."

"It *did* work," Rhodes marveled as they bellied up to the counter like two gunslingers who'd just taken out all the black hats. "The controlled environment of the lab was one thing. I was worried that we were rushing it and—"

Upton hushed him. "There's the quick and the nonfunded in our world, son. It's not like the university labs. We're in the real world, fighting the real shit. If the boss wanted us to rush it and present it, then we rush it and present it." He turned to the frowning clerk. "Double serving chocolate, extra nuts and, yes, add the m&m's."

"Just a single scoop vanilla," Rhodes said.

The clerk turned to his task.

Upton lowered his voice. "Six years they were working that guy. And we did it in a minute. If we'd have been done a couple years earlier, we'd have been the ones who got bin Laden, not that CIA bitch. It was like turning on a spigot." Upton smiled, truly happy, a rarity for him. "He'd totally lost the ability to lie or even withhold the truth. He'd have talked until it wore off." He looked at his watch. "He's probably still blabbing away as they haul him back to whatever hole they're keeping him in here."

"We need to follow up on that," Rhodes said. "Make sure the controlled parameters are matched in the field." He ran his tongue along his upper lip. A slight sheen of sweat covered his forehead.

The clerk handed Upton his heaping cup of ice cream, then went to get Rhodes's single scoop. Rhodes frowned as Upton shoveled a spoonful of ice cream, nuts, and m&m's into his mouth.

Rhodes shook his head in disgust. "I'm surprised you ordered the double with nuts *and* with m&m's considering your ass is busting out of those pants. You and Riggs. Two big fat pieces of shit."

"What?" Upton muttered around all the material in his mouth.

"Your. Fat. Ass." Rhodes emphasized each word. "You've gained like what, forty pounds just since I've been on the project?"

The second spoonful paused on the way to his mouth. "That's not funny," Upton said.

Rhodes snorted. "I bet Linda just hates the thought of fucking you. That's if you can even get it up around her. She's a whale, too."

The clerk was holding out Rhodes's single serving and Upton slapped it out of his hand as Rhodes reached for it. Upton grabbed a mask out of his coat pocket and slipped it on.

"What the fuck?" Rhodes demanded. "You treat everyone like they're your servant. I did *all* the work on Cherry Tree. The general saw that right away. It was my idea. He saw through you right away. Your stupid show. You son of a bitch . . ."

As Rhodes rattled on, Upton simply muttered "Oh, shit," as he pulled out his cell phone to call in a contain team.

━━━━━━━━━

Twelve blocks away, General Riggs's armored limo paused outside a Washington restaurant. The general stared at Brennan seated across from him. "Still seeing her?"

"Yes, sir."

Riggs shook his head. "I don't trust politicians."

"She's not a politician, sir," Brennan replied, reaching for the door handle. "Her father is the politician."

Riggs leaned over and grabbed his hand for a moment, halting him. "What we just saw is a game changer, Brennan. You get that, right?"

Brennan settled back in the seat. "What do you mean, sir?"

"Think of the power. The power of the truth. In World War Two, Winston Churchill said that 'in wartime, truth is so precious that she should always be attended by a bodyguard of lies.'"

Brennan was used to the way Riggs worked. Impulsive, prone to overreact, the general had taught himself discipline and surrounded himself with a handful of key people whose job it was to keep him from taking precipitous action. Brennan was one finger on that hand, which was short a couple of fingers to begin with.

"Sir," Brennan began, skating out onto the thin ice of confronting Riggs's single-minded vision of the world, "drugging the Russian ambassador with a truth serum might not be a wise course of action. Especially at this delicate time. Could be a Gary Powers sort of moment. The president wants SAD. Congress wants this treaty. Most importantly, the American people want this treaty."

"You might like his daughter," Riggs said, "but the president is deluded and the American people are naive. We have the upper hand on the Russians, the Chinese, and everyone else who has a nuke. Why level the playing field with this treaty? It flies in the face of our national strategy and interest. We've been sucking hind-tit for decades on this, when we're the lead fucking horse."

"SAD greatly reduces the risk of nuclear accident," Brennan said, "and of terrorists getting their hands on one. Plus, we can't keep telling other countries not to develop nuclear weapons when we have more than the rest of the world combined. *And* we're the only country that's ever actually used them."

"That's exactly why we *can* tell them not to develop them," Riggs said. "I've been a soldier for a long time, Brennan. Let me tell you something. If I were a Russian general, I would have a gun to my president's head, telling him to get us to sign the treaty even as we continued to build our own arsenal while the Americans reduced theirs."

"That's a bit paranoid, General." For a moment, Brennan was afraid he'd crossed a line, but Riggs, surprisingly, laughed.

"You aren't paranoid if they are indeed out to get you, son. And believe me, those Russian and Chinese bastards are out to get us. That Upton might be a pompous shit with his little show with the needle, but Cherry Tree is special. I can feel it in my bones.

"We have a way to strip away our enemies' bodyguard of lies. Are we just going to use it on pieces of dirt like that man in the chair and get information that's six years out of date? Or are we really going to use it? We've sat on our nukes for over sixty years and what good has it done us? We could have taken out Russia early in the Cold War with minimal casualties. LeMay knew the numbers. He begged presidents to act and they all ignored him. None of the rest—Vietnam, the Gulf, Afghanistan—would have happened if we'd done what he wanted."

Brennan frowned at the leap of illogic into the cesspool of paranoia, but knew the ice after his brief rebuttal was too thin to challenge the general anymore. "Sir, even if the treaty gets signed, it will take years to implement."

"We don't have years," Riggs said with surprising anger. "I swore an oath to defend this country with my life and by God"— his fist slammed into the leather seat—"I am going to do just that. Your father understood. He worked with LeMay on Pinnacle. Time is running out on that and time is running out for me."

"Time is running out on Pinnacle," Brennan said. "The missile in Nebraska was a close call. We were lucky Masterson's Nightstalkers were on top of it."

"Bullshit," Riggs said. "The damn thing was a dud. No maintenance on it in decades. What the hell is to be expected?"

"We're maintaining the stockpile as best we can. Outlier weapons . . ." Brennan shrugged. "We don't even *know* where some of those are. We didn't know about this one in Nebraska. That got lost somewhere along the line because of the secrecy."

"The problem," Riggs said, "is Masterson's people are trying to get on top of Pinnacle now. Some idiot left the name in the LCC there."

"It's inevitable that word will get out about it," Brennan said. "It's a program that's outlived its usefulness. Masterson has tried to penetrate Pinnacle before and failed. But our luck won't hold. Maybe we should just abandon it."

"Pinnacle is a program we need now more than ever, with the treaty coming up. Nebraska was an oversight." Riggs shifted his bulk on the seat. "There's something the president is leaving out of all of this and the public doesn't know. The Rifts. We don't know what the hell is on the other side of those things. Everyone is so focused on the Russians and the Chinese and Iran, the few who are in the know are forgetting about that. In the beginning, we formed Pinnacle inside the military to prepare for *that* threat."

"But LeMay co-opted that," Brennan pointed out.

"LeMay was a hero!" Riggs snapped. Just as quickly, like a summer thunderstorm passing, Riggs smiled, showing shiny white teeth above his square jaw. "Go join your fiancée, Brennan. Give her my best."

"Sir, I can't help you if you don't fill me in on what's really going on."

Riggs fixed Brennan with his Beacon Hill stare. "The Russians aren't the real threat. Don't get me wrong, I know the treaty has to be derailed and we can use Cherry Tree for that. But when I saw the DORKA blurb about Cherry Tree in the daily intel summary last week, I knew there was potential."

Brennan's eyes widened. "You made them do that demonstration."

Riggs nodded. "Squeezed the balls on the idiot who runs DORKA. You should see the file my people have on him."

"But why?" Brennan knew the answer. "The treaty."

"Yes." He leaned forward. "There are people other than the Russians I need to get the truth out of. We're in the eye of the storm, Brennan. People are asking questions about Pinnacle. We can't have that made public. And at the same time, we can't lose it. The best way to fight having a secret revealed is to learn other people's secrets." He laughed. "Mutually assured destruction by truth.

"Pinnacle and the treaty are tied together. And we can't lose the first and have the second. Too many good men over too many years put everything on the line to defend this country and keep it safe. Not just our country, but our world, from whatever is on the other side of those Rifts. I'm not going to see that undone. Do you understand?"

Brennan knew when to retreat. "Yes, sir."

"Good, good." Riggs smiled. "Give your fiancée a kiss for me. Go now."

Brennan blinked at the abrupt about-face. "Yes, sir." He fumbled for the door and opened it. As soon as he was out, the armored limo was pulling away, the door slamming shut with a solid thud.

Brennan paused outside the restaurant and took a couple of deep breaths. He was getting sick and tired of the general. In fact, he was getting sick and tired of a lot of things he had to put up with. He opened the door and entered the pub. Debbie liked to eat at what she called "common folk" places, although he knew her true motivation was to stick out like a sore middle finger and get the admiring glances and muted whispers of admiration that she had graced the common folk with her presence.

Brennan frowned, surprised at the thought, because it had never occurred to him before. They'd always eaten at places like this, ever since first dating sophomore year in high school. Brennan spotted the Secret Service agents before he spotted Debbie and, already simmering over Riggs's diatribe and off-kilter by his own thoughts, his attitude took another sharp turn in the wrong direction.

Debbie was staring at her phone, oblivious to the world around her. She had the agents to take care of that for her, Brennan thought as he sat down across from her. She didn't look up for four seconds.

He knew because he counted, just like when they used to play touch football as a kid after the ball was "hiked" and before you could rush the passer—one Mississippi, two Mississippi, three Mississippi, four Miss— Well, okay, just under four seconds, but that was three too long.

"Hey," she said with less enthusiasm than Brennan desired. "You're late."

"I was with the general."

Debbie rolled her eyes, which he really hated. "How is the old Lightning Bolt?"

"We just had a most interesting experience, very positive," Brennan said, forcing some cheer into his voice. "Let's order champagne to celebrate."

She raised her eyebrows. "In the middle of the day? How daring of you!" she added with a laugh. "That's my old Bren. You've been much too serious lately." She reached across the table and placed her hand over his. "What was so interesting and positive?"

Her touch sucked the anger right out of him and he actually relaxed. "Big breakthrough on the DORKA front."

"Ah, the geeks. What have they invented now?"

"It's a secret."

She pulled her hand back. "I'm not fond of celebrating something that I don't know."

"If I told you, I'd have to kill you, cut your head off, and stuff it in a safe." He said it with a smile on his face and an edge in his voice.

Debbie, in turn, pointed at the two Secret Service agents. "I don't think they'd take that as a joke." She picked up her fork as a waiter deposited a salad in front of Brennan. "I know you don't mind. I ordered when you weren't here on time. Last time you never showed and I never ate. I'm learning boundaries. At least my shrink says I am."

Brennan got the waiter's attention. "Champagne. Your best."

The waiter scurried off, probably trying to figure out if they even had champagne in this dump, Brennan thought.

Debbie put the fork down. "I'm sorry, Bren. I've had a difficult morning and I don't mean to take it out on you. My mother is all atwitter about their last Christmas in the House. She wants it to be extra special so people remember it. Like, who's going to remember? And the secret thing bothers me because that's the way my dad is all the time. Drives my mother crazy too. It's hard to be understanding when you don't have the information to understand, if you follow?"

Brennan nodded, but he noticed that one of the Secret Service agents was looking at his cell phone. Wasn't he supposed to be watching the area?

Debbie's phone next to the breadbasket vibrated.

"Who's that?" Brennan asked before even the second vibrate.

"I don't know." Debbie hit Ignore without even looking at the screen.

"No. Who was it?"

Debbie sighed. "You have *got* to stop this jealous thing, Bren. It's getting old."

He snatched the phone off the table. "Who the hell is Daniel? And why does he have your number?"

"Daniel? I don't know a Daniel."

He looked closer and grimaced. "Okay. Danielle. Who's that?"

"She's in my spinning class. What is wrong with you? You're acting crazier than usual."

"How usual crazy am I? What did Danielle want?" he asked, trying to pretend he wasn't being a complete fool.

She grabbed the phone from him and read the text. "She says Daniel is going to be on a bike in front of me tomorrow morning and he has buns of steel and what a lucky girl I am."

"Very funny," Brennan muttered.

"I try." She reached across the table once more. "I *do* try."

Brennan noticed that one of the Secret Service agents was smirking and Brennan felt a surge of anger that the man was listening and judging him.

"That agent seems too involved in your life," Brennan said in a low, taut voice. "Shouldn't they be standing near the door and pretending to be statues or something?"

Debbie laughed. "Oh, he's just acting weird because I blew him in the car on the way over. Happy?" She waited for him to laugh, but when he didn't, she shook her head with more than a hint of disgust. "I'm going to the ladies' room. Here, knock yourself out." She handed him her phone.

He didn't even wait until she was out of sight. He scrolled through her call record, thinking she was acting way too open, just like someone with something to hide. Then he noticed that the one Secret Service guy (and did they ever think about the fact that their initials were SS?) was staring at him with an odd look on his face.

Yes, there was something in that stare.

Riggs might be paranoid about the Russians and the Chinese, Brennan thought, but he knew the real danger was people. Couldn't trust 'em. Especially women. His mother had gone out of the house when he was eight, not for the proverbial pack of cigarettes, but for tampons at the PX. Or so she said, and never came back.

Debbie was cheating on him. He was certain of it. They had finally settled on a date, the first weekend in April, when the cherry trees should be blossoming in DC, and with that thought, he giggled, sensing the irony.

They had a history and it wasn't all written in large, beautiful scrolling letters. There were some dark chapters. Maybe she was getting in some last bangs before the big day. It was a thought that had occurred to him more than once. He checked her text messages.

The waiter, a bit out of breath, came up with a bottle of not-too-bad champagne. It never occurred to Brennan that the man had run down the street to a liquor store and bought it.

Exasperated, Brennan tossed her phone back onto the table next to her glass of bubbly.

Debbie came back and saw the full glass and mustered a smile. "Bren, you've known me forever. Why do you think I'm doing something? Don't you trust me?"

"I trusted you," Brennan said, "but how can I trust you in this new reality?"

"What new reality?"

"You don't get it, do you?" Brennan didn't wait for an answer. "It's all going to end. Do you have any idea what's really going on? Not just the treaty. But the experiments. The things those scientists are working on? And how just plain fucking-ass stupid some of them are? The Rifts? The Fireflies!"

"What Rifts?" Debbie asked. "Fireflies?"

He didn't hear her. "The clock is ticking. It's just a matter of time before it's all over. And then there's the general. Fucking Pinnacle. Stupid idea that should have gone away a long time ago. If he had his way, we'd all be blown back into the Stone Age, speaking of blowing."

Debbie picked up her glass. "I think the only clock that's ticking is the one until April and you're having cold feet."

He snorted. "Just because you're the president's daughter doesn't mean you get to know everything. In fact, what you don't know is far outweighed by what I do know." He stared at the Secret Service agent, uncertain if the man was staring back because of those damn sunglasses they always wore.

Debbie followed his gaze and put her flute of champagne down. "Not that again. We've been engaged for three years and dating since high school. Why do you make a big deal out of nothing?"

"How do I know it's nothing? Five years ago your father wasn't president and you didn't have all this."

"You think because Daddy got elected my love for you went out the window? And remember, your father was always so much more important for all those years and I never thought anything different about you."

"He was in your hotel room in Chicago."

Debbie blinked. "What? Who?"

"That agent. I remember him. I came in and you just had a towel wrapped around you and he was in the room."

"Fully dressed. I told you, I was taking a shower and something fell and he was checking."

"Right. Nice story. Very convenient."

Debbie rolled her eyes once more. "This is like the quarterback in high school, isn't it? The one who wouldn't give me the time of day except when he asked to cheat off me on the algebra final and you were convinced that cheating meant *cheating*. I don't even remember his name."

"You remember he was the quarterback."

"We ended up not going to the prom because of that. You only get *one* prom, Bren. And you caused us to miss it."

"Oh geez. Not the prom thing again. You bring that up every time we fight."

"I bring it up," Debbie said, "every time you get jealous for no reason. Don't blame me. You trigger it. I don't cheat and I don't lie, Bren. Accept that." She pointed at the agent. "You planted that seed, not me."

Brennan blinked, because thinking of planting reminded him of Cherry Tree.

"What is wrong with you?"

"You're right," Brennan said, with a tremor in his voice, the anger gone. "I know you didn't do the quarterback."

"How do you know that?" Debbie demanded.

Brennan started to cry, startling her. She'd never seen him cry. "I made it up and pushed it onto you because I'd been with Mary McCarthy. She told me I couldn't go to the prom with you if I wasn't going with her."

Debbie stared at him. "What do you mean 'been with Mary McCarthy'? The girl with the braces in senior year?"

Brennan glumly nodded. Between sniffles: "She gave me a blowjob in the chem lab after school one day when we were making up an extra-credit project."

"At least someone got a blowjob," Debbie said. "Surprised she didn't rip your dick off with those braces. In fact, I'm kind of wishing she had."

"It was the best blowjob I've ever gotten." With that Brennan grabbed the tablecloth in panic, knocking over both flutes and stuffing his napkin in his mouth to shut himself up. He started giggling insanely, having no idea why he was saying these things to her.

Debbie's jaw dropped, then a flush of anger over years of accusations and missing the prom flooded her face. And the projection of betrayal, which hit deepest of all.

"I hope you got the extra credit in chem!" she said as she threw her napkin down and jumped to her feet.

And at that moment, Brennan's cell phone chimed, the tone that meant the text was Top Secret, no bullshit, check it the fuck now.

Brennan spit out the napkin as he read it. "Oh no, no, no!" Brennan cried out as he accepted he had just admitted his darkest secrets.

A couple of them at least.

Give him some more time and the rest would come, but luckily for him, time was up. The Secret Service agents had begun moving when the flutes went over and now they were hustling Debbie toward the limo, screeching to the curb. Like Brennan was some nutcase standing outside the Washington Hilton. All he'd done was knock over some glasses.

And tell the truth.

Brennan was stunned for a moment too long, enough to let Debbie get halfway to her waiting Secret Service car before he bolted out of the seat and ran after her. "Stop! I can explain!"

The agent—the smirky one—who slammed him to the ground seemed to take a bit too much relish in doing so. The other agent grabbed Debbie over her protests and pushed her into the limo.

The car door thudded shut and Debbie was whisked off to the White House while Brennan was whisked off to wherever it is the Secret Service whisk people off to.

CHAPTER 7

Where they whisk people off to is a place named Deep Six.

Not very subtle, but who said you had to be subtle? The facility was run by contractors who, interestingly enough, were all non-American. They were from countries that did not have extradition treaties with the United States. Besides their excellent pay, part of their contract guaranteed them a helicopter ride to an airport, from which they would be flown to a place where they could retire in style should the need arise.

Deep Six was part of a large facility in a part of the Pennsylvania countryside called Raven Rock. After the Russians exploded their first nuke in '49 and the US no longer had a monopoly on blasting the hell out of another country, those in power in Washington decided they did not want to get blasted to hell (or heaven, depending on their optimism and beliefs).

Since Shangri-La, as it was nicknamed by President Roosevelt (Eisenhower changed the name to Camp David in honor of both his grandson and father), was located just over the Maryland border, someone suggested looking for a site near there. They found a mountain made of granite, Raven Rock, and started blasting and digging, and then blasting and digging some more to the tune of almost a million cubic yards, ultimately hollowing out a large part of the mountain.

Then they built office buildings inside. Because a government runs on bureaucrats and bureaucrats need offices. Or cubicles, depending on rank. There were also tunnels going hither and thither. Some say there's a six-mile tunnel from Raven Rock to Camp David, but the government denies it.

It also denies there's an Area 51.

One of those first tunnels used to end at a massive underground reservoir because man does not live on bread alone. Except as the facility grew, as many government facilities have a tendency to do (like weeds), there was a demand for more water. Another, bigger reservoir was built for potable water. And then another one for industrial water—cooling, waste, sewage, waterboarding, etc. The original reservoir developed a crack during some of the adjacent construction and all the water eventually leaked out, leaving a dark, damp, dank, disgusting cavern.

The perfect place to put a prison for prisoners whom the government didn't want to admit it had and who would most likely never see the light of day. Plus, they had all that industrial water for the waterboarding nearby.

Primarily, it was a very secure place.

After his interrogation in Springfield, Wahid had been whisked back to Deep Six by a contingent of contractors via helicopter. They landed at the helipad on top of the peak and then were hustled into an elevator, dropped down into the bowels of the mountain, and taken along tunnels to a thick steel door that barred the way to Deep Six.

Those who worked in the other part of Raven Rock and caught glimpses of armed men dragging hooded subjects along the tunnels were smart enough not to stare or ask questions. What happened in Deep Six, stayed in Deep Six.

By the time they got Wahid back in his cell, he'd already infected one-third of the guards.

Colonel Sidney Albert Johnston sat in his office, deep inside DORKA, ignoring the blinking lights on the phone as he checked to make sure his 9mm pistol was loaded, then tucked it in his belt. He imagined this is what Robert E. Lee must have felt when his scouts told him Hooker's Army of the Potomac was approaching Chancellorsville and had twice as many men. It was not a time for timid action. It was a time for audacity.

Perhaps his imagination was being a bit overly dramatic, but he was from the South, he was in a crisis, and he was in charge.

"Sir?" Upton intruded on Johnston's martial thoughts and earned a steely-eyed glare.

Johnston picked up the slender file folder Upton had brought to his office: the After Action Report on the lab trials of Cherry Tree. "You don't know dick about this thing your people invented, do you?"

"I told you we didn't have time for—"

He didn't wait for more, because he knew Upton was going to cover his ass. "You don't know possible vectors, do you? How did Rhodes get Cherry Tree?"

"It can't be airborne," Upton said, "or you and I would have it."

Johnston looked at the screen where a team was working on Rhodes wearing masks and gloves, sticking needles in both his arms. The clerk from the ice cream store was there too, but so far, he seemed all right.

"Then why are they wearing masks?" Johnston asked.

"Precaution," Upton said. "We think he must have jabbed himself with the needle accidently and—"

"Bullshit," Johnston snapped.

First, the stupid dog and pony show Upton had pulled, then the lie about the first test. He'd locked the lab down as soon as he got the contain call, and on the video monitors he could see white-coated scientists milling about in confusion and muted anger. Upton had arrived minutes ago with Rhodes in tow, but it hadn't been handled right. You think scientists could handle a contain correctly?

But everything at the DORKA lab out in the Virginia countryside was focused on keeping things from getting out. Upton coming in with Rhodes had not been planned for and they'd bungled it because, in reality, they didn't quite know what they were dealing with.

The scientists hated being told what to do by the government, but that didn't stop them from cashing their government checks every month and using the top-notch facilities here at the innocently named Department of Research & Kinesthetic Application. He'd sensed some warped humor in the cover name when he was first assigned as the liaison, and he'd learned that they were doing nothing at all about kinesthetics (he'd had to look it up), which is what a cover name was supposed to do: misdirect.

He'd found the scientists to be the greatest bullshitters he'd ever run into, and he had twenty-three years in the army, which meant he'd often been neck-deep in it. When they weren't flat-out covering their asses, they reverted to science-speak like word camouflage. The bigger and more remote the word (like kines-thetic), the bigger their shit-eating grin as they flashed that superior smile of a PhD in the lab talking to a civilian. Or even better, a dumb soldier.

Johnston was sitting ramrod straight in his chair, as taut as a plebe during meals at West Point, but he became even more rigid as a flash of Robert E. Lee inspiration connected synapses in his brain. It was very simple, the way Lee had split his army at Chancellorsville; Johnston had to split his own force. Turn the truth against the lie.

"How much Cherry Tree do you have left?" he asked Upton.

The scientist pulled the wooden case out of his lab coat pocket. "We've got three needles loaded. And there's a supply in the vault."

"We've got to know the vector," Johnston said. He could see that two of the scientists working on Rhodes were arguing. The "patient" was babbling something, some childhood trauma he'd never even disclosed to his shrink.

"Shit," Johnston muttered. He jumped out of his chair and left the office, Upton in tow. They entered the chamber where Rhodes was strapped to a table. The half-dozen geniuses who'd worked on Cherry Tree were clustered around the table.

"You fucked up," Johnston said without preamble. They all spun about.

"My father cheated on my mother," Rhodes was saying. "I saw him. In the garage one day, when I came home early. With my best friend's mom."

"Shut him up," Johnston ordered and one of the white coats slapped a piece of tape over Rhodes's mouth, which was another tick mark confirming what Johnston feared.

"You're a dick," the only woman in the room said to him, pulling down her mask, and that checked the last box on the list of his fears.

"You're infected. You all are."

They all stared at each other, and then began talking at once.

"Shut up!" Johnston screamed. "Do you have any idea of the clusterfuck you've initiated? The question is, how did you get infected? How did Rhodes get infected? And who the fuck else is infected? For once I want to hear the truth," and even as he said it, he realized he was going to get exactly that, a classic catch-22 if there ever was one.

He held up two fingers. "One. Vector? How did you all get infected? Two. How do we stop it? Is there an antidote?" He extended another finger as a thought occurred to him. "Three. How far can it spread?"

"Ah, the questions three!" one of the scientists said with a giggle, which made them all start laughing. Johnston glanced at Upton, noting that he wasn't joining in as the six white-coats babbled, in amazing sequence, with Monty Python snippets, several with falsetto voices.

"'What is your name?'" the first asked, nudging the one next to him.

"'What is your quest?'" asked the second, who passed it to the third.

"'What is your favorite color?'"

Johnston was getting ready to pull his 9mm and quiet the room down as the fourth went:

"'What is the capital of Assyria?'"

"No, no," the female cried out. "'What is the airspeed velocity of an unladen swallow?'"

At which point someone argued she had jumped over things.

Johnston fired a round into the ceiling, which a part of him knew destroyed the sterile integrity of the room, but he was convinced this wasn't airborne. That stopped everyone for a moment, allowing Johnston to get a question in.

"How is this vectoring?" he demanded. "How did you people get infected?"

They all stared at the woman, who apparently was the vector person.

"How the hell should I know?" she said.

"Take a guess," Johnston suggested.

"I ran a simulation while you guys were out showing off. We knew it wasn't airborne so I wanted to check my parameters and—"

They couldn't even stop the bullshit when they had to tell the truth, Johnston realized.

"What was different this time?"

The woman frowned. "Well, factoring in the differentials and the parameters from the original experiments to this one, the only difference was we weren't wearing hazmat."

Johnston closed his eyes briefly. "Why? Why did you test it again?"

"None of the rats grew another head, did they?" she asked. "According to Deep Six, the first prisoner we tested yesterday has recovered completely. And John," she nodded at the guy next to her, "agreed to give it a shot, literally, pun intended, so we could get his first-person data."

"You didn't have authorization," Johnston said, and they all giggled.

"We do lots of things here without authorization," the woman said, "because you don't have a fucking clue how to run a lab."

"I liked you all better when you lied," Johnston said.

"That's because the truth sucks," she said.

"How long does it last? Still four hours?"

One of the scientists began waving his hand, like he was in school. "I know. I know."

"No, me!" Another was waving his hand. And then they all began talking at once and the best Johnston could extract from the babble was four hours still appeared to be the medium.

He fired again, a bit of plaster falling down and hitting him on top of the head.

Through their laughter he got in another question: "How come Rhodes is infected and not Upton or me? We were all in that room."

"Direct contact," Upton said. "The prisoner grabbed Rhodes's arm. We didn't touch him and he didn't touch us."

The woman was nodding. "Yepper. We all touched John." She giggled. "But not like John wants to be touched, right, bad boy?"

"Do we have an antidote?"

"We barely have Cherry Tree," Upton said. "And why worry about that when it simply wears off?"

The woman was running her hands over John and one of the other scientists was getting mad. Johnston expected a scientific brawl to break out any moment, which didn't worry him much because they weren't much of a physical threat. Maybe they'd take each other out and he'd have some peace.

"That's why we experimented," one of the scientists not interested in the woman said. That caused a pause in their focus and everyone started talking about the nature of an experiment and the exact definition.

"You guys make way too much money," Johnston muttered.

That caught their attention for the moment.

"Sure we do," the woman said. "We laugh about it all the time. We laugh about it and you and the government and all the waste. A lot."

Johnston tapped his gun against his thigh. "You know why we pay you so much?"

Surprisingly the woman smiled. "So you don't have to kill us."

"Exactly," Johnston said.

The woman frowned. "Are you going to have to kill us now?"

"I wish," Johnston muttered. "How much contact did it take to vector?"

"Not as much as I wished." The woman turned back to the men surrounding her. It was like watching a white-coated, fully clothed orgy as she ran her hands over her colleagues. They'd all been down here way too long.

Johnston closed his eyes and played back the scene in the interrogation room. Who'd touched who?

His eyes flashed open. "We've got to get ahold of Brennan. And the interrogators. This thing is out!"

He ran for the door and the one scientist not participating in the chaste orgy ran after Johnston and grabbed his hand just before he could make his escape. "'Do you mean an African or European swallow?'" he said, then collapsed laughing, letting go.

Johnston stared at his hand for a moment, swallowed hard, then went out the door, locking it behind him, ignoring Upton's protestations that *he* wasn't infected.

Yet.

Johnston locked himself in his office. He picked up the special line—the one that he'd always known that if he had to use, his career was over—and dialed 666.

CHAPTER 8

Moms hated the Pentagon. Literally, although she wasn't too fond of it figuratively either. In its brochure and press releases, the Department of Defense boasted that a person could get from any one place in the Pentagon to another in seven minutes or less.

Unless they were a person like Moms.

Going to a place only someone like Moms wanted to go.

She'd already passed through three security checkpoints, all on the supposed lowest level. That didn't bother her as much as simply getting in from the parking lot to the first checkpoint. All the rank irritated her. They had full-bird colonels here doing the work of secretaries. One-star generals fetched coffee. The place was so top-heavy with eagles and stars it was amazing anything got done.

And the ribbons. Every officer's jacket uniform was so laden with them above the left breast pocket, she was surprised they all weren't walking tilted over. She'd been out of the "real" army not that long—okay, a while—but she didn't recognize what some of the awards were for. Most of the ribbons indicated combat duty, and it was rather easy to tell the difference between those in this building who would rather be there than here. This was a world away from where the soldiers on the ground implemented the policies that flowed out of the building.

She turned down a hallway and another desk blocked the way. Two military police, honest-to-God soldiers, not contractors, stood behind the desk, which was manned of course by a full-bird colonel. He looked up at her, noted the civvies, ran his eyes up and down her body, checked her hand for an Academy ring (she never wore her West Point ring), then sighed as he mentally slotted her: another military person turned play-spook.

"Can I help you?"

Moms took out her real ID and flipped it open.

The colonel popped up. There was no rank or name on the ID, just her clearance and a QR code. It was enough to get him to his feet, because he only saw that clearance a couple of times a month, even three security checkpoints in. There were fewer than fifty people in the country who held it, and only a few visited the Pentagon. And when they did, they normally came in the VIP entrance through the underground parking lot, whisked by two-star generals to whatever briefing they were to attend by a four-star general.

Moms still hadn't said a word. The colonel took her ID and scanned the QR code with a handheld device. It beeped green. Then he picked up another handheld device.

"If you don't mind, ma'am?"

Moms stood still as he shone it in one eye, then the other, checking her retinas. It flashed green.

The colonel waved her through, the two MPs stepping aside. She walked down the hall and then a set of stairs to a sublevel that wasn't supposed to exist according to the brochures and press releases. None of the doors were open. There was no bustle of people going about. The work down here was done behind closed doors, in hushed tones, with a minimum of what the army called "dissemination of information."

She reached a desk set in an anteroom, behind which sat an elderly man peering at a newspaper through glasses perched on his bulbous nose.

He looked up and smiled. "Good day." He waved the paper. "Got a mudder running the fourth tomorrow, but don't know if the weather will agree. You play the ponies?"

"I'm afraid I don't."

"Smart girl."

Moms couldn't remember the last time she'd been called girl.

"Who do you want to chat with?"

"Pay."

He nodded sagely. "No one gets paid enough that comes through here."

"I'm getting paid too much."

A frown crossed his wrinkled face. "That's not good either."

"No, it isn't."

"You'll be wanting to talk to Mrs. Sanchez then." He glanced at his computer screen. "Moms, is it?"

"Yes." The odd single name, no salutation, seemed not to bother him in the slightest.

He pulled open a drawer and extracted a thick, brown file. He broke the seal on it, reached in, and pulled out a stapled set of purple paper. Moms recognized the paper and the handwriting on it.

He ran his finger down it. "Fourth-grade English teacher?"

"Mr. Carletti."

"Name of the second street you lived on?"

"Same as the first street," Moms said. "Taylor Lane."

He smiled. "That was one of those they told you to mix up, eh?"

He asked six more questions, two of which also had mixed answers. Eight questions and answers out of the five hundred on the purple paper that she'd filled out many years ago when she'd first been submerged into the world of Black Ops. It was the last check and balance. Technology could be fooled, scanners could be overridden, but the human memory checked by another human and then twisted by deceit was the final obstacle. She knew there was probably some sort of weapon in the man's other hand and was certain there were guards behind some of the doors scattered about, watching this play out on video screens, ready to burst in at the wrong answer. If she got it wrong, they wouldn't be cuffing her and reading her rights.

"Very good," he finally said. He placed the purple paper back inside the folder and slid it back into his desk. He hit a button underneath his desktop and a door swung open, revealing a room the size of a telephone booth.

It didn't have a telephone. Just a chair.

"Enjoy the ride," he said.

Moms got in and sat down. The door hissed shut. There was a slight jolt, then she was moving sideways, which was a bit disorienting. She came to a jarring halt, and then she was moving backwards. She thought of a horror movie she'd watched on Netflix in her bunk at the Ranch one night, *The Cabin in the Woods*, and how all these creatures from nightmares were kept in little cubicles deep under a government-run facility. Each cube could be moved about as needed. That's what the subworld of the Pentagon reminded her of.

Except she was the one being moved about to go meet someone in one of those cubicles. If she was Nada, she would know what that made her, but being Moms, she'd long ago accepted that the world needed people like her and places like this. Nada accepted it also, but it just depressed him.

With another jerk, the booth came to a halt and the door swung open. Moms stepped out.

A chest-high counter, like the DMV, awaited her. Except there was no "take a number and take a seat." That was the job of the old man reading about horses. They couldn't have the people who came to this part of the Pentagon seeing each other and perhaps recognizing that person on a mission or while walking through the mall with family. It was called Black Ops for a reason.

An older woman was waiting for her. She was dressed in Southwestern casual, white hair flowing loosely around her sharply angled face. A younger woman, dressed similarly, was sitting at another desk, gaze fixed on a computer screen. She didn't even look up at Moms's entrance.

"Good afternoon, Moms. I'm Mrs. Sanchez." She had an identification badge dangling from her denim vest with a purple band across the top.

"Afternoon," Moms said. She reached in her pocket and pulled out a bank statement and held it out, along with her ID. "I'm getting paid too much."

Sanchez took the bank statement and ID. "That's a complaint I rarely get."

"I've called, but naturally no one would talk to me about it over the phone. Even a secure line."

Sanchez waved. "Come around the counter." She led Moms to her desk. The walls were decorated with hung rugs and etchings of the desert.

Sanchez scanned in the QR code.

"I like your jewelry," Moms said.

Sanchez paused, met her eyes, and smiled. "Thank you. My daughter makes it. She's very talented."

"She must be."

"You've been complimented, dear," Mrs. Sanchez called out.

The younger woman tore her gaze from the computer screen and gave a flicker of a smile. "Thank you."

"You're welcome."

Mrs. Sanchez reached into her desk and pulled out a thick brown folder. It had yellow paper inside: Moms's pay records. Once someone went Black, they no longer existed on the computer except for security checks and cover identities. All other paperwork was paper, just one copy as needed. Paper couldn't be hacked into, could be locked in secure places like this, and could also be shredded, meaning someone really, truly, disappeared.

It happened.

"How long has this stipend been going into your account?" Mrs. Sanchez was flipping pages in the folder.

"Six months," Moms said. "This is the first chance I've had to get here."

Sanchez nodded as she got to a certain page. "It's a survivor's benefit."

"From who?"

"I can't tell you that."

"Who can?"

"The comptroller might be able to." As if on cue, a portion of the wall behind Sanchez's desk slid open and a colonel entered. He had no ribbons, just a Combat Infantry Badge above his left pocket.

"It's my old friend from the real army, now an event horizon," he said with a grin. "In so deep, you suck all light with you."

"Bill." Moms got up and shook his hand. "You went in pretty deep, too." He perched on the edge of Sanchez's desk, who leaned back in her chair and folded her arms, watching and listening.

"Been a long time," Bill said. He glanced at Sanchez, then back to Moms. "Afghanistan, just a couple of weeks after 9/11. I gave you a bunch of money."

Mrs. Sanchez's daughter spoke without glancing over. "Six million, four hundred thousand, five hundred and thirty dollars. Moms returned one point four-two-six-five of that with her country clearance voucher. Managed to account for every single dollar, which less than twelve percent of those in your situation were able to do."

Moms glanced at Mrs. Sanchez, who was beaming proudly. "She has a good memory."

"Seems so," Moms said. "Made my ruck a little heavy, although we spread it out among the team."

Bill nodded. "Bought off the Northern Alliance."

"Bought goats, and horses, and technicals, too," Moms said, referring to pickup trucks with machine guns mounted in the cargo bay. "One of my guys got hit and he had so many wads of bills in his vest, they stopped the bullet before it even got to his body armor."

"That's always nice to hear," Mrs. Sanchez said. "We rarely hear of the direct results of our actions in the field."

Moms shifted uncomfortably in the chair. "Where are all your ribbons, Bill?"

He laughed. "We don't do those down here. It's like sticking your DD214 on your chest and advertising everywhere you've been and everything you've done. I like to keep my past a bit more private. Like you."

"A CIB, though," Moms said.

"Could have gotten that anywhere."

"Not really," Moms said.

Bill reached down and tapped his right leg below the knee. There was a hollow sound. "Got both the same place. Why I ended up in the puzzle palace here."

"Sorry."

"Lots have suffered worse."

There was a moment of silence, one all veterans observe when touching on the subject of comrades that would never see another day. It also brought Moms back to the reason she was here.

"Why am I getting a survivor's benefit? I wasn't married last I checked."

"Never married," Bill said. "Not that you didn't get offers."

Even Mrs. Sanchez's daughter stopped typing for at least two seconds before going to work.

Bill reached out and Mrs. Sanchez handed him the folder, with the appropriate page open. He frowned as he read. "Well. I'm afraid we can't tell you. Compartmentalization and all that. You don't have to be married to get a survivor's benefit," he added as he flipped the folder shut and handed it back to Mrs. Sanchez. "You know all those forms you fill out before a major deployment? The one for the benefit? You just list the people you want to get a slice of the pie and we get that slice to them."

That made Moms think about whom she'd listed on her form when she'd in-processed at Area 51.

Mrs. Sanchez slid the folder back into her desk.

"What kind of benefit is it? A gratuity spread out?" Congress, as the first combat casualties were being carted out of planes at Dover after 9/11, had initiated a "death gratuity" one-time payment of $100,000.

How one could put a price on a life was beyond Moms.

"No," Mrs. Sanchez said.

"When will it run out?" Moms asked.

"It won't," she said. "As long as you're alive, you get it." She cocked her head. "Your benefactors get the same. Didn't you read the form?"

Moms shook her head. "I thought it was the same as the army."

Bill laughed. "Is your unit the same as the army?"

"No."

"Why would you think your benefits are?" Bill asked.

"It's the best our government can do for those of you in the field," Mrs. Sanchez said.

Her daughter spoke up. "Black Ops survivor benefits account for less than point zero-zero-zero-zero-eight of the entire Black Ops budget. Statistically almost insignificant." She paused, seeing the reaction, then quickly added, "But only in terms of numbers."

"Is there anything else we can do for you?" Mrs. Sanchez asked, and Moms realized that while Bill wore the uniform and held the title of comptroller, she was the person in charge down here. Then, sliding into a Nada Yada, she wondered if Bill worked here at all and whether he was really the comptroller. Or if, as she went through the various layers of security, they'd found someone who shared a past link with her and brought him in to divert attention from Mrs. Sanchez and what was really going on.

Moms wondered how Nada could stand to get through the day with his paranoia.

Moms stood. "I just wanted to make sure everything was legitimate."

"You can count on us," Mrs. Sanchez said.

And at that moment, Moms's cell phone began to play "Lawyers, Guns and Money."

She snatched it from her belt and looked at the text message. Then at Mrs. Sanchez. "Can I get to the White House from here?"

———

Neeley was doing her best to ignore the family. The steady rumble of the C-130 turboprop engines was a sound she was more than familiar with, but the excited Pakistani voices *still* bitching were getting on her nerves. They'd been in the air for a day, stopping briefly at Rhein-Main in Germany and were now somewhere over the North Atlantic. The pill had run out hours ago and all Neeley wanted to do was sleep.

Some people were never satisfied that you'd saved their lives.

The woman was now at the forefront, waving her arms and shouting at the interpreter.

"Enough!" Neeley finally yelled.

"*You speak Pashto?*" the wife asked, stunned. Neeley ranked the question up there with asking whether she was breathing oxygen, since she'd just done it.

"*It's been over a decade we've been at war there,*" Neeley said. "*I could've learned Latin and Greek in that time.*"

"*Why did you not speak to us?*" the wife asked.

"*All you do is argue. I didn't have time for it on the ground and I don't want to listen to it now.*"

The words were like water breaking on rock. Ignored. "*Where are you taking us?*" the wife demanded. "*What will happen to us?*"

Neeley sighed. She hated dealing with amateurs. "*What exactly did you think would happen when you gave up bin Laden's location?*"

The man finally spoke up. *"They said we were safe. That they had a, how do you call it, a cover story."*

"Yeah," Neeley agreed. *"They even made movies about it. Better than admitting a pissed-off garbageman gave up the world's most wanted terrorist simply because the asshole was using proper tradecraft technique and burning all his trash and not paying the local to haul it off. He didn't think that one through. Should have paid you off* not *to get his trash."*

"I have a noble profession—" the man began, but Neeley didn't have the patience for it.

"What did you think you were going to do with twenty-five million in Abbottabad?"

"We have received only a very small portion of it," the wife argued. *"We have been waiting—"*

"You bought the nice fridge," Neeley said. *"You didn't think people would notice? Didn't you ever see* Goodfellas?*"*

The little girl spoke for the first time. *"What is* Goodfellas?*"*

Neeley didn't have the time or inclination to fill the girl in on the Lufthansa heist and what happened after. She'd have a chance to see the movie in the States.

"But we had no *refrigerator,"* the wife argued. *"It was just a small one. We have been waiting very, very patiently."*

"Your new place will have one, I'm sure," Neeley said. They didn't understand the fundamental truth that the only thing that had kept this family alive so far was the cover story and the dribbled-out payment. And the only thing that kept the CIA looking good was projecting that its hard work had located bin Laden's compound, not this wreck of a man. The combination had forced the case officer handling the informant and his family to keep them in place, trying to gain as much time as possible.

Neeley, having spent many years in Black Ops, also suspected, deep down, that the CIA was hoping the bad guys would find out about the informant and wipe him and his family out. Save money on the reward, and they could still maintain the cover story: *Yeah right. A garbageman gave up bin Laden?* She could hear the laughter now if the bad guys tried to publicize it. And they'd get laughed at too. All in all, these three were a loose end and an embarrassment to everyone involved. Which also might explain why the mission had obviously been compromised. It would not be the first time the CIA had given up an asset they considered expendable after the fact. If that were the case, and Hannah found out the identity of the person who did it, they would not be long for this earth.

And this family still didn't get it.

"*And the rest of our money?*" the man asked.

Neeley glanced at her watch. "*The money is gone.*"

The man stood, swaying with the plane. "*What do you mean it is gone? We did our part! I was the one! It was me!*"

"*And I'm sure the United States will forever be grateful, even though no one will ever know.*" Neeley shook her head. "*I wouldn't be telling anyone else what you did, even in the States.*"

"*You are cheating me!*"

"*Not me. I saved you.*" Neeley spread her hands, indicating the plane. "*You think this was free? I'm sure the balance of the twenty-five million is being sucked out of an offshore account right now by Mrs. Sanchez. It might just pay for the cost of running this op, which means the books will be balanced and by golly, she's going to balance those damn books. The government might run on a deficit but not Black Ops.*"

"*That is not fair!*" the wife screeched.

Neeley reached in her pocket and pulled out some gum and handed it to the girl, tuning the parents out as they turned on each other, screaming, as if the one who went louder would be righter.

Neeley knelt and looked the girl in the eyes. *"They're learning the only fair in life has a Ferris wheel and cotton candy."*

The girl was confused. *"What does that mean? How is cotton candy? Whose wheel?"*

Neeley pressed a hand against the side of her head, sensing a headache coming on from the parents arguing. She wondered how people could stand to raise children. She'd never gotten that memo and it hadn't been in Gant's set of rules. She'd rather run an op.

"Don't worry," Neeley told the girl. *"You'll be fine. Just not rich and not so close to getting your heads chopped off every day. Things are actually turning out as well as they possibly could for you and your parents."*

"I told you this would happen!" The wife was shaking her husband's shoulders. *"Did I not tell you this would happen? That CIA man you trusted kept telling us wait, wait. And we waited. You said trust him. Trust the CIA. Trust the Americans. And now? See? See? Why do you never listen to me? Why do you swallow your mother's words as if they were gold, but you throw mine out like they are the garbage you collect? You should have said nothing! Nothing!"*

The husband sat down, head in hands, as his wife continued to berate him.

"I'm afraid you're going to have to listen to this for a long time," Neeley told the frightened girl. *"I can just save your life. I can't save you from your family."* Neeley put a hand on the girl's shoulder, trying to conjure up something she'd never experienced on the other end as a child. *"It will all be fine."*

She looked past the girl as the crew chief came down the cargo bay. He held out a headset as he plugged it in an outlet. "Priority message for you, ma'am."

Neeley turned away from the girl and her distraught family. She put on the headset. "Neeley."

She recognized Hannah's voice. "I'm diverting your 130 to the closest airbase where there will be a chopper waiting to get you back here ASAP. You've got a new mission. There seems to be a window of opportunity. Are you aware of Deep Six?"

"Yes."

"There's someone in there. General Riggs's science adviser, named Brennan. He's being held there. There's been an accident with a DORKA experiment and he's infected."

"That's Nightstalker territory," Neeley said.

"They've been alerted," Hannah said. "But I want you to get to Brennan and ask him some questions."

"Break into Deep Six?"

"It is designed primarily to keep people out," Hannah said.

"Is this a Sanction?" Neeley asked, which meant she had permission to use deadly force at her own discretion.

There was a moment of silence, then the reply. "It is a Sanction. I think Brennan knows about Pinnacle. As much as anyone knows. We can finally end this."

"Roger that."

Neeley expected to hear the click, meaning the transmission was over, but static lingered. "Hannah?" she finally asked.

"Yes."

"What's going on?"

"The accident at DORKA. It's some sort of truth serum called Cherry Tree. It hasn't been contained yet. It's gotten loose in the White House and is spreading. I'm not sure how or what the long-term effect is, but this could get out of control. And when things get out of control . . ."

"Murphy's Law," Neeley said, a maxim that was more ancient than Gant's rules. What can fuck up, will.

"Be prepared to move to the White House on an adjunct mission as needed after you get to Brennan and find out as much as you can from him." Hannah made it sound like breaking into a highly secure, underground facility was a fait accompli.

"Roger that."

"Be careful." And then the click.

Doc looked at the menu, trying to find something he would be willing to eat and could afford. The woman hadn't shown up yet and part of him hoped she wouldn't. The place was way too expensive for him by his lonesome, never mind with a date. Not that he wanted to call her a date, but it was obvious that's what she thought when they talked on the phone, so splitting the check probably wasn't an option. He wondered why he let his sister do this to him. He always agreed when she set him up and it always turned out badly. She always said this next one was perfect, *the* one, and he had a growing suspicion that there was no one. That his job, his passion for knowledge, was and would forever be his first and only love.

But one has to humor a sister, especially when she is the only family one has left.

Still. Sixty-nine bucks for a steak? This was Vegas. One could get a steak for two dollars with ten dollars' worth of chips at most of the lower-class casinos and they might even throw in the start of a lap dance. Doc only knew because Roland had dragged him out one night, and Doc had had the honor of watching Roland wolf down fourteen bucks' worth of steaks at seven different places.

Besides the base pay, combat pay, danger pay, Black Ops pay, jump pay (not worth it), and various other streams of income as a Nightstalker, it was barely making a dent in the student loans required to get the four PhDs he boasted about so much.

Even with those PhDs, including one in physics, Doc had no idea what fusion meant when it came to food. Why would anyone want to fuse sushi and Indian food? Could that even be fused? He mused on that for a moment, as Roland had mused on *spear* vs. *arrow*. Wasn't the point of sushi the opposite of Indian food?

Doc sighed. He'd have to order something and push it around. Doc ate for energy and he understood very much how calories translated into force. He had never understood eating for the flavor, especially when the flavors were so weird. He was so caught up in the energy trail from food to calories to energy to how much energy the brain required that he failed to notice the woman until she sat down across from him.

She was a bit older than he had expected, but other than that, exactly what he anticipated when he'd walked into her favorite restaurant and scoped it out, the way Nada had taught him to "scope it out." For most men that meant checking out the women, but for a Nightstalker it meant first assessing the potential threats, the security, then the emergency exits, both marked and those other avenues that could be made into an exit with a little bit of ingenuity. Then for things that could be used as field-expedient weapons and cover; Roland had taught him that, constantly pointing what could be used to burn, impale, explode, maim, slash, and otherwise damage the human body. Roland had also explained what a table could be composed of and the depth needed to stop various caliber rounds when you flipped it up for cover. It had all been rather complicated and confusing but also intriguing, even for Doc, with all his PhDs. Roland was only good with certain numbers, but on those, he was worth listening to. He was an encyclopedia of calibers and armor and entry wounds and exit wounds and ricochet angles that would make the best quant on Wall Street run screaming to Hell's Kitchen.

But it was Nada who'd said you can judge people by the surroundings they chose. Like the woman. The restaurant was too polished, meaning the food wasn't going to be that great and neither was she. The food was going to be art, not sustenance, like some people.

"Doctor Ghatar," the woman said, nodding her head in greeting, her expensive earrings glittering in the candlelight.

For a moment he wondered who she was referring to, then he realized she only had his last name from his sister. A name that was fading away from him with every year in the Nightstalkers.

"Yes. And you must be Gay." He did not phrase it as a question, but the name got his mind going. Having a name that projected a mood meant you rarely lived in one. (Frasier, Ms. Jones's one-eyed shrink, had told him that.) But still, Doc had to cut her some slack. Applying Nightstalkers' templates to civilians might not be fair. For all he knew Gay could be a fun and lively person who was straightforward and down to earth and laughed off gentle criticisms and accepted compliments gracefully.

But he doubted it. She looked too perfect, like the restaurant. It was why Roland never went to those top-tier strip clubs. He said the women's bodies were too perfect and that they'd cut you. Doc had never quite grasped that last part.

"You are as your sister said you were," Gay said. She too was Indian. Despite their years in the States, his sister could not imagine marrying outside of the home country.

One part of Doc's brain worked on trying to untwist the meaning in that statement while he evaluated the net worth she was covered with. He thought it ironic that people spent so much time and money on things in an attempt to show others who they were. She had perfect hair, expensive clothes, and a watch that cost more than his car. But one could buy all that with a loan, or from an ex-husband's alimony. Or they could all be fake, which is the first conclusion he knew Nada would jump to, and then it really bothered him to be channeling Nada.

Real things that no one could take a loan on and buy seemed to have little value. Doc knew he was overthinking this, but the last mission, time running out, had brought him a bit too close to the black void. Like most who gazed over into that chasm, one tended to get a little introspective.

Or they were a psychopath and never thought of it again.

"As are you," Doc finally replied.

"Do you have a first name?" she asked.

Doc lied.

"And what do you do for a living?" she asked. "Your sister was very vague."

That's because his sister had no clue. Doc told her a very elaborate lie, the same one he'd been telling ever since joining the Nightstalkers and getting his cover for status. Which was different than cover for action, Nada had patiently explained to him during his in-processing.

The good thing was there were no student loans tied to all the training the Nightstalkers had given him in tradecraft and field-craft.

The bad thing was there was a high probability of getting killed being a member of the team even if one were perfect with tradecraft and fieldcraft. Murphy was always waiting to screw things up.

She asked more questions. He was beginning to miss Ms. Jones's in-briefing and "why we are here" speech because he had no clue why he was here. He batted back the conversational shuttlecock and asked her all the required questions in return.

She was lying too. She had a little twitch on her left eyebrow. Mac had taught him how to look for tells. She'd have been a lousy poker player.

Doc knew he was lying, but he had a good reason; he had to keep secrets larger than himself. In his business, one learned that a secret could only be protected by lies. She was lying because she'd already made a decision to never meet him again. He'd known that from his first look, and he knew it was because he had not been paying attention, anxiously awaiting her entrance and not pulling out her chair for her.

Some women need that chair pulled out. She was one. She knew if he wasn't focused on her from the start, she could never get that focus.

He did give her points because she'd accurately judged him so quickly and just as quickly made her decision. Decisiveness was good.

"And your credit score?" she asked after their salads arrived and before the meal, as the shuttlecock was drifting lazily toward the floor.

"My what?"

"Credit score?"

"I do not know."

The tell was twitching and he knew that was the wrong, wrong answer. At that moment Doc would rather have been anywhere and, despite knowing what it meant, he actually was glad when his phone began playing "Lawyers, Guns and Money."

"Good friends help you move," Mac said. "Great friends help you move a body."

"I'm hoping it won't come to that," Kirk said, pulling back slightly on the slide of his MK23, making sure there was a round in the chamber. It was a glaring sign of the nervousness held by the other three in the black SUV because they'd all supposedly checked their weapons before entering the vehicle.

But it was also a reminder.

"Eagle?" Mac asked.

Eagle sighed, but didn't reply. Kirk reached across and drew Eagle's pistol. He pulled the slide back and confirmed there was no round in the chamber. He pulled it all the way back, chambering one.

"Make sure it's on safe," Mac said, "'cause we don't want Eagle shooting his dick off."

"My finger is my safety," Roland said, the refrain of all shooters in Special Ops. "And really, really good friends help you make a body."

"And your dick is going to kill you," Mac said. "How much did you blow in Vegas this time?"

"Not much," Roland said, but he was shifting into action mode and even Mac couldn't needle him out of that.

Eagle was driving, because Eagle always drove. Kirk was in the passenger seat because this was his turf, northwest Arkansas, just above the Ozark National Forest and below the loop of the Buffalo River National Park. Roland and Mac were jammed in the backseat, Roland's knees shoved into the back of Eagle's seat, which bothered him, but it wasn't like Roland could make himself shrink. And Eagle needed as much legroom as possible.

If Nada was there, he would have made Roland and Mac switch places. But Nada was with Zoey, a story none of them believed, because no one believed Zoey was real, so who the hell knew where Nada was?

They'd left the Snake in an isolated field twelve miles back, a place Kirk said it would be safe, but like any good driver, Eagle had shut all the hatches and put on the security system. Anyone touched the Snake, they'd get zapped with enough volts to put 'em out but not kill 'em. They'd still be lying next to the aircraft by the time the team got back from its vacation mission.

If they got back.

"This is a town?" Eagle asked as they approached Parthenon.

"I thought Texas had some real shitholes," Mac drawled, "but you boys up here got us beat."

"Reminds me of home," Roland noted with all sincerity and perhaps a twinge of longing, angling his commando dagger in the sunlight, checking the edge.

"This isn't Senators Club," Eagle said, referring to the gated community where they'd run their last Rift mission.

A sign warned that Highway 327 did a hard juke to the left at the stop sign. It was as best they could tell since bullet holes had chewed most of the sign off. The stop sign, which seemed to anchor the town to the intersection, was also riddled. The place was more an intersection than a metropolis.

"Take a right," Kirk said, taking them off the two-lane hardball onto a one-and-a-half-lane paved road that had seen better days.

"I remember the plan and the terrain," Eagle said, but gently, knowing Kirk was nervous enlisting them on a personal mission. But who better to help you than the comrades you entrusted your life to?

The paved road gave way to a single dirt-rutted lane.

"Mac?" Kirk asked.

"Roger," Mac said. Eagle tapped the brakes and Mac was out the door with his pack and rifle case and into the underbrush on the north side of the road. Roland put half of the backseat down and assumed the prone position, trying to get out of sight. Combined with the tinted windows, it was a bit of overkill perhaps, but Roland was going into combat mode and the word *overkill* never applied.

It wasn't easy, given he had body armor on and his combat vest. He'd argued he should be the one with the rifle on overwatch, but this was Kirk's op. Kirk knew Roland would have more value standing behind him as a presence. He'd also be less likely to start shooting people by misjudging threats through a sniper scope. Mac was more levelheaded with bullets. He fired them like he owned them and each one cost a lot.

Eagle continued on and they reached a stream. There was no bridge and Eagle plowed into the water. They roared up out on the other side.

They reached a fork in the road and Eagle turned right. They switchbacked up a slight rise and then Eagle stopped the SUV. Not part of the plan, but there were two men standing in the road with AR-15s aimed at the windshield. They wore Arkansas formal attire, meaning they were draped in one-piece camouflage hunting outfits and wearing beat-up baseball caps.

Kirk got out, hands up. "I need to talk to Ray."

"I remember you," one of the men said. "You Pads's oldest boy." He walked a couple steps closer to the SUV and peered at the tinted windshield. "Who's your friend?"

"Buddy from the army."

"You got bad choices in buddies," the man said as he spit tobacco into the dirt. "We don't like his kind 'round here."

"You mean intelligent?" Kirk asked.

"Don't get smart with me."

Kirk laughed. "That's called irony."

The other man spoke up. "What you want with Ray?"

"It's between me and him," Kirk said. "Family business which ain't your business." Kirk was falling back into the lingo of Winthrop Carter, the man he'd been before the Nightstalkers and before the army.

The first man shook his head. "Not if I don't let you go talk to him."

"It's about the kid and your sister," the other man said. "Ain't it?"

Kirk nodded. "Yes."

The second man shook his head. "You can go talk to Ray, but you gonna see he ain't listening to people much anymore. No matter who it is or what they say. He ain't the same as you remember. He ain't the same as anyone remembers."

"What's wrong with him?" Kirk asked.

The second man shrugged. "Don't know, but he's in charge now and no one is going to ask him. He's mean as a cottonmouth if you confront him."

"You packing?" the first man asked.

"I am."

"Leave it here."

"I won't."

The man aimed right at Kirk's face. "I said leave it here."

"I was issued my weapon by the government and I won't be leaving it here," Kirk said. "And ask your buddy to take a look between your eyes."

The second redneck glanced over and saw the flickering red dot resting between his buddy's eyes. "You got a shooter out there?"

"Got a couple of shooters," Kirk said. "I don't mean any trouble for Ray but we have to talk. You know you can't stand between family."

The man indicated for his partner to step aside and they waved for him to pass. As they went by, that guy pulled out a cell phone and made a call.

Kirk got back in and Eagle drove through the roadblock, Roland still crunched down in the back.

"I could kill them," Roland said. "'Don't like his kind'? Let me kill him."

"Don't worry," Kirk said over his shoulder. "He's TDTL. Someone will do that soon enough."

"TDTL?" Roland asked.

"Too dumb to live," Kirk explained.

"I do appreciate the offer though, Roland," Eagle said. Then he began humming the theme from *Deliverance*.

"Funny," Kirk muttered, but he was focused on what was ahead. A large ramshackle house, which had obviously been added to bit by bit, sat on top of a small knob. A barn was to the right, except the barn looked to be in a lot better shape than the house, with a new metal roof and all the windows covered with heavy wood shutters. Several smokestacks punched through the roof, with smoke lazily drifting forth. "They're cooking," Kirk said. "And it's a big operation. Bigger than what was here before."

"I thought your uncle didn't use?" Eagle said.

"He didn't, but a lot's changed here since I been gone."

Nodding at the house, Eagle said: "I bet you the inside looks better than the outside." The SUV stopped in front of the house. Kirk got out while Eagle stayed in the driver's seat, engine running.

"I got two shooters upstairs," Eagle informed Roland, looking down at the display. Instead of a GPS it showed the input from a thermal camera mounted into the molding on the front bumper. "Windows A3 and A5." Kirk had laid out the building to them the previous night and they'd designated sides, floors, windows . . . everything, so that they could quickly designate targets.

Google Earth helped.

The front door swung open and Kirk's uncle Ray came out, his left arm looped over the shoulder of a woman. Three men fanned out behind him, staying on the porch, their boots creaking down the worn wooden planks, two ARs and one pump-action shotgun being brought into play. The barrels were pointed down.

For now.

Ray had a large .357 Magnum tucked in a holster on his left side. The woman helped Ray down the three stairs to the dirt path. An incongruous white picket fence about three Mark Twain stories short of a new paint job separated him from Kirk, who halted at the gate.

"Ray."

The older man had his head cocked slightly to the left. He nodded. "Winthrop. Been quite a while since you've been home."

"I've been busy, Ray."

"Fighting other people's wars," Ray said. "Told you it was dumb. Fought in Vietnam. For what? Now we buy furniture from the same gooks we used to bomb."

Kirk spread his hands. "What's going on, Ray? What are you doing up here in Woodrell's place?"

Ray laughed. "Ain't no more Woodrell. He's in the swamp. Got tired of him pushing, so I pushed back."

Kirk shook his head. "I don't get it, Ray. Meth took my dad and you helped keep it away. Now you're running it?"

"Meth didn't take your dad," Ray said. "Being stupid killed your dad."

"You told me you'd take care of—"

Ray cut him off. "Never said such a thing."

"Ray, listen—"

"You got shooters out there in the woods?" Ray asked.

"Yes."

"I got shooters too," Ray said.

"You promised to look after my sisters and brothers."

"I am," Ray said.

"You got Parker working up here," Kirk said. "How is that looking after him? Dee said you slapped her when she came here to get him. You don't slap women, Ray. You know that. Especially not my sister."

Kirk could see the woman wasn't window dressing. She was supporting a good portion of Ray's weight. She was like many women in the hills, possibly aged beyond her years. She could have been an old twenty-five or a young fifty.

"What's wrong with you?" Kirk asked.

"Nothing's wrong with me," Ray said. "Tell your nigger friend to get out of the car."

Kirk blinked. His uncle had never used that word even though it was more than common in the area. Deep in a dark drunk, Ray had told Kirk several times how his life had been saved twice in Vietnam by his best friend, an African American (which is the term Ray had always used) from Atlanta.

Eagle got out of the SUV and walked up beside Kirk.

"Couldn't find the shooters," a voice called out from behind as the two men who'd been blocking the road broke out of the tree line on the right, twenty yards away. "We looked, Ray."

"You didn't look good enough," Ray said.

"I know he's kin," the man continued, "but look who he come down here with. We don't"—the man didn't get another word out as Ray pulled the Magnum and fired. The bullet hit the man in the shoulder, the large round pirouetting him 360 degrees.

At the sound of the gun, Roland came out of the back of the SUV, his M249 at the ready. A red dot centered on Ray's forehead as Roland aimed at the house.

Kirk held his hands up. "Hold on, hold on! Everyone just calm down."

"I never promised you nothing," Ray said.

"He thinks he's telling the truth," Eagle said in a low voice to Kirk.

"What?" Kirk was confused, but Roland was ignoring both of them, his light machine gun at the ready. And the red dot was steady on Ray's head.

"Ray," Kirk said in a louder voice. "Come on. This isn't you."

Ray laughed and tapped the side of his head. "I see things now, Parker. I see the way things need to be."

"I'm not Parker," Kirk said. "I'm Winthrop."

Ray blinked, and there was a window into him through his eyes. Kirk looked at the woman, then the other gunmen. "You let him do this? To all of you?"

The woman spit. "Shut your trap, boy. Your uncle is the toughest son of a bitch this here county ever made. You don't be talking trash about him."

"He doesn't know reality," Eagle said in his low voice. "Prefrontal cortex is fried. Wet brain, given what you say about his drinking. They all don't know it. He's fabulating."

Roland caught that last part. "He's what?"

"He's inventing his own reality," Eagle said. He took a step closer to Kirk, but spoke in a voice they could all hear. "You would never hit Dee, would you, Ray?"

Ray blinked, more twitched. "I never hit Dee."

Kirk closed his eyes briefly. "Dee would never lie to me."

"It just gets worse," Eagle said to Kirk. "There's no cure."

"Get away from him!" Ray yelled as a young girl ran to the man he'd wounded, trying to tend to his wound.

"Ray!" Kirk caught his uncle's attention. "You're sick. Let me help you."

"Girl," Ray said, lifting his pistol toward the young girl who was pressing down on her father's wound. "You git, or I'll—"

Kirk lifted his arm and fired before anyone could react. The bullet hit Ray in the left thigh and knocked him down like a hammer.

No one else fired as Roland swept the muzzle of his machine gun back and forth.

Kirk walked forward. He knelt next to his uncle. "You're sick, Ray. I'll get you care."

Ray was shaking his head, eyes blinking in confusion. "I didn't do nothing wrong. I didn't."

Kirk cradled his uncle's head in his lap. "I know. I'll get you care. The—"

His next words were cut off as Roland's cell phone began playing "Lawyers, Guns and Money," followed by Eagle's, then in the distance Mac's, and lastly Kirk's.

"We got to go," Roland said.

"I've got 911 on the way," Eagle said. "He won't be hurting anyone, anymore. And it isn't his fault."

***

"It stinks," Zoey said.

Nada couldn't argue with his niece's assessment of the La Brea Tar Pits. He felt uncomfortable in his civvies, never mind not having body armor. He did have his MK23 in a hip holster under his loose jacket because he'd as likely go somewhere unarmed as not breathe. They were seated at a bench facing the pits. It was a sunny, Southern California winter day.

"It's got history," Nada ventured, glancing at the brochure he'd taken from the museum lobby. "A lot of animals have died after getting stuck in there. They still do. Birds and things."

"Gross," Zoey said while Nada considered a tar pit as a weapon. He looked out at the black goo and imagined camouflaging it with a layer of sand and leaves. Static, but effective as an obstacle. A person could channel an attacking force using such an obstacle. He remembered the quicksand in Malaysia where he'd been sent from Delta Force to go through a tracking school run by former headhunters. They had pointed out how game moved around such obstacles in predictable patterns.

At least they said they were "former," but Nada had had his doubts. Lots of people said they were former whatever, but in the long run, one tended to go back to one's roots.

"I'm hungry," Zoey said in a voice pitched about a year less than her five, which any parent would take as a warning sign. But Nada wasn't trained in those familial arts. He had picked up that his brother hadn't wanted to let the two of them go out alone, but it had never crossed his mind it was because of him, not Zoey.

As she got up and began spinning and twirling, another sign of wanting to move on from the bubbling black graveyard, he thought of Scout and he felt a pang of something.

A more normal person could have told him he missed the young girl from North Carolina who'd helped him on their last mission. Nada figured it was the hot dog he'd eaten.

"Can you do a cartwheel?" he asked Zoey.

She paused and looked at him. "I think so."

"On the grass," Nada said, having at least that much kid-sense to get her off the paved path.

Zoey gave it a pretty good attempt, ending up in a ball on the grass. "It still stinks," she noted as she got to her feet.

"I'll help you," Nada said. "You have to keep your legs straight."

Zoey was less than enthused but gave it a try. As she cartwheeled to the right, her hand came down on a dead bird buried under the leaves. She instinctively tried to pull her hand back as her body toppled over and Nada lost his grip on her ankles. She landed in a heap, saw the bird, and gave a little girl shriek, the kind that carries much farther than tiny lungs should be capable of.

"Easy, Zoey, easy," Nada said. "It's dead. It can't hurt you." He leaned over and tried to pick her up, but she was scrambling away from the body, now crying and hyperventilating.

"You okay, little girl?" A young man stopped jogging and was walking over.

"She's fine," Nada said.

"You her father?" the man asked suspiciously, because Nada looked like no one's father.

Nada hated being asked questions, especially by strangers. "Go back to your run."

Zoey got to her feet, crying and looking totally forlorn.

A few more people were being drawn in and Nada tried to put his arms around Zoey and comfort her.

"You know this man?" the jogger asked Zoey.

Nada ignored him and leaned his head close to hers. "Scout, it's just a bird."

She shoved herself out of his arms. "My name is Zoey," she shouted. "Not Scout!"

"Somebody call the cops," the jogger yelled, taking a step to get between Nada and his niece.

Nada's instinct was to run, to avoid the confrontation, but he couldn't leave Zoey. He had his federal ID and could clear it up with the cops. And that depressed him, to realize that he was going to have to use his false identification to prove he was what others take for granted. Because he knew he wasn't an uncle, not in the real sense. He was the outsider, the weird one, and because of that, he was going to have to be the one doing the accommodating in this, the normal world.

"I'm her uncle," Nada said to the jogger, raising his hands slightly and spreading them in the universal sign (in Nada's world) of "I won't kill you right this second."

The guy didn't appreciate the gesture.

"He's got a gun!" the jogger screamed, spotting the MK23 in its holster, and then more people screamed and everyone began running away. No heroes here, especially not with someone who looked like Nada who had a gun, not even for a little girl like Zoey.

Maybe it was an LA thing.

Nada sighed as he heard the distant siren coming closer and pulled out his real fake badge and ID. A clusterfuck.

And then his cell phone began its distinctive ring, "Lawyers, Guns and Money," and as he sprinted away to the call of duty, no time to talk his way out of this, knowing the cops would reunite Zoey with his brother, he realized the irony of what he'd always told the team:

Zoey leads to getting Zevoned.

CHAPTER 9

An Hour Earlier

"Trust no one," the president said.

The Keep had her quill pen poised over the latest page in the book, but didn't write his words of wisdom down. "That's been on every president's list."

"Maybe they should highlight it?"

The Keep carefully laid the pen down and flipped through some pages in the book. "It's been highlighted and scored and given extra stars and exclamation points. You read it years ago when I in-briefed you after you took office."

"Maybe it needs its own page?"

"Good idea, sir," but it was apparent she wasn't going to make any special note about it.

"I'm surprised JFK didn't put that on a separate page," the president said.

"He didn't make it to this meeting," the Keep said. An awkward pause followed that. "Terribly sorry, sir. I shouldn't have said that."

She picked up the quill and held it carefully and with respect. Its original owner, after all, was Thomas Jefferson. It was antiquated and archaic, exactly the way it should be as she entered the president's observations from his four years in office in the Book of Truths with ink and quill from the third president.

The quill was archaic, not the ink, although it was specially made with the same formula Jefferson had used centuries earlier.

Templeton smiled sadly. "How about this: Especially don't trust someone who tells you not to trust anyone? I learned that the hard way."

The Keep nodded. "Very good." She wrote in large, flowing letters, almost calligraphy, and he wondered if that was part of why she'd gotten this job or if she'd been taught it after getting the job.

Everyone in the White House thought the Keep was part of someone else's staff. She wore the same type of bland business attire, had an access badge that gave her the highest clearance, and kept a low profile. In housekeeping, they thought she worked for the social secretary. In social, they thought she was a senior staffer at housekeeping. The cooks (chefs, since it's the White House) thought she worked for maintenance.

There was only one other person on the top floor of the White House, seated too far away to hear, a shadow that always was behind the president, even when the sun didn't shine: a military attaché who carried the "football." Technically, it was just a metal briefcase. It weights forty-five pounds and a satellite antenna pokes out of the side. It is not locked to the aide, as many commonly thought, since they were in the relative safety of the White House. The case holds the key ingredients needed for the president to annihilate any enemy at a moment's notice: a transmitter (never used); a black book listing options for nuclear strikes based on current threat analysis and updated at least daily, more often in times of crisis (peered at several times by presidents with reactions ranging from morbid interest to shock and dismay, but never used); another book containing options of classified sites the president could be taken to in case of emergencies (used on 9/11/2001); and most importantly, a three-by-five card with the authentication codes for launch (never used). There is also a sat phone and a pistol, the latter an object of speculation as to whom it was to be used on and why. The dark humor was it was the attaché's last way out if the case had to be used.

The Keep had told Templeton four years ago during the in-brief that several presidents, most notably Jimmy Carter and Ronald Reagan, had preferred to keep the code in their jacket pocket, indicating a strange combination of need for power and lack of trust. This had led to Carter sending the authentication codes for a nuclear holocaust out to get dry-cleaned along with the jacket while on a trip one time.

After that, the Secret Service began checking laundry.

Then it had ended up on the emergency room floor in discarded clothing after Reagan got shot.

After that, the Secret Service really tried harder to keep the president from getting shot.

The Keep had recommended following protocol and leaving the codes in the case.

Templeton thought the constant presence of the officer in range of the president was more than just a practical thing. It was a reminder of the seriousness of his job, for despite four years in office, he'd never been able to zone the guy out of his sphere of awareness.

He couldn't comprehend carrying those codes in his pocket. Sometimes, late at night, he pondered what it would be like to have that briefcase opened and give the codes. Then he usually took a Xanax to get back to sleep.

The president heard his wife's angry voice echo up the stairwell and sighed. "Why is Christmas so damn important around here?" he asked.

The Keep responded to the president's question, because she did more than just keep the book. She was also fluent in White House and presidential history. "Christmas didn't become a national holiday in the United States until 1870, during the administration of Ulysses S. Grant. One might think this would have something to do with the separation of church and state, but the same bill also made New Year's, the Fourth of July, and Thanksgiving national holidays."

President Templeton snorted. "Maybe Grant just liked days off and to party? He supposedly liked to take a drink or two. Or maybe the Founding Fathers were too busy for the first century or so to worry about national days off?"

The Keep nodded. "Possibly. But contrary to popular myth, Grant was not a great imbiber of alcohol in quantity. He simply had no tolerance for alcohol. So when he did drink, the results were, shall we say, not fortunate for him. As far as Christmas in the White House, Abigail Adams threw the first Christmas party here and it was quite the smash."

The president was slouched in a chair in the solarium on the third floor of the White House, the uppermost level, while the Keep sat at a large round table, a large, leather-bound book in front of her. The president's Secret Service detail was one floor below, quite irritated not to be on the same level even though they also had two guys on the roof, as always.

Somehow the Keep was able to overrule even the Secret Service inside the White House. Which made the president suspect there was more to her than just taking care of the big book. But in four years, he'd never seen her do anything except occasionally brief him on incidents that the covert world she represented dealt with. Incidents that never had After Action Reports typed up on computers, or paper; only verbal briefings, one on one. Incidents that didn't even make the Top Secret daily intel briefing. Incidents that scared the shit out of him and caused him to take more Xanax than he probably should.

"Adams was from Boston," Templeton said. "I thought they were all uptight hard-asses, like General Riggs."

"Not Abigail," the Keep said, making it sound entirely plausible that she was on a first-name basis with a long-dead First Lady. "She threw a great party."

The Keep did not look the part. Midthirties, pale skin, with short dark hair. Athletic, slender build, and just barely over five feet tall. It was easy to see how she was rarely noticed. Templeton didn't even know her name, only her title and first name, Elle, which no one used but was on her ID badge with Keep as her last name.

She'd been important the first month he was in office, and she was important in this last month, but for the rest of the four years, he had no idea what she did except for the incident briefings. Apparently she also brushed up on White House history. The last time he'd seen her was six weeks ago, giving him the summary on a Rift incident in North Carolina. The very existence of Rifts and Fireflies was just one of several secrets she'd briefed him on when he took office.

She had a tiny office down the center hall on this floor, where a cluster of the staff worked. Now that he reflected on it, Templeton realized he'd never seen her office. In fact, there were a few rooms in the White House he'd only glimpsed on the quick tour four years ago.

Templeton shook his head as the sound of the preparations rose through the floors below. Even here in this private sanctum they heard the clamor of hammers banging and voices shouting. "Does it have to be such a big deal? The money could be better spent in other ways."

The Keep shrugged, such goings-on of little consequence to her. "Christmas at the White House has evolved into what it is with each administration adding their own special touch."

It had indeed. As the decades and centuries rolled by, Christmas at the White House grew from Abigail Adams throwing a great party (according to the Keep) to an elaborate, drawn-out affair lasting from Thanksgiving through New Year's, so significant that there was a year-round full-time staffer planning the event.

She probably had an office next door to the Keep, the president mused, and like a holiday vampire only rose at the appropriate time of year.

This year, the last in President Templeton's term, the holidays had an added urgency to it, a feeling not quite of desperation but perhaps resignation. Christmas in the big house for a lame-duck president is an awkward event for the First Family, knowing they're going to get the boot in less than a month. Why put up decorations when you're going to be packing everything in a few weeks? Most people wouldn't do it, but most people weren't the First Family and subject to the obligations of tradition and the expectations of the "people," whoever they might be.

"Do you think the treaty lost me the election?" Templeton asked. He was putting off the task the Keep was here for, but in reality, he was actually putting off going downstairs to the chaos of the preparations and the meeting with the press in the Entrance Hall in front of the tree. He could expect to be barraged with questions about the treaty, not good old St. Nick. And, of course, he also didn't want to face the demands of the Oval Office over in the West Wing.

The Keep spread her hands, long slender fingers covering the book that was the purpose of this meeting. The Keep had started the meeting by asking him simply: "Tell me what you learned here."

And he'd laughed and said: "Like what did I do during the summer?"

She had not laughed. "Lessons learned, to be passed down the line."

And he'd had to begin to dredge up memories, many bad, a few good.

The Keep answered his question. "Your opponent did a good job of equating the treaty with being soft, Mister President. Of caving in."

Someone telling the truth. That was a rarity in this building, Templeton thought. But the Keep had nothing to gain or lose by doing so, unlike most others that surrounded him. When he and his administration went packing, she would still be here, dumping on the next poor schmuck who had "won" his job.

"I think it was the name," he said.

A furrow of confusion crossed her forehead. "Name, sir?"

"My middle name. Armstrong. What do you think of when you hear it?"

"Neil Armstrong, sir. First on the moon."

"Ah yes, the little hop, as my wife once called it in one of her fouler moods while we were watching the Discovery Channel. It takes a lot to impress her. But that's not how my opponent played it. Armstrong. Middle name. Just like you know who, who got it at Little Bighorn. How can they make that leap, then leap to the treaty leading us into another massacre? And, of course there's Lance Armstrong. And what that's about, I have no idea. There's absolutely no connection."

"There rarely is with politics, Mister President," she said. "Human beings, while irrational, are predictably irrational. In fact, note how you went from hop to leap without consciously realizing it?"

Templeton laughed. "How come you weren't working on my campaign?"

She tapped the book on the table, drawing them back to task. "I have a job, sir."

Templeton straightened up in the chair and sighed. "You know, you scared the heck out of me that first month when you briefed me here, in this same room, with that damn book of yours. And not just the top ten lessons learned by every president, but all the rest. Especially the stuff about the Rifts and the Fireflies and the other near disasters."

"I'm sorry, Mister President. I didn't mean to."

"You know what I call you in my head," he said. "I call you the Heartbreaker."

She nodded. "Your predecessor came to the same conclusion, and I understand all previous Keeps have been called the same in one form or another. We prefer realists."

"I couldn't even tell Helen or my chief of staff how you broke my heart and turned me into a liar for so many of my campaign promises. You and that damn book hog-tied me long before I got to this point of being a lame duck." He shifted in the chair and stared her in the eye. "Do you know why they call it a lame duck?" He could tell she knew, but he didn't care. This was his chance to bitch and by God he was gonna take it. "Birds molt a few feathers here and there, but ducks drop them all at once like a dirty bathrobe and have to sit around naked and vulnerable because they can't fly for weeks. We should have a duck as the national bird, not an eagle."

"Would you like me to write that down, sir?" she asked, and he knew she wasn't jerking his chain. It was her job.

"Very funny." He looked about, because he could use a drink. "Heck, Franklin fought against using the eagle as the symbol of our country, didn't he?"

The Keep nodded. "Yes. He called the eagle a bird of bad moral character that did not make his living honestly. That an eagle was a carrion bird, which isn't quite true as an absolute. He wanted the turkey as our national bird."

"You know," he added as he spotted nothing to drink in the room, "if I'd been reelected I was going to switch to pot. Easier on the liver. Enough states have made it legal. What the heck? Don't drink, smoke pot. You can write that one down."

The Keep smiled. "What a good idea. We've lost too many fine men and women to the bottle."

"And a few bastards," the president said. "McCarthy drank himself to death after losing to the army in his hearing. I remember there was a section in there from Ike about how, in retrospect, he'd realized he'd handled McCarthy the wrong way. Should have squashed him like a bug right from the start. What do you think of that?"

"I don't judge or evaluate, sir. I just copy it down."

"No," the president said in a sharper tone than he intended. "After you copy it down, you read it to the next poor sap who inherits this house and shit on his head. Then you copy down what he's learned four years later for the next poor sap."

"It's efficient," the Keep said. "It preserves institutional knowledge."

He stared into her deep blue eyes, so full of intelligence and a keen quickness that bothered him in a way he couldn't define. "You should brief anyone who thinks they want to get the nomination from either party. I bet it would send some home before they even got started."

"That wouldn't be secure, sir."

"So you trust all the former presidents to never speak of these things or write about them in their memoirs?"

"Will you, sir?"

"No."

The Keep seemed to take that as sufficient answer to his own question. "You are joining a very unique club, sir. It's why former presidents get along better than most people expect. You share something very special."

"And you share it with no one." It was not a question. "Why does the Keep have to be a woman?"

"We've learned that men respond better to women bearing bad news, sir. Less testosterone and less desire for the alpha to be right, regardless of cost."

"Now that the new president is a woman, are you losing your job, too?"

"No, sir. She'll have to resign herself to me like you did, until I pass the job along."

"So are you a duck?"

"No, sir. I'm an eagle. I always hold on to a few feathers. No pun intended," she added, quill in hand.

"That's the funniest thing you've said," the president noted, "and it's not that funny. You might be considered carrion, feeding off my dead carcass now that the country has discarded me."

To that, the Keep had nothing to say.

"How many presidents have you served?"

"You're the second, sir."

"How'd you get this job?" he asked.

"I was selected, sir."

"By who? My predecessor? Your predecessor?"

"No, sir."

Templeton waited for amplification, but the Keep only seemed a font of information regarding history and secrets. He was so sick of it all.

"Who selected you?" he pressed.

The Keep's face showed the tiniest glimmer of . . . was it irritation, the president wondered?

"Hannah chose me."

"Of course," the president said. "Who else but her." It too was not a question. "How on earth does she find someone like you with the weird combination of knowing just about everything and reading the secrets in that book but having no desire to tell anyone?"

"It's Hannah's gift to find people with certain talents, sir."

"And how do you get replaced?"

"I don't know, sir. It's on the last page of the book if I feel a need to replace myself."

"You haven't read it?" he asked in surprise.

"No." She seemed genuinely confused. "Why would I read it? It's to be read when I need to replace myself if need be."

"What if you get hit by a bus?"

"There's always Hannah, sir." She shook her head, as if trying to figure out how to explain something to an ignorant child. "What you've never understood, Mister President, as no president before you has ever really understood, although some came close, is that the United States of America is like a finely tuned engine. It runs because there are those who maintain it in the shadows, on the inside. For my part, we run on information. We take it in, we give it out."

"And the Cellar takes action when need be. Sanctions."

She frowned that he even dared mention the name and the term, even here in the sanctity of the White House. "We have operatives who take action at Hannah's directive."

"But you're not one of those operatives?"

"I keep the book, sir."

Templeton got up. He walked to the table and took the book, turning it to face him, and looked down on a page where the Keep had been writing in longhand, adding Templeton's comments to its contents. "The Book of Truths. Really torpedoes campaign promises and lofty goals when you walk in the room and lay it out."

"It doesn't have to, sir," the Keep said. "It just makes the world real."

"Same thing. Blew Kennedy's missile gap right out of the water when he read the truth about the numbers in this book. There was a gap all right, but it was the opposite of what the Pentagon and the CIA and the defense industry was telling everyone."

"It was the truth," the Keep said. "It helped him make the right choices during the Missile Crisis."

Templeton shook his head. "This shouldn't be called the Book of Truths. It should be the Book of Secrets. Why don't we just publish the thing and let the American public know all the truths in it?" He didn't wait for, or expect, an answer. "That's why they're secrets."

There was a loud crash from downstairs and voices raised in alarm.

The president headed for the door. "'What fresh hell is this?'" he quoted. "Shakespeare always had a good line for any occasion."

"It's not Shakespeare," the Keep informed him as he left the room to investigate. "Dorothy Parker."

"Great," the president muttered. "Can't even let me get Shakespeare right."

Just a minute earlier, Debbie Templeton had bolted from her Secret Service limo and darted into the Entrance Hall, two stories below where her father was. She immediately ran into some stewards who were carrying boxes of ornaments that flew out of their arms and onto the pink and white marble floor. The sound of breaking glass and ceramic filled the hall, followed by gasps of dismay from both stewards.

One of them fell to his knees, as if he could magically reassemble that which had been broken beyond repair. "They're so old and precious!"

"Irreplaceable," the other steward said in shock.

"Precious?" Debbie hissed in her best Gollum imitation. She shifted to her regular voice. "What the hell is wrong with you? They're just balls of glass. Balls like your balls, if you had any." She found this quite amusing and cackled maniacally.

This trumped the broken ornaments and the entire Entrance Hall froze in shock: the stewards touching up the decorations on the towering tree that dominated the room (adding ornaments from the states of a delegation of congressmen coming later in the day, pulling ones from states not represented), the carpenters adding to the gingerbread house display (produce from same states being featured, removing said produce from same nonrepresented states), and the waitstaff cleaning up after a reception for some group and preparing for the next.

Never a dull moment.

"Debbie!" The First Lady's voice was pitched in a tone everyone recognized. She strode across the hall like she owned it instead of borrowing it for four years. She gripped Debbie's upper arm in a vise grip and hauled her out of the hall and toward the State Dining Room, cutting a hard right and shoving her into the elevator. The door shut before the First Lady's own two Secret Service guards could enter, so they sprinted up the stairs next to the elevator.

Inside the elevator, Helen Templeton pressed her daughter against the wall. "What has gotten into you?"

Debbie was laughing and crying at the same time, which basically made her a mess. She started blubbering. "Brennan, Mom. They took Brennan away. He cheated on me."

"He cheated on you? Who took him away?" Mrs. Templeton handled the statements in her view of the order of priority.

"In high school! That's why we didn't go to the prom. He got a blowjob. From Mary McCarthy of all people. Can you believe that?"

The elevator doors opened on the top level revealing the president, the Keep standing behind him, thick leather book in her arms, and farther in the distance the aide with the football. Seconds later, two winded Secret Service agents came dashing out of the stairwell to their right.

"I always knew that boy was no good," the First Lady said.

"Oh, Helen, give the girl a break," the president said instinctively. "What boy? Brennan?"

"You don't even know what's going on," the First Lady snapped at him. She spotted the Keep in the background. "What's *she* doing here?"

The First Lady had gone on a purge the first months in the White House and any woman she considered attractive, aka a threat, was banished from the main residence. She'd forgotten about the Keep, whom she'd added to the list. Everyone, it seemed, forgot about the Keep.

It was also why a female officer never carried the football, something the president hadn't noticed.

The president ignored his wife and removed her hand from his daughter's arm. "What's wrong, dear?"

Debbie collapsed into his arms, heaving with sobs, yet bursts of laughter poked through. "Brennan. He always accused me of sleeping with that stupid quarterback who cheated off me all senior year. Turns out he was the one who cheated. And all these years he'd been putting that on me. How shitty is that?" Just as quickly, her mind jumped tracks as she looked over her shoulder at her mother. "Do you think you have enough Botox, Mom? Really? For God's sake, you haven't been able to smile in years."

"Debbie," her father said.

"What are Rifts?" Debbie asked. "Fireflies? Bren seemed upset about them. More secrets?"

In the background, the Keep was startled, which meant she clenched her left fist tight and dug her fingernails in to prevent showing any sign of being startled.

"And Pinnacle?" Debbie said. "He said something about Pinnacle?"

The president swallowed, ignored the questions, and misdirected, the way four years of dealing with the White House Press Corps had taught him. "I don't care how upset you are, that's no way to talk to your mother."

Debbie pushed out of his arms and looked at him. "You're not much better. Look at all the makeup you have on."

"I have to address the press and the cameras wash you out so—" Templeton began to explain what he knew she already knew, but she cut him off by placing her hands on his face and trying to rub off the fake rose on his cheeks.

"Stop that!" Helen cried out. "It took that girl"—the First Lady rarely remembered any of the staff's names, relying on "that girl" or "that guy"—"twenty minutes to do your father's face."

"I'm calling the doctor," the president said as he gripped Debbie's hands and pulled them away. Several Secret Service agents hovered in the background, uncertain what to do. Was this a threat to the First Family from the First Family, or was this a family squabble? Who, exactly, were they to protect from whom?

Their job sucked.

"Yes!" Debbie screeched, struggling against him. He was so surprised he let go. "Call the doctor," Debbie continued, "and have him check out this loon you married."

"I won't stand for this!" the First Lady snapped. "Who do you think you are? I know you're upset about Brennan and whatever he did, but it's hardly fair for you to attack us about it. I told you a long time ago to walk away from him."

Debbie ignored her. She looked at her father, perfectly calm for a moment. "Why did you marry her? She hates you, you know. She only cares about the power and she always wanted to live in this house and she saw you as the ticket. She helped get you here, but now what? What's she going to do for an encore?"

The president took a step back, as if the words hit him with physical force. He spotted the Keep standing there, observing, book in her arms, and he knew this escapade would probably fill half a page. That made him angry. Something about presidents not having been divorced and remarrying, although hadn't Reagan been married before Nancy?

He pointed at one of the agents, the female one. "You take care of her. Get her to the doctor. I've got a country to run and a press conference." With that, he stepped into the elevator and hit the down button, then the close button several times hard.

The doors swished shut and he was free of the scene.

"I've never seen you treat us this disrespectfully," Helen said mournfully, shaking her head sorrowfully, a nice show for the spectators. "It's rather sad, Debbie," she added, just in case no one had picked up the shake and tone.

"It's not sad," Debbie said. The female agent was at her side, reluctant to make a move. "You run this family like a corporation and you're the CEO and all that matters is your bottom line. The world according to Helen, and we all must bow to you."

Helen's face flushed red. "You prim tight-laced little bitch. You think I don't know exactly who you are and how you've tried to undermine me with your father since the day he brought me into his life? I've tolerated your condescension and little snips toward me since then, but not anymore. I will not stand for it!"

The Secret Service agents were swiveling their heads back and forth as if watching a really nasty tennis match with hard green exploding grenades instead of soft green bouncy balls.

Helen took a threatening step toward her stepdaughter, so threatening the female agent actually took up position in between them and got bumped by the First Lady into her daughter.

"I can't believe I didn't make him ship you off to boarding school!" Helen hissed. "Things would have been so much easier around here without you around."

Debbie blinked, stunned in a moment of clarity. A horrified look crossed her face. "Helen! How old are you?"

"I'm fifty-two. And what of it? I look forty."

"Oh my God," Debbie whispered, the fight gone out as awareness washed over her.

"What, you self-important whiny baby? You think I look older?"

"You've never told anyone your real age before," Debbie said. "Even when asked, you always change the subject."

"So what if I haven't?"

Debbie broke and ran for the stairs, screaming for her father, the Secret Service hot on her heels, all the while screaming: "We can't lie! We can't lie!"

They caught her just as she reached the top stair and it took three of them, one from her restaurant detail, to subdue her. All the while she protested: "You've got to stop him. You've got to stop my dad!"

Helen snapped her finger at another agent and he produced a cigarette and lighter, apparently well trained at the finger snap. She fired it up and regarded her stepdaughter. "You've gone over the edge now. Finally. When it does me no good."

The Secret Service guy from her detail shook his head as he looked into Debbie's eyes. "You look so sweet but I always thought you'd be a great lay."

Debbie stopped struggling. "We're all up shit creek now." And then she kissed him, lips full on, mouth open.

Helen laughed. "See. I always knew what you were. Just like me."

And in the background, the Keep had her special cell phone out and hit autodial one: her direct line to Hannah to inform her of the situation, part of which Hannah was already reacting to, the Cellar having intercepted the contain Protocol call from Upton earlier and the 666 call from Colonel Johnston at DORKA.

President Templeton walked past Chief of Staff Louis McBride without acknowledging him. He was in the Cross Hall en route to the Entrance Hall where he was to address a handpicked group of reporters in front of the Christmas tree about some bullshit—he couldn't remember what exactly—but the speech would be on the podium, carefully written and vetted by the worker bees in the West Wing. Just the thought of more Christmas bullshit made the president furious. Plus there was whatever the hell was up with Debbie. The day had begun bad and was continuing to get worse.

"What's wrong with your face, Mister President?" McBride asked, reaching out and trying to slow his charge. "You can't go out there looking like that."

The president pushed him aside and walked up to the podium, the tree looming behind him. He cleared his throat, glanced at the notes already in place on the podium. He picked them up, then tossed them away. He stared straight at the camera while McBride hovered just out of view. "My fellow Americans. You are so naive. Do you have any idea how difficult it is to deal with your total lack of understanding, your inability to process information, your willingness to believe whatever garbage some cable news channel spews out like so much—"

"Cut the feed!" McBride screamed. "Cut the feed!"

Except it had never been live.

Hannah's reach from her office deep underneath the National Security Agency was long and efficient.

"We're in lockdown! Security code bravo-tango-six-eight-two." The tall woman stalking down the Cross Hall emanated total command.

The Secret Service hesitated at the lack of recognition.

"Move, people!" Moms snapped, holding up one of her real fake badges. "Listen to the security code for the day! Bravo-tango-six-eight-two. Seal off the residence from both wings and the outside. NOW! We are in one hundred percent lockdown and isolation.

"We have a contagious pathogen loose in the White House. No one gets out!"

CHAPTER 10

Brennan had always thoughts tears would eventually run dry, but he had not stopped sobbing during the trip.

The Secret Service agents had whisked him to a helicopter with no markings at the helipad behind the White House. The chopper was waiting for them, blades turning. The smirker had shoved Brennan, still cuffed, out the door, causing him to fall facedown on the concrete. Two contractors, black balaclavas covering their faces, picked him up and tossed him in the back of the chopper. It lifted off immediately.

That was his first hint he was in more serious trouble than Debbie knowing about the blowjob he'd gotten from Mary McCarthy in the chem lab. He started to beg and they gagged him and put a black hood over his head. They were speaking to each other in some language he could only guess at but remembered from the interrogation room. They were on the radio and seemed concerned about something they were hearing.

After a flight of indeterminate length, but not overly long, during which Brennan's mind kept replaying over and over all the many mistakes he'd made and people he'd harmed, the helicopter landed. He was dragged off and hustled along through doors he could hear clanging into an elevator that dropped fast and far, then out of the elevator and through another door that slammed shut with a very solid thud.

One of those thuds that seemed to intimate the door would never, ever open again.

Between the thud and the screams and arguments echoing ahead in what was apparently a large chamber, Brennan knew he was in very, very deep shit.

Then there was also the burst of automatic weapon fire.

From helicopter to military jet with afterburners to Area 51, Nada had made it from LA to Nevada faster than a degenerate gambler snorting coke off a whore's ass on a private Learjet. At least that's the way Roland dissected it.

That it made little sense meant it was pure Roland. Everyone was very impressed that Roland knew the word *degenerate*, although Kirk privately bet Mac that Roland had no idea what it meant. Mac reminded him that Scout had used the term during the "Fun in North Carolina," and Kirk argued that still didn't mean Roland knew what it meant.

The rest of the team had come in on the Snake just before Nada landed on the Area 51 airstrip. The Snake was being refueled and they were mission prepping around the craft, waiting for Ms. Jones's voice to brief them on the mission, which was unusual.

Unusual in that they were at Area 51; unusual in that Moms wasn't with them; unusual in that they were waiting after an alert. Nightstalker Protocol, called Standing Operating Procedures elsewhere, was Nada's Bible. Every team member carried an acetate copy on their person. He had twenty-three items in the pre-op load Protocol. He'd erase the checks when they got back in order to be ready for the next mission.

Nada was busy making sure the team box in the cargo bay of the Snake was fully stocked, directing each man to check their part: Roland weapons; Mac demo and engineering; Kirk commo; and Doc medical.

Mac carried the heavy plastic demolitions case into the cargo bay and secured it next to the larger team box that stayed in the Snake at all times. That box held a wide variety of gear, from climbing ropes to arctic clothing to chemical/biological protection suits, parachutes, dry suits, spare radio batteries, two million in gold coins for barter, etc., etc.; someone with an extremely paranoid and inventive mind had packed it. And then repacked it. The contents changed slightly after every mission as they went through a detailed After Action Report.

Doc was checking his med kit, making sure everything was up to date.

Roland easily carried a machine gun in one hand and a Barrett .50-caliber sniper rifle in the other while his ruck bulged with ammunition for both, along with other deadly goodies. Roland slapped the machine gun into a mount that could extend when the back ramp went down. He slid the Barrett upright into a sheath along the forward bulkhead, then checked his MP5 submachine gun while Kirk dialed up the proper frequency, linked his PRT with the radio, and did a satcom check, locating the nearest Milstar satellite to bounce a signal off of. Then he found two backups, just in case. He updated the current set of codes.

All they knew was that there was no time to go back to the Ranch. Wherever they were going next, they were launching from Area 51.

"Better not be another nuke," Mac groused as he flipped shut his pocket-size team Protocol, satisfied his gear was ready. "So much for peace on earth."

"I bet it's not a Rift," Kirk said as he looked over the latest frequencies and security codes, which changed daily. He looked up at Doc. "Right? You're on top of everything that goes on in the Can," he added, referring to the device buried deep under their feet that gave warnings of a Rift beginning to form anywhere on the planet. Kirk had his suspicions about Doc's motivations regarding research into the Rifts, unsure what Doc's end game was.

"There has been no muonic activity," Doc said succinctly, zipping shut his med kit. "I called Ivar and he said everything is quiet."

"So it's not a Rift," Kirk said, over-making his point, but that was lost because they were all a half step off, being pulled in from the points of the compass where they'd just been and the unusual circumstances in which they'd been involved.

Eagle came walking up the ramp, satisfied the Snake was topped off. He gave a thumbs-up to Nada, who used his black felt-tip pen to make a check mark in his acetate Protocol. Those check marks accumulated until every box was checked and they were ready to lift and fly.

"Where's Moms?" Roland asked, frowning over the new M249 light machine gun resting on his lap. He missed his old one already. This one lacked the worn sheen of heavy action and hadn't been test fired, coming right out of the crate. That made Roland very uncomfortable, as if he were going on a first date with a virgin. He was hoping for some action but uncertain how good it was going to be and what the results might be.

"I don't know," Nada said. "All I got was the recall and nothing further." He looked at the other five. "Any of you hear *anything*?"

Five shakes of the head.

This too was unusual.

"Maybe she's at the Ranch getting briefed?" Kirk suggested.

"Then why are we waiting *here* to get briefed?" Nada asked. "We should be picking her up. Meeting at the Barn at least." He looked at Eagle. "You guys didn't come from the Barn, did you?"

Four sets of boots shuffled uneasily on the metal grating.

"What were you up to?" Nada asked.

The speaker above them crackled and they all looked up, even though there was nothing to see. Ms. Jones's voice crackled out. "They were up to no good. An indiscretion that will be dealt with later. Ms. Moms is in the White House." She quickly briefed them on the little that was known:

Cherry Tree. The president infected.

"Moms has containment at the White House," Ms. Jones concluded. "She's also done a good job on concealment."

"But what about overall?" Doc asked. "How is this thing spreading? It had to come from somewhere."

"It came from the DORKA facility in Virginia," Ms. Jones said. "How exactly it made the leap to the White House isn't clear yet."

"I can research it en route," Doc said. "If—"

Ms. Jones cut him off. "By the time you get to DC, it will be too late one way or the other. Moms has the White House under control and is working with the Secret Service to ensure containment and keep up concealment. The DORKA facility outside DC that originated the pathogen has been externally locked down, so that's contained."

"Fucking DORKA," Nada muttered. There were several entries in the Nightstalkers' Dumb Shit Scientist Protocol dealing with incidents initiated by a DORKA screwup somewhere in the world.

Ms. Jones either didn't hear or most likely pretended not to hear as she continued. "We're uncertain how it made the leap to the White House but we're checking on it. Another agency is also working on that."

Everyone in the cargo bay glanced at each other. They had a standing wager going whether there were other Nightstalker teams out there. If so, how come it always seemed this team got the crap missions? And then why were they being called in from leave? Then again, they knew there were other secret units who had different missions.

"If you don't need us for containment," Nada said, "what do you need us for?"

The Nightstalkers worked under the doctrine of the Three Cs:

Containment. The first priority was to always make sure whatever the problem was, it didn't spread.

Concealment. Keep the civilians, and in some cases the authorities, from knowing what was going on to avoid panic. Pretty much everything the Nightstalkers dealt with would cause panic if people found out about it. Nada always pointed out to each new team member the effect "War of the Worlds" had on citizens. And that was just a made-up show on radio. Nightstalkers dealt with the real shit.

And finally, Control. Which had three levels: damp, dry, and wet. Dry was something that could be contained and concealed without the need to destroy it. Damp was something to be contained, and maybe even studied, but the decision was always made to err on the side of caution, so damp usually went wet, which meant that whatever the problem was, it was to be utterly and completely destroyed.

Wet didn't seem to be an option in this case since destroying the pathogen meant wiping out everyone infected, from the president on down.

Ms. Jones continued. "The missile in Nebraska on your last mission. The 'Clusterfuck in Nebraska' as Mister Nada has so elegantly described it . . ." When Ms. Jones cursed, it didn't sound like a profanity. Perhaps because English was her second language, perhaps because she didn't put the proper emotional inflection in it. "It wasn't a simple oversight that left it there. We believe it was deliberately left in that silo."

Nada frowned at the *we*. Ms. Jones never talked in the plural, unless including the team.

"It also had two predetermined targets programmed in its guidance system back in 1962. Actually, it had a primary target before 1962, and then a secondary target was added that year."

They all waited, then finally Ms. Jones continued.

"One, of course, was Cuba. That was the one added. The primary target was where you are standing."

Roland looked down, a frown on his forehead. "The Snake?"

"Geez!" Mac exploded.

Roland poked a finger the size of a baton into the smaller man's chest. "Got you."

A flash of anger raced across Mac's face at being suckered by Roland, but he got it under control quickly.

"Who would target Area 51?" Nada asked, shaking his head at the two.

"That does not make sense," Doc added. "There are nuclear safeguards, a nice way of saying bombs, already in place here. A self-destruct sequence in case of a catastrophic event."

"Like an uncontrolled Rift," Kirk added, staring at Doc.

"Yes," Ms. Jones said, as if they were discussing the weather rather than nuclear weapons. "But that self-destruct is under my control."

"Fuck me to tears," Nada said as he realized the implications and Eagle articulated them.

"*D-O-D.*" Eagle said each letter clearly and with absolute certainty.

"Very astute, Mister Eagle. We have known for a long time that there was an element in the Department of Defense that has been secretly stockpiling nuclear warheads. Whether taking ones slated to be destroyed or acquiring them by other means. The first known incident where we became suspicious was in 1950."

"The first nuke that went missing in Canada," Eagle said. "Off that B-36."

"Correct. Your predecessors, on one of the early teams, jumped into Canada and investigated. They never found a trace of the bomb but they did suspect that someone got there before them. As if the entire thing were planned and someone was waiting for that bomb to be dumped and that plane to go down."

"Ten more warheads have been lost since then," Eagle said. "At least that's the official count."

"We believe they were not all lost," Ms. Jones said.

"Are there other missiles in other silos aimed here?" Kirk asked.

"We don't know," Ms. Jones said. "We believe there is a central stockpile of most of these warheads."

"It does not make sense," Doc said. "That missile was sealed in. It couldn't have fired."

"We believe this program, code-named Pinnacle, has been so covered and compartmentalized that they've actually lost track of some of their own secrets over the years. Some secrets die with those who hold them tightest."

That might have sounded crazy to a normal person, but to the Nightstalkers, so immersed in the covert world, it had the perfect ring of logic to it.

"'Three may keep a secret if two of them are dead,'" Eagle quoted.

"Didn't Moms say that?" Roland asked.

"Benjamin Franklin," Eagle corrected.

Nada, once again, more familiar with Ms. Jones than any of the others, sensed uncertainty on her part. An unwillingness to cut to the chase. "If we're not joining Moms in DC, and we're not going to the DORKA facility, can I assume we're going after this stockpile?"

"You assume correctly."

"And where, exactly, is it?" Nada asked.

"I don't know yet. But we're working on it."

We again, thought Nada. This was bigger than the Night-stalkers.

CHAPTER 11

The person who was supposed to find out that information was on board a Nighthawk helicopter, flying around Washington, DC, toward Pennsylvania. Neeley was seated in the back, peering at an iPad screen, scrolling through the scant amount of information Hannah had managed to forward her about Deep Six. An Asset was sitting next to Neeley, pointing at images, diagrams, and maps as they came up. He filled her in on what he knew about Raven Rock, having been stationed there for six years in the signal battalion that manned the main facility.

Where Hannah had found him on such short notice didn't matter. It was what Hannah did. Hannah had also made sure a duffel bag full of gear was waiting on the floor of the chopper along with the iPad.

The Asset came to a halt as the scrolling did, when they were somewhere over Frederick, Maryland.

"You've never been inside Deep Six?" Neeley asked.

"No one I know has been inside their vault door other than the contractors. Those guys are crazy. No one messes with them." He shook his head. "You're never going to be able to breach the security at the Rock in the first place."

"I'm not going to."

The Asset pointed at the iPad. "I can show you where the ventilation shafts are. You might be able to—"

"Why would I want that information?" Neeley asked as she opened up the duffel bag, revealing all sorts of weapons and war gear.

"To get in. As I said, security is very tight. Lots of armed guards at all the entrances to Raven Rock." The Asset had seen too many *Mission: Impossible* movies.

"I'm not worried about getting in the main facility," Neeley said. "Raven Rock, the overall facility, is run by the Department of Defense, correct?"

The Asset nodded.

"Then I can get in," Neeley said as she considered the various "covers" she had and which was best to deal with a DOD facility.

"They closed Fort Ritchie," the Asset said, "which used to be the supervising post for Raven Rock."

"Who is Deep Six's higher command?" Neeley asked.

The Asset frowned. "I don't think Deep Six has a higher command; they definitely didn't fall under the military. I'm not even sure the CIA has a handle on those people. It's all foreigners. They never mingled with us. We provided logistic support as required but no one I know ever went inside and I never saw anyone come from DOD or any government agency to check on it."

Neeley had suspected as much. Deep Six was a top-secret facility inside of a secret facility, and to ensure deniability no one wanted command of it. After Abu Ghraib, no military officer in their right mind would want to be anywhere near this. And the CIA had Guantanamo, which allowed them to do as they pleased in Cuba. But here, on US soil, deniability ruled.

"Deep Six is in what used to be the old reservoir, right?" Neeley said.

The Asset nodded.

"Let me see those schematics again. It's a prison. It's designed to keep people from getting out, not getting in."

Secure in his office, Colonel Johnston watched on screen what had gone from groping to a complete, naked orgy down in the lab.

It was not a pretty sight watching a bunch of scientists go at it with their deepest and darkest fantasies freed of inhibition.

Upton had joined in. Johnston shook his head in disgust. They all had nothing to lose down there. There was a good chance they might get wiped out when whoever was on the other end of the 666 line got here. It *was* why they all got paid the big bucks.

But not Johnston. He got O-6 pay, straight up.

He turned off the monitor.

All his outside lines were dead, but not before he'd learned that Brennan had been taken to Deep Six, and it was highly likely the First Daughter and General Riggs were infected.

Who knew how far Cherry Tree would blossom?

There was no doubt that the cutoff was the result of the 666 call. DORKA was in external lockdown and when it was unlocked after Cherry Tree burned out here, he was going to be the one in the line of fire. He wore the rank, he was responsible. He'd lived his life by that code.

The White House.

The Pentagon.

This was bad.

Johnston hit the button on the side of his pistol, ejecting the magazine.

He knew he'd never make O-7, get that star. When he'd been given this assignment, running herd on a bunch of geeks, it was implicit. This was a dead-end, an end-of-the-career, get-ready-for-retirement slot.

All the years he'd given the army and this was his reward. To be undone by a bunch of geeks who'd never seen a day of combat.

Johnston took off his coat and carefully hung it on the hanger on the back of his locked door.

Johnston pulled open one of his drawers. He pulled out a single 9mm round.

He'd saved it for more than two decades, from the First Gulf War.

He laughed bitterly over the fact that it was now called the *first*. What had been the point if they'd had to go back and do it all over again?

This bullet had been in his pistol when he'd left his company CP to take a leak during the heady days when they had the Iraqis on the run.

But not all of the Iraqis had run.

A kid in an ill-fitting uniform, maybe seventeen, but no more, had run into the alley with just a bayonet in hand.

Dick still hanging out, piss dribbling, Johnston had drawn the pistol, finger on the trigger, but not been able to pull it.

It was just a kid. But he kept coming, screaming something, bayonet glinting.

Johnston had still been frozen when the kid stabbed him, knife sliding off the body armor covering his chest and slicing into his arm, causing him to drop the pistol. As the kid stabbed him again, this time in the gut, just below the end of the armor, Johnston had finally reacted, grabbed a piece of cinder block and swinging it, hitting the kid in the head, stunning him.

Then he'd kept swinging until the kid wasn't moving anymore, his head a bloody pulp.

Johnston had slumped against the wall, bleeding from two stab wounds, the kid's mangled head cradled in his arms, weeping. For how long he'd never known, but it couldn't have been long, because he was able to finally compose himself, stand up, zip up, and make it back to his CP, blood dripping from his wounds and his chest and face drenched in the kid's.

Johnston looked over at the rows and rows of medals lining the jacket chest.

He'd gotten the Purple Heart for the knife wounds and the Bronze Star for killing an enemy combatant in hand-to-hand combat. He still remembered an interesting tidbit about medals, although he could no longer recall the source: Napoleon was credited with inventing the modern version of medals, pieces made of ribbon and metal, awarded for bravery. In medieval days, bravery was rewarded in real terms—with land, with riches, with titles that were worth something. But now a man was supposed to be satisfied with just a piece of cloth?

Of course, it wasn't that simple. It was what the cloth represented.

Johnston stared at the two ribbons at the top of several rows of awards.

What exactly did they represent?

He hadn't thought of that incident in Iraq in years. Not consciously. A secret buried deep inside, in the depth of his soul, that he'd wanted no one to ever know about, least of all himself.

It was a visceral revulsion of himself.

The truth.

He pulled back the slide on the pistol that locked it and dropped the bullet in the chamber. Then he hit the release, slamming the receiver in place.

Loading it.

Locked and loaded.

Johnston got up and turned the uniform jacket around, hiding the medals.

Then he put the gun to his temple.

His military aide had stomped out in a huff because General Riggs had just told him he was the most worthless human being ever and to find Brennan. It was strange that Riggs had told the full-bird colonel off like that because, like all aides, he was something important to someone important (a nephew, an important wife, holder of some good blackmail) and that mattered more than if they could do the job.

Still it was kind of funny that Riggs had finally bothered to tell him what he'd always thought. Outside of that aide who had been foisted upon him, every member of Riggs's inner circle was intensely loyal to him, owing their careers to his rising star. As he went, so went they. They also shared his philosophy that the military needed to be given a freer rein to deal with the problems in the world, that the civilians could fuck up a soup sandwich.

Let the aide sulk. That just proved the point that he was useless, taking things personally. The damn idiot was an aide to the vice chairman of the JCS. Didn't he realize his ticket was already punched by some rabbi somewhere who had the strings to get him that job? Riggs might be number two in the Department of Defense but he knew who controlled the purse strings and also knew who got the lucrative contracts and could offer jobs to retiring generals to make lots of money.

The game was rigged, and it disgusted Riggs, but like the Robert Heinlein quote hanging on his wall said, "Certainly the game is rigged. Don't let that stop you; if you don't bet, you can't win."

The key, of course, was that each man's idea of winning was different. Money, unlike most people, interested Riggs not in the slightest.

Riggs prided himself that he'd never been anyone's aide. He'd worked his way to this position. He was a good soldier and a smart soldier, meaning he did the damn job, not aided someone else to do it. Although, technically, he was number two to the chairman, Riggs was the one who did the real work.

Like the whole Cherry Tree thing. Think the chairman would go within a mile of that?

His intercom crackled. "Sir?" The terse inquiry still emanated hurt feelings.

Fucking loser, Riggs thought. "What?"

"I've got news. It's important."

"Get in here."

Riggs shoved the last bit of candy bar into his mouth as the door opened and the colonel rushed in.

"The White House is in lockdown!"

It didn't occur to him to ask the first question most normal people would ask: Why? "What about the Emergency Operations Center?"

The aide shook his head. "Just the main building. They've cut off the East and West Wings. The only news came from

McBride—something about a surprise emergency exercise by the Secret Service to test the security system."

"Bullshit. Where's Brennan?"

"The Secret Service took him into custody after he attacked the president's daughter."

Riggs smiled. "Finally grew a pair, did he?"

But that was also a preemptive strike, he suddenly realized.

It was adding up. They were coming after him. Locking the president in and coming after the only man who could save the country.

"Who's got the football right now?"

The aide blinked. "Sir?"

"The Duty, dammit." Said that way, with a capital *D*, got through to the aide.

"Major Preston, sir."

Riggs nodded. "Good, good. He's a good man. Reliable and knows his priorities. He's one of ours. Where's the vice president?"

"With the chairman, sir, in Scotland, working on SAD."

"So no one's in charge."

"Sir, the—"

"Get my car. Assemble the staff. We're going to the PEOC."

"Sir, we—"

Riggs fixed the man with a withering stare and he scurried to get the car.

Riggs hefted himself, with difficulty, out of his chair.

Time to face his destiny.

He opened his drawers and pulled out what he would need: his pistol, a copy of the Constitution, a Bible, and four Snickers bars.

Once Moms got them moving and they understood the threat was a pathogen, the Secret Service inside the White House reacted with precision and alacrity. The corridors leading to the East and West Wings were sealed. All doors leading in and out were also shut just after the two agents who'd dumped Brennan at the helipad returned. The president, along with the First Lady and First Daughter, had been hustled upstairs to the private residence, all shouting at each other.

It seemed the First Family had a lot of unresolved issues.

"What about tunnels?" Moms asked McBride, who seemed to be the one who knew who did what here.

"We've shut all the doors below," McBride said. "I've got an agent on each one. The head of the Secret Service is outside and he's got people in hazmat right up against the building on an interior line and then an exterior line working both ways. What the hell is going on?"

Moms took a deep breath. The building was secure for the time being, and McBride had issued a cover story for concealment about a no-notice security exercise. How long that cover story would last, she had no idea. There were a lot of people milling about, at a loss what to do now that the routine of preparing for Christmas at the White House had been interrupted.

And the president and his family had apparently gone insane.

They'd lined everyone up and made them dump cell phones and any other communication devices into a large barrel. All trunk lines in and out were shut off. Complete blackout.

"Get these people occupied doing something," Moms said to McBride.

"Hold on," McBride said. "What's wrong with the president? I need to know what is going on."

So Moms spent two minutes and twelve seconds telling him about Cherry Tree and that somehow it was loose here in the White House. The color drained from McBride's face when she told him what Cherry Tree did: A politician's worst nightmare had just been thrust in his face.

"You mean he can't lie?" McBride asked when she was done.

"From what I understand, it's worse than that," Moms said. "Whoever is infected can't stop telling the truth. And the problem is we don't know how many people in here have been infected. You need to quarantine anyone who has had physical contact with the First Family. His daughter brought it in here, so start with her."

McBride shook his head. "That's not going to be easy."

McBride turned to the crowd of Secret Service agents, stewards, staffers, media reps, chefs, maintenance personnel, and others who were now trapped inside and began to try to make sense of this insanity as they backtracked to the moment Debbie Templeton left her lunch with Brennan and entered the White House. Each person he thought she might have had physical contact with was hustled into the State Dining Room.

But Moms was focused elsewhere, also trying to stay physically distant from everyone. A woman was sitting in a chair near the staircase up to the residence. She'd been hovering near the president when Moms interrupted the already cut-off news conference. The woman seemed quite detached from all the turmoil tornadoing around her. From the appearance of the chair it was supposed to be one that was admired, not sat in. The fact this woman felt secure enough to do that said something on top of her lack of alarm.

She had a large leather-bound book on her lap. It reminded Moms of her mother's photo albums. The ones with the little black corners holding everything together. As the chief of staff tried to put a lid on a pot inside the White House that was beginning to boil with Cherry Tree, Moms wondered how different it was now that pictures all seemed to be on hard drives or in the cloud, not tangible, not in a book like real memories. It made memories seem less real.

As Moms made her way around the crowd toward the woman, she considered the fact that people probably still made scrapbooks, even if they were electronic and could be wiped out with the flash of EMP from a nuke. (Nebraska wasn't that far away in her own memory scrapbook.)

Her mother's scrapbook had been full of pictures of her brothers, all younger, all of whom were now leading normal lives—doctor, salesman, actuary, and the youngest taking over the farm. Moms had never really considered that there were no pictures of her in that scrapbook. Did that mean she didn't exist?

Moms could make out more as she got closer. The woman wore a nondescript business suit and had the tag on the chain around her neck that everyone else who belonged here had. The color indicated the highest security clearance.

The woman was too aware, yet detached at the same time. It took one to know one, and Moms had a good idea this woman came from the same dark world she did. Moms didn't like people with their own agenda on her mission. This woman was up to something and it most likely wasn't the same thing Moms was up to, so therefore she was a potential problem.

Moms stopped in front of her and the woman stood, book clutched to her chest. Exactly the way suicide bombers almost always took off their bomb-laden backpacks and clutched them to their chest before pulling the fuse. It was a level to which Freud had not dared go, clutching that which meant life and death closest to your core, your heart.

"What are you doing in the middle of my op?" Moms asked.

The woman smiled. "You must be Moms."

It wasn't the smile that relaxed Moms slightly; it was the way her eyes matched the smile. Nada always said, "watch the eyes." Moms had been face-to-face with lots of dangerous people and those who wished her harm, and this woman was neither.

Not directly. But she was something and Moms needed to know what that was.

And she knew her Nightstalker name, which was a bit disconcerting.

The woman, Elle Keep, her nametag said, was still a problem, but probably not a dangerous one. A loose thread in a big building full of loose threads. Moms needed to cut this one or reel it in so she could move on to the next one. That plan unraveled with the woman's next words:

"It's *my* mission. Even better, and more professionally, we could call it *our* mission."

Nada watched the eyes, but Moms had another way to evaluate. She looked down at the woman's shoes. Shoes told you a lot about a person. These were expensive but functional. Which meant she knew how to fit in, but also how to be practical.

"What's *our* mission, Elle?" Moms asked.

The woman shook her head. "Call me Keep."

Frak me, Moms thought. "Keep?"

"More correctly, *the* Keep. I'm from the Cellar. I always wondered if I'd ever meet a Nightstalker. I wondered, but hoped not to because of the circumstances that would be inherent in such a meeting." The Keep looked past Moms at the media people screaming about their rights to the chief of staff and two chefs on the marble floor wrestling because they had finally let loose on each other about whose dessert POTUS liked better. "But I certainly could not have imagined this."

"We usually can't imagine most of our missions," Moms said as she processed *Cellar*. Mac had always bet the under, saying it was a myth. Sort of the way people in Black Ops always said, "I thought you guys were doing that!" and the other person said, "No, we thought you were doing it!" But everyone always hoped there was something like the Cellar, which really was supposed to be doing "it." Because "it" needed to be done.

"Good point," the Keep said. "You work for Ms. Jones, and I hate to be rude, but she works for Hannah. As do I."

Nada wins again, Moms thought. "And what does the Keep do?"

The Keep rolled her fingers on the book she held so tight. "This book. I know you have to keep containment here and I don't want to be an inconvenience, but above all, we must protect this book. It's more important than the president."

CHAPTER 12

The Secret Service that had been on duty was holding a perimeter, keeping the main building secure. Inside of them, a cordon of security in hazmat suits was at every possible exit: doors, windows, underground tunnels. As Cherry Tree blossomed inside, the uniformed senior officer outside, confused but resolute, kept the line. He'd called in everyone on the roster and also had the members of the Tactical Response Team doing an exercise around the House for the sake of the media that had gathered outside.

It was a ruse that would only last so long, but now that information was starting to clarify on Cherry Tree, it was a ruse that only needed to last so long.

Then, as always, things got worse.

General Riggs's convoy pulled up to the rear of the White House. His armored limo rode heavy, followed by five black Chevy SUVs with tinted windows. Riggs's staff piled out and the general bulled his way forward, halting just short of the senior Secret Service agent.

"Sir, we're conducting a security training exercise and—"

"Bullshit," Riggs said. "What's really going on?"

"Sir, we're conducting a security training exercise—"

"I'm the vice chairman of the Joint Chiefs of Staff," Riggs said. "The chairman is in Scotland. That makes me the ranking military officer in the country. I have the highest security clearance in the country. What is going on?"

The senior agent did his best. "Sir, it's a confusing situation, but the White House is in lockdown because some sort of pathogen is loose. We don't believe it's fatal or even physically harmful, but information is still coming in on it."

"We've been attacked." Riggs said it with absolute certainty. "The White House has been attacked and we've been decapitated by a biological attack."

The Secret Service agent shook his head. "No, sir. I don't think so, sir."

"You're not paid to think," Riggs said. "You're not paid to command. I am."

A reporter who had been lurking outside the barriers shoved against a couple of agents and shouted, "General! What's going on? Who's running the government? If this is an exercise, where is the president?"

Riggs paused dramatically, feeling his destiny welling up in his chest, and turned to face the reporter. "There's no need for alarm. As for now, I'm in control now and will be until we can"—he held up a meaty fist with the rolled-up copy of the Constitution in it—"make sure things are running smoothly again. That is"—he said—"pending the return of the White House . . ." But fuck that, it wasn't true. "Gentlemen," he said to no one in particular, but everyone within earshot, "I am in charge."

He turned and strode toward the East Wing, his staff crowded around him. The head of the Secret Service watched them walk away, then turned to the reporter.

"It's all part of the exercise," he assured the confused man. Then he returned his attention to his priority: the building containing the president.

Riggs burst into the Visitors Foyer, noted the blocked doors to his right and the Secret Service guards, and turned left, down the East Colonnade. He went past the Family Theater (and they gave the military shit about waste?) toward the East Wing of the White House, the lesser known of the two flanks. It contained the First Lady's offices, *like anyone gives a rat's ass about that bitch*, Riggs thought as he waddled into the main corridor. It also had the calligraphy office, because that was the way they ran shit over here with their sense of priorities.

A military guard stood at the entrance to the elevator that led to the PEOC: the Presidential Emergency Operations Center. Most people knew about the Situation Room under the West Wing where the Oval Office was, but the PEOC was the real deal. Where the commander in chief would go when the shit hit the fan. Where the armed forces of the United States could be commanded and controlled.

Except the shit had hit the fan and as far as Riggs could tell, the president was cowering over in the Residence.

The marine on duty at the elevator popped to attention and snapped a salute. Riggs acknowledged him by tipping the Constitution to the brim of his cap. As many of his staff as possible (not many, given his girth) crowded in with him; the rest would have to wait for the next ride.

The PEOC had been built during World War II for President Roosevelt. During the Cold War it had been boasted that the center could survive a direct ICBM hit. As Riggs descended in the elevator through earth and the steel-reinforced concrete that covered the bunker, he knew technology had outstripped the outmoded facility. A modern targeted nuke would bust this bunker wide open.

He didn't plan to allow the Russkies and the Chinese the opportunity to do that.

Riggs giggled at the thought. Those pinched in around him tried not to eye him, staring up at the ceiling or at the walls. The elevator rumbled to a halt and the doors slid open. The duty staff, a half dozen officers, and NCOs who manned the PEOC hopped to attention as Riggs entered.

"At ease, gentlemen, at ease."

Riggs went to the head of the conference table, which took up most of the room. It was where Bush had eventually arrived on 9/11. Of course, Riggs knew the real deal, because he'd met the officer who'd had the duty that day, when America was attacked. Bush had been reading aloud to a group of second graders, continuing even after being told one, then two planes had hit the World Trade Center.

Then they'd finally managed to get to *Air Force One*, took off, and had no clue where to go since there was concern Washington, DC, was under attack. They eventually landed at Barksdale Air Force Base and then flew on to Offutt where the president was secreted in the Strategic Command Underground Command Center. There he communicated back to the VP in this very room until it was deemed safe for the president to return to Washington.

In essence, Riggs's destiny was to make sure scared-shitless politicians didn't screw things up again. Once more the White House was in chaos, but this time Riggs was going to pick up the slack.

He placed the items he'd brought with him on the table. First the copy of the Constitution, which he rolled out flat. Then he weighed the top end down with the Bible. When he drew his pistol and placed it on the closest end, silence descended in the room.

The elevator opened and the rest of his staff entered.

Riggs looked at the twenty-some-odd military men gathered around the conference table in the PEOC. He raised his hands. "Gentlemen. The country is being attacked. We, in this room, are the last line of defense. The president and the White House are under attack by biological agents. The vice president and the chairman are out of the country and we must assume, compromised. I am in charge."

"Technically, sir," one of the officers who'd been on duty and was not part of his staff protested, "the line of succession is—" He paused as Riggs lifted the gun off the bottom of the Constitution and pulled the slide back, chambering a round.

"Sergeant Major," Riggs said, indicating his senior enlisted man who had followed him through all those assignments over the years and owed his career to him. "The next man who speaks out against me is speaking out against the country and committing treason. Feel free to shoot him."

The Sergeant Major drew his own sidearm, locked and loaded.

General Riggs lowered his arms, put the gun back down on the Constitution, and stretched a hand out to the officer on either side of him. "Let us pray, gentlemen, and then let us take action."

Everyone in the PEOC linked hands and Riggs led them in a heartfelt prayer.

And spread Cherry Tree throughout the room.

———

Inside Deep Six, Brennan cowered in the corner of his cell. In the adjacent cell, Wahid was staring at him, arms folded, waiting.

"I'm sorry," Brennan said. "I didn't invent the stuff. Really."

Wahid said nothing, Cherry Tree having finally worn off, while Brennan was still in the throes of it.

"I know it's wrong," Brennan said. "But—" He was cut off as another burst of automatic fire echoed through the cavern. The muzzle flashes were like a strobe light in the dim lighting. They came from the far end of the cavern where the guards were quartered.

Deep Six consisted of the empty, original reservoir for Raven Rock, over three hundred feet long by eighty wide. Cages for prisoners were set in clusters along the floor. The walls and tops of the cages were built from industrial fencing, laid over steel pipes. The floor was the original rock of the reservoir. The only item in each cage, beside the prisoner, was a bucket for sanitation purposes.

The mercenaries who ran the place were quartered in several wooden huts. Lighting came from bulbs spaced far apart on electrical cords stretched along the ceiling. The entire atmosphere was one of gloom, darkness, and the end of life as those here had known it.

The guards were a mixture of former thugs from various security agencies in Eastern Europe and the Middle East. Most were wanted men in their home countries. They were here for the pay and the promise of moving on to a nonextraditable country with enough in a Swiss account so they could live out the rest of their days.

Most of them, anyway.

But a good percentage were here because they liked what they did. Sadists.

A metal chain had been looped around Brennan's neck by the two guards who'd brought him in. Attached to it was a yellow card with nothing on it. He noted that Wahid had a red card.

Seeing the glance, Wahid smiled and finally spoke in surprisingly good English. "Yellow means you are not to be tortured. Not yet. Red means they can do what they want. Torture. Rape. Kill me if they please, now, because I told all I knew during your experiment. Before that, my card was black. Do anything they want, but don't kill. I do not expect to last another day here. I have heard there is a card colored green which means one is to be out-processed and released. I am told no one in here has ever been given this green card."

More firing from the vicinity of the barracks.

"Then again," Wahid said, "I think the guards are more interested in killing each other right now than prisoners. There are ancient ethnic and religious differences among them. Christian. Muslims of various sects. Men from tribes that hate each other. Whoever survives will eventually get to us, I'm sure." Wahid cocked his head, considering the cowering Brennan as he might an object of interest and slight disgust.

"Tell me, since you must tell the truth. Do you really believe what your country is doing here is right?" He waved a hand, taking in the cavern.

"No." Brennan couldn't stop from giving the answer, even though he'd always agreed with Riggs that America's enemies had to be dealt with harshly.

Brennan was on the rock floor, knees drawn up to his chest, as far away from Wahid as he could get. In the cage on the other side, a naked man was strung up from a metal bar holding the mesh that was the roof of their cages. He wasn't moving, his feet dangling limply. Brennan feared the man was dead.

"These monsters here tortured me and tortured me and I never talked," Wahid said. "Until your science. So are you going to use this Cherry Tree for interrogation, as you use drones to attack from above? So clean, so sterile, for those who implement it. Not so much for those on the receiving end. You have this Cherry Tree in you and you ended up here. How does that feel?"

"Terrible," Brennan said. "I didn't do anything wrong."

"I think you've done many things wrong," Wahid said. "Haven't you?"

Brennan sobbed. "Yes. Yes, I have."

"I think this weapon, this Cherry Tree, is much more dangerous than your scientists who invented it realize."

"It is!" Brennan cried out. A single pistol shot echoed and someone screamed in a cluster of cages about thirty feet away. Brennan could see a guard walking along the cages, peering in. The guard stopped, pointed his gun and fired. A scream from inside the cage.

"He is not shooting to kill," Wahid said. "He is taking pleasure in wounding. I have seen such men. It does not matter what side one is on or what the cause is, such men exist everywhere."

"It's out," Brennan couldn't stop himself. "Cherry Tree. I infected the president's daughter, I think. I don't know who else is infected."

Wahid sneered. "Blowback. Your great country is excellent at that. You send death and destruction out into the world and then are amazed when it comes back on you. Now it seems you are sending truth out into the world. It will be most interesting to see what comes back."

"They can't shoot me," Brennan said. "I work for the vice chairman of the Joint Chiefs of Staff. My father commanded NATO!"

"I think the rules," Wahid said, "your status, who your father was, the colors on the cards, aren't going to matter soon. If the truth becomes the rule in here, those who enjoy the kill, the pain, they will take over. Because in crisis, the ruthless almost always prevail over the good." Wahid took a step closer to the grating that separated Brennan from him. "But if I get the chance, I will kill you with my bare hands and my teeth. I will rip your throat out."

Wahid spit through the grating.

Roland fired a long, sustained burst from the M249, chewing up the target silhouette until he separated the top from the bottom. He sighed contentedly as he lowered the smoking barrel. It wasn't the same as his old companion, not having tasted combat yet, but it was an all right first date.

The target had been set up along the edge of Groom Mountain, so the rounds went through and into the side of the rock. Everyone had checked and rechecked their weapons, gear, and ammunition. Eagle had walked around the Snake a half-dozen times. Mac had ordered extra demolitions, assuming that wherever they were going, the nukes were going to be well secured. He wasn't going to be caught in a tunnel waiting on Roland's muscle to open a door this time. He was checking an array of shaped charges, arranging them in order of strength and yield.

And Nada and Kirk were seated in the cargo bay. Kirk was maintaining the secure satcom link to Milstar and had a printout of frequencies, call signs, and code words on his lap, ready to supply as needed to Nada.

Ms. Jones had told them the White House was locked down with Moms inside. And that General Riggs had secured himself in the Presidential Emergency Operations Center.

"*Seven Days in May*," Eagle said, stopping his pacing about for the moment as he heard the last part.

Nada looked up from the radio. "What?"

"A classic," Eagle said. "Published in 1962. About a military coup being planned because the president was signing an arms reduction treaty with the Russians. The author wrote it after meeting General LeMay, who scared the shit out of him."

Nada had radio calls to make, but he respected Eagle's knowledge.

"It was made into a film that premiered in '64. Burt Lancaster and Kirk Douglas. The Pentagon opposed making it. Kennedy gave his approval."

"Kennedy got killed in '63," Kirk said.

"No shit," Eagle said, the profanity unusual for him. "If these Pinnacle people have been stockpiling nukes, what do you think their endgame is?"

"Their endgame comes tonight," Nada said.

Neeley got into Raven Rock via the front door as she had told the Asset. She didn't have to use the clearance she'd displayed at the Pentagon to see Mrs. Sanchez, but one that was a level below that. Even though she was rigged for combat, with body armor, MOLLE vest festooned with the weapons of death, an HK416 in her hands and a new thumper on a lanyard along her side, the guards let her in. After all, she had placed her eye on the retina scanner and the light came back green.

That's the way the government worked. She figured an orang-utan in a clown suit would be allowed in if it passed the retina scan.

She had multiple magazines of 5.56mm ammo for the HK in the first row of pockets on the front of her MOLLE and a dozen 40mm grenades, special rounds she'd handmade, looped along the side of the vest.

"Deep Six?" she asked the two military police armed with just pistols. If the Asset thought this was tight security, he had never experienced tight security.

Before they could answer, an officer wearing silver oak leaves came striding up the tunnel leading into the mountain, a pained look on his face. "Are you here to deal with the incident?"

"What incident?" Neeley asked.

The officer was looking her over, not in a sexual way, but searching for rank, unit identifier, anything he could latch his military mindset on to.

There was none. Except for the weapons and the security clearance she obviously had.

"There's been firing going on in Deep Six. The door is sealed."

"Let's walk and talk," Neeley said, nudging him into the tunnel. One of the MPs followed, hand wavering uncertainly over his holster.

The lieutenant colonel filled her in on what little he knew. "They brought in someone not long ago, shut the door, and since then, we've heard firing echoing out."

They turned a corner and the main cavern that made up the core of Raven Rock came into view. Several three-story office buildings were packed into it. All the windows seemed to be blacked out.

"Anyone get an office with a view?" Neeley asked as they moved along the edge of the cavern.

"The interior of the windows are painted over with landscapes," the officer said. "The shrinks say it helps."

"Does it?"

"No."

At the far end of the cavern another tunnel beckoned. They headed down the path and Neeley heard a distant shot.

"See?" the officer said, as if she had doubted his ability to hear shots. "It's quieted down, but it sounded like a hell of a firefight for a bit."

"Let's hope it was," Neeley said.

They came up to a steel door. A keypad was to the right.

"No one knows the code?" Neeley had to ask, because there were no stupid questions in covert ops. For all she knew the nighttime cleaning crew knew the code.

"Negative." The officer shook his head. "They're not even American in there—the guards. And we hear screams all the time. It's muffled but . . ." He shook his head. "I sent a memo up the chain of command and got a phone call from a general in the Pentagon who reamed my ass and told me to mind my damn business. And—" He paused as something occurred to him. "You're not from that general, are you?"

"No." Neeley was looking at the keypad. One thing Gant had emphasized was that high tech often hid low tech. She slid her knife out of the sheath and jammed it between the back of the keypad and the door frame. She applied leverage and the pad popped off.

"Blue wire, green wire, or red wire?" she said to herself.

Another shot echoed through the door and the lieutenant colonel started nervously. "You don't know?"

"Joking," Neeley said. She slashed through all three wires with her knife, then stripped the ends off the green and red. She sparked them together and there was an audible click as the lock disengaged.

Neeley edged it slightly open, before turning back to the officer. "I assume they rely on Raven Rock for power?"

"Yes."

"Cut it."

The lieutenant colonel pulled out his radio and gave the order.

A drunken guard came staggering down between two clusters of cages, bottle in one hand, pistol in the other. He paused outside Wahid's cage.

"No more black card," he slurred. "Too bad for you." He lifted the pistol.

"No!" Brennan cried out. "I am the assistant to the vice chairman of the Joint Chiefs of Staff. I order you not to execute the prisoner. He has valuable information that is needed."

The guard laughed. "You are in cage. You give no orders. I think I just shoot you first, then him."

The muzzle of the gun turned toward Brennan and he'd never seen anything as large and threatening as the gaping hole at the end of the barrel.

What amazed him, and gave him the smallest moment of pride, was that when faced with death, infected with Cherry Tree, the honest core of himself was able to face it with open eyes. He slowly got to his feet, the gun tracking him. He even took a step toward the guard.

"This place," Brennan began, "is a disgrace to the United States. You, sir, are a disgrace to humanity."

The guard blinked, surprised at the outburst from a prisoner. In the next cell, Wahid was also amazed.

The surprise didn't last long. The guard's finger curled around the trigger. "Fuck you."

And then everything went dark.

"Stay back," Neeley said. "Open it in five minutes with armed guards backing you up. If I'm not standing there, kill them all."

"What—" The colonel didn't get a chance to say anything else as Neeley flipped down her night-vision goggles and slid into Deep Six, the door shutting behind her.

The odor was the first thing she noticed. Dank, dirty air. Unwashed bodies. Through the night-vision goggles, she could see everything in a greenish tint: clusters of cages, shabby barracks at the far end, rock walls curving to a rock ceiling.

Move fast and hit hard. Gant's voice echoed in her brain and she did just that.

A pistol fired to the right, the muzzle flash like a flare in the goggles. Neeley swung the muzzle of the HK416 in that direction and fired twice and the figure crumpled. Voices cried out from the cages as she rushed forward, but she didn't think prisoners were a threat.

She passed two bodies, automatic weapons in hand.

She was reminded of the battle of Cirith Ungol in *The Lord of the Rings*, how Gant had laughed when she read that part to him, the two types of orcs fighting each other and pretty much wiping out the place's defenses.

When one employed scum, one got the results.

Neeley fired at a man running to her right, M4 in his hands. He crumpled to the ground.

The sharp crack of a pair of bullets passing close by caught her attention. She zigged to the right, putting some cages between her and the muzzle flashes. Sorry about that, prisoners, but whoever had fired had been moving also based on the spacing.

She sensed for a split second someone dropping from above—and then impact.

No one ever looks up, she heard Gant's voice in her memory as she was slammed down to the rock floor, dropping her rifle. She rolled with the impact, pulling her knife and slamming it home in the man's chest. He grunted from the force of the blade, foul breath washing over her. She stabbed him again. She grabbed his balaclava-covered chin and sliced the knife deep across his throat, severing both carotid arteries. The last beats of the mercenary's heart sprayed her with blood, but she was off him, searching for her HK.

She abandoned the search as two men came charging forward, shouting something.

Still kneeling, Neeley pulled up the thumper and fired.

The round was one she'd labored over: a mixture of small fléchettes and buckshot, in effect making the result a very large and lethal shotgun shell once fired.

Both men went down.

Neeley slowly got to her feet. She heard panicked voices calling out in a mixture of languages: Arabic, Pashto, and a range of others.

"Brennan!" she called out.

Someone fired from a window in the nearest barracks, the round wild and ricocheting off rocks. Neeley broke open the thumper and loaded a different shell, high explosive. She fired, the round going through the window, and the shooter wasn't a problem anymore.

The resulting explosion blinded out the goggles for a moment.

"Brennan!"

"Here."

Neeley followed the voice.

"Who are you?" Brennan asked. He was standing by the gate for his cage. "Let me out. Please."

"Where is Pinnacle?"

"Oh," Brennan wailed. He beat his fists against the side of his head as if he could smash the truth that was being forced out. "The Dark Side. It's the Dark Side."

"Dark Side of what?"

"Yucca Flats, Nevada. East of it. In the Nevada Test Site. No one can go there." He giggled. "Actually, no one thinks they can go there, but you can."

"What exactly is Pinnacle?"

And when she heard the answer, Neeley knew this was a much bigger problem than they'd thought.

CHAPTER 13

Of course, problems come in threes, or at least twos. Rarely onesies.

Major Truman Preston could hear the First Family screaming at each other and could care less. What worried him was that the White House was in lockdown, the president seemed a bit off his rocker, and he couldn't get an outside line on his Department of Defense–issue cell phone. He needed to check in with his supervisor at the Pentagon, but neither cell nor landlines were working.

So he sat on the second floor of the Residence, tucked away in a corner, a position he was more than used to, and held the football on his lap. Forty-five pounds of deadweight, with the emphasis on the *dead*. The surface of the case was dinged and battered and bruised from years of traveling. The damn case was older than he was. You'd think someone would have made the decision to swap the old thing out for a new case. Although the interior was updated with the latest electronics, never the outside.

Tradition mattered, even in apparently trivial ways.

Despite the turmoil raging and the lack of communication, Preston was his usual calm self because they didn't fob off forty-five pounds of worldwide destruction on people who panicked easily. He'd already had a Top Secret clearance from his work in the army. Then he had to get a Yankee White clearance in order to even be near the president, but that wasn't that hard because it required an SSBI—Single Scope Background Investigation—same as his TS had.

But then had come the psych screenings. Don't want a loon or potential loon carrying the football.

Don't want someone who runs around the aisles of *Air Force One* screaming, *"We're all going to die,"* when they encounter heavy turbulence. Or like that guy in *Aliens* who kept whining. Preston would have put a bullet in that fellow right from the start.

In essence, as the not very good joke went, they were looking for the human equivalent of yellow dog, a Lab that could sleep at the president's feet with its tail in the fire and show no sign of concern.

Nope, nothing much bothered Truman Preston.

But the sight and sound of the First Family raging at each other made him a bit uncomfortable. The First Daughter, Debbie, had just stormed away from her parents, dragging a Secret Service agent by the tie into her bedroom, door slamming shut behind them. If he didn't know better, he'd swear they were having loud, angry sex, with her parents still right next door accusing each other of all sorts of things—the stuff people really only said to each other in that last argument before divorce, when darkest feelings and truths were uttered that one could never come back from.

Except a lot of people in the House were confronting each other, just like the First Couple.

And people were running about. That was the most disturbing thing. No one ran in the White House. Not even children, although he'd heard that Kennedy's kids had, but look how that turned out for all of them. It only took a few weeks here before everyone took on the slow, purposeful stride of power the White House exuded and they became part of the conveyor belt.

Yet he'd just seen a junior press secretary being chased by a pair of Secret Service agents as she tried to wedge open a window and climb out. They'd grabbed her, kicking and screaming, back to the others on the first floor.

So people running in the White House was not something Preston had planned for today and he, more than anyone else in the building, thought of life as a plan. A slow, deliberate relay in which he carried the baton for a while and then passed it off at the end of his shift and then got it back. Routine. Normal.

One thing he was certain of: It wasn't going to hell in a hand-basket on his watch.

He heard the president scream at the First Lady that she was a castrating bitch. A vase came flying out of the open door to their room and Preston ducked as it shattered on the wall near him.

That, too, was not normal. Preston had been around the president and his wife for four years and the harshest thing he'd ever heard the old man say was, "Gosh darn, double toothpicks!" Preston had no clue where it came from, but it meant POTUS was upset. But now they sounded like two sailors on shore leave. And that vase had been around since Dolley Madison (he remembered every detail of his in-briefing to the building, another trait necessary to his job), so there was something up with that. The First Lady had a fit if it was even turned in the wrong direction, and now she had just smashed it.

Reluctantly but realistically, Preston got up and moved farther away, out of the thrown porcelain line of fire. (There was a lot in that room.) He wasn't sure where was safe right now in the White House, but any place was better than where he had been. He felt a physical wrenching in his gut, a loneliness, as he moved away from the man whom he never left while carrying the football.

The football seemed heavier than usual and the room seemed to close in on him, but no one had prepared him for this. He took a seat farther down the hallway and fidgeted.

"Major Preston."

A lesser man might have startled at the quiet voice just behind him, as if she'd snuck up on him. He recognized her and knew she always moved quietly. She had so little presence few ever noticed her, but she carried that big book, and because he carried the big briefcase, he'd felt a kinship from afar.

"Yes, ma'am?" There was also the fact that during that inbrief, he'd been told that she was the only person he was never, ever to interrupt when the president was with her.

"*But what if—*" he'd started to ask, and he'd been cut off at the knees.

"*NEVER!*"

So who the hell was she?

"Sit back down," the Keep said as she settled into the chair next to his, placing the leather-bound book flat on her lap. "But please, make no attempt to touch me. Or anyone else for that matter. You haven't had physical contact since you came into the House for your tour of duty, have you?"

"No, ma'am. The Secret Service already asked." People never got close to him, even in normal times, he suddenly realized. As if he were a leper. "Why?" he added.

"Should you have passed your security check, Major?" the Keep asked.

Preston blinked. "Of course. Well, I mean, I did. So yes."

"And the psych evals?"

"Yes."

"What about ethics?" the Keep asked.

Preston realized he was now holding the football to his chest.

The Keep gave a sad smile. "It gets heavy when you're no longer carrying it for someone else, doesn't it, Major?"

Preston realized his palms were a bit sweaty and he tried to remember the last time they'd been like that outside of the gym. He was one of those who only sweat after extreme exertion. He really didn't understand the intent of her question. What was comforting, though, was that despite the chaos in the White House, she seemed calm enough.

"What's going on?" Preston asked.

"I have a message from Smedley Butler."

"Who is that?"

"And you're a marine." The Keep seemed disappointed. "You've heard of Chesty Puller, right?"

He nodded, a warm feeling washing over him at the name of the famous marine general.

"John Basilone?"

Preston's chest swelled. "Won the Medal of Honor and still went back into combat. KIA at Iwo Jima. A hell of a marine."

The Keep nodded. "But Smedley Butler won *two* Medals of Honor as a marine, yet you've never heard of him. Interesting, don't you think?"

Another piece of something shattered and the First Lady was cussing up a storm. Something about a lack of testicles on the president's part. He supposed it was a follow-up to his comment about castration.

The Keep tapped a finger on her book. "*War Is a Racket.*"

"Excuse me?" Preston said.

"Smedley served in the marine corps for thirty-four years, got out in 1930. Then he wrote a book with that title: *War Is a Racket*. Old Smedley said he could give Al Capone some hints on how to conduct business since the gangster only ran three districts in Chicago and Smedley was part of rackets on three continents in his long and storied career. But you've never read the book, have you?"

"No."

"Never heard of him."

"No."

"If you want to know who someone is," the Keep said, "one of the easiest ways is to study what they read. What they study. What their hobbies are. Background checks are one thing. One can't be absolutely right about everyone, but for your job, we do have to be right. So the best way is to know what people read in their downtime. E-books help a lot with that. No longer have to do those tedious inventories of who checks out *Catcher in the Rye* from the library or what you used your credit card for at Barnes and Noble. What people do when no one is watching is when you get to know who they really are. But someone is always watching, Major. Someone is always watching those people who hold something like that"—she indicated the case once more—"in their hands. And when you least expect it. Makes sense, doesn't it."

The last was not a question.

"Is there a point to this?" Preston asked.

"Just passing time, out of the way, like you," the Keep said. "If we stay still and quiet, maybe everyone will ignore us."

And that's when the case buzzed in his hands.

"And you have the only outside line left here in the White House," the Keep said.

Preston ignored her. He reached inside his shirt, pulled out the key on his ID tags, and inserted it in the lock on the case. One of the locks. The other had a code that changed with every shift. He was the only one who knew the code. He dialed it in.

"Smedley was the *only* marine ever to win two Medals of Honor," the Keep said as Preston worked, "and the Marine Brevet Medal. Of course they don't give that one out anymore. Yet after he retired, he, like Eisenhower a generation later, warned of the military-industrial complex and complained he'd just been a gunman for all the businessmen who got the government to send marines into places like Honduras, the Philippines, China, Mexico . . . a list so long, even he had trouble remembering all the countries he'd had boots on the ground in."

Preston flipped the latch on the briefcase and pulled out the satellite phone, turning away from the woman. He listened to the brief instructions, then turned the phone off, stuck it back in the case, removed the pistol that was always in the case, and latched the case shut.

"You're sweating," the Keep noted.

Preston stood, the briefcase very heavy in his one hand, the pistol in the other. "Why are you giving me this history lesson?"

The Keep stood. "We've found that confronting someone, especially a soldier like you, usually reinforces their initial attack impulse and rarely, if ever, causes them to change their mind. I'm trying to get you to change your mind about what you're about to do by telling you about one of the greatest marines there ever was who changed his mind."

"You've said your piece." He gestured with the pistol. "Now I have to do my duty."

"To who?" the Keep asked, but he was already moving.

And that was how Major Preston abandoned his post at the order of the vice chairman of the Joint Chiefs of Staff.

The vice chairman of the Joint Chiefs, meanwhile, was leaving nothing to chance. While he waited for Preston to heed his call, he was typing on a keyboard hooked in the secure military Internet. The only problem was his fingers were almost too wide to hit only one key at a time. Other than that, he was just rocking along as the letters appeared on the laptop screen.

>>PINNACLE URGENT

There was a pause, a couple of seconds too long in Riggs's judgment, then a reply.

<<PINNACLE HERE

Riggs nodded. Finally, finally, finally, it was time. "Payback is a medevac," he muttered as he began typing.

"Excuse me, sir?" the closest officer asked.

"Shut the fuck up," Riggs muttered as he focused on his typing, never one of his stronger suits, even when his fingers were single-key-sized.

>>PINNACLE INITIATION BY ORDER RIGGS VCJCS

This time he slammed a fist onto the conference tabletop as it took at least five seconds for a response.

<<REQUIRED AUTHORIZATION CODE REQUIRED

"No shit, dumb fuck," Riggs muttered. He reached into his coat pocket where the flask used to reside and pulled out the acetate card that had been passed from general to general, starting with General Curtis LeMay in 1951. How it was passed, and whom it was passed to, was an intricate study of trust, paranoia, and patriotism with a bit of socio-pathology thrown in that could provide enough fodder for hundreds of PhD dissertations.

Except not a single word of any of this was in any report.

The only document regarding Pinnacle that ever existed was this authorization card.

It had never been sent out with the laundry.

Riggs knew he needed to be very careful. He'd only get one shot at this. No second chances allowed. He extended his right pinkie, small enough that it could tap a single key. He held his breath and typed:

>>ELCANNIP

So, okay, they had never been very imaginative from 1951 and forward through Ortsac. But the cursor remained blinking for ten long seconds and the response Riggs yearned for came:

<<PINNACLE INITIATED

———————————————

But Major Preston wasn't the only one who had a means of communication out of the White House.

Moms had to make a decision. This was like Whac-A-Mole with Cherry Tree. No matter how hard they tried to isolate those infected, the efforts to keep runners inside the White House was infecting more. There seemed a tremendous urge among those infected to get out, to tell someone the truth. Whether it was a spouse, a child, a parent, someone they had wronged, someone who had wronged them . . . whatever. That was more dangerous than Cherry Tree.

They had seventy-two people isolated in the White House and at last count, twenty-two were infected. The latest news from

Ms. Jones, via Hannah, via some operative the Cellar had, was that Cherry Tree burned out in four hours.

Moms sat down in the Pantry on the first floor, as isolated as she could get, and reached in her pocket and called Ms. Jones on her satphone.

"Yes?"

"I need to talk to Doc," Moms said without preamble.

"Certainly." There was a series of clicks and then Moms heard Kirk's voice.

"Moms! Are you all right?"

"Get me Doc. Hell, Kirk, put me on the team net so I can get feedback."

"Wait one."

A few seconds later, Doc's calm voice came over the net and Moms realized how much she missed her team, not only for mission support, but just support.

"Everyone else there?" Moms asked.

"Roger," Nada said, followed by Eagle and Mac.

"I need help here." In her usual succinct manner, she laid out the problem in the White House ending with: "I don't think we can keep a lid on this forever. Either someone is going to get out, or the story is going to go on so long that no one will believe it's an exercise. Plus, even though the president and First Family should be through their four hours soon, it will look awkward bringing them out and yet continuing to isolate others.

"On top of that, we've got a bigger problem. There's no way we can keep seventy-two people quiet after they come off of Cherry Tree. The shit is going to hit the fan. Thoughts."

There was just static for a few moments, then Doc spoke. It only took him a minute to outline the solution to the spread of

Cherry Tree, but Moms nodded when he was done. "Excellent idea. And for the second problem?"

And as she had hoped, it was Kirk, who had cheated his way through Ranger School, who had the answer.

"Outstanding," Moms said. "Nada. What's the status of your mission?"

"We're waiting for target location," Nada said. "Then we'll go take care of our little problem."

"Do you have enough support?" Moms asked.

"Definitely," Nada said. "You need to take care of your bigger problem there."

"Roger. Out."

If there was a hell on Earth, the Nevada Test Site was it. It was definitely the deadliest location, with many places so radioactive, a human being wouldn't last ten minutes. Large swathes were splattered with subsidence craters from underground nuclear explosions crowding each other out for space.

Seven hundred and thirty-nine nuclear devices had been exploded in the Nevada Test Site. Lagging way behind were Alaska (three), Colorado (two), and Mississippi and New Mexico duking it out with one each. The rest were places like the Marshall Islands where the US government had paid out $759 million so far to say, oops, sorry we nuked your islands. Even obliterated one.

The Department of Energy, which technically controls the site, likes to say *devices* and not *weapons*, because there were those who had tried really hard to harness nuclear explosions for things other than death and destruction.

Which was why the largest man-made crater was there: Area 10's Sedan Crater, part of the Plowshare Program, was 1,280 feet wide and 320 feet deep. Plowshare's concept was to use nuclear warheads for peaceful purposes, aka Isaiah 2:3–5: *"And he shall judge among the nations, and shall rebuke many people: and they shall beat their swords into plowshares, and their spears into pruning hooks: nation shall not lift up sword against nation, neither shall they learn war anymore."*

They tried. A Pan-Atomic Canal across Nicaragua was one concept. Detonating twenty-two nuclear bombs to clear the way for I-40 in the Bristol Mountains was another.

So they blew a 104-kiloton bomb on Yucca Flats that produced the Sedan Crater and also sent a radioactive dust plume across the country that reached the Mississippi River.

After $770 million spent, it was decided Plowshare sort of, kind of wasn't the smartest idea a bunch of scientists had come up with.

But the weapons testing went on until 1992 when a treaty was signed halting all nuclear testing, the diminutive grandfather of SAD.

Left sitting out in this wasteland were the facilities and devices being prepared for further tests. Orphaned, they were snatched up by Pinnacle, which to that point had been using abandoned missile silos and a scattering of "retired" bombers kept in barely flyable condition at the Tucson "Boneyard."

Pinnacle was consolidated at Icecap, a large tower that housed the drill needed to tear into the desert floor and position another device for testing. Alongside Icecap stood a warehouse with the gear needed to support the project. Three four-mile-long sections of rail track extended out from the tower, going nowhere in particular. Their purpose was to allow the three diesel engines in the tower to pull their flatbed carrying an ICBM missile out to launch. There was also a missile on the top of the drilling platform, just underneath the retractable roof.

That gave Pinnacle the ability to launch four missiles, which was double the number ever used in actual war. Which meant Pinnacle had the ability to start a war.

The entire facility was manned by three men but defended by an array of automated defenses that had been skimmed from developmental programs over the past decades.

The ultimate defense, of course, was the radiation. The three men were ensconced in a shielded bunker fifty feet under the desolate landscape. Housed above them were twelve other nuclear warheads, all primed with self-destruct. The men spent one month on, two months off, rotating with two other crews. They were all paid top dollar and they were all committed to the cause.

The really scary thing that Neeley had learned from Brennan was that this facility, while the heart of the Pinnacle, wasn't all there was to it. There were other nuclear warheads wired into it, the exact number even Brennan or the men manning it didn't know. The years had buried the locations and numbers with the men who'd held the secrets.

The one in Nebraska had been one of those. How many more were out there was anybody's guess.

With General Riggs delivering the correct password, the tall doors on three sides of the drill house slid up. The automated diesel locomotives began powering up. At the top of the drill house, the roof slid aside, revealing an ICBM.

A button was pushed and the preparation for launch sequence began.

"With the White House compromised and the PEOC occupied by General Riggs," Ms. Jones said, "we do not have our usual last-ditch backups."

"She means cruise missiles armed with nukes," Mac said to Roland by way of explanation.

"We should receive word shortly on the location of Pinnacle," Ms. Jones continued, "and the optimal solution would be to wipe it out completely, unless, of course, it's located among civilian targets."

"I doubt that," Eagle said. "They've hidden this stockpile somewhere deep and inaccessible would be my estimation."

"I concur," Ms. Jones said. "But I still believe we are going to have to be surgical with our strike when the time comes. We don't want word of this to get out. It would cause considerable consternation among the populace to learn there's been a rogue nuclear arm to our military."

"It would be a clusterfuck," Mac said to Roland. The big man smacked the smaller man on the back of his head.

"I get it," Roland said.

"Yes, Ms. Jones," Nada said, "but we have to assume they've got a self-destruct. They had one in Nebraska. And I don't think we're going to get lucky again."

"Mister Nada . . ." Ms. Jones began, but hesitated.

Everyone turned to look at the team sergeant. Ms. Jones never hesitated.

"Yes?" Nada prompted.

"I need you to get something from the Vault."

Nada was on his feet. "Yes, ma'am. And that is?"

And when she told him, they all knew why she'd hesitated.

But Nada didn't. He gestured at Eagle. "You drive."

And the two of them headed for the Humvee parked nearby to drive into the bunker built in the side of Groom Mountain where the Vault containing the Nightstalkers' support was located.

The breach team General Riggs sent down the tunnel to the basement of the White House outnumbered the Secret Service guards in hazmat suits three to one. They also had superior firepower. They also wore the uniforms of the US military, which caused the Secret Service agents to hesitate. The soldiers did not.

Within seconds the three agents were flex-cuffed to a pipe that ran along the wall, cursing at their fellow federal employees and warning of infection as they opened up the barricaded door. Standing on the other side was Major Preston, an unconscious Secret Service agent at his feet.

Preston stepped through and the door was shut again. The party made its way back to the Presidential Emergency Operations Center.

"General," Preston said as he put the football on the conference table in front of Riggs.

Everyone in the room fixated on the case.

Riggs smiled and touched a blue button set into the tabletop in front of him. The entire wall along one side of the room split apart, each piece rumbling to the side to reveal a massive screen. It was currently dark.

"Good job," Riggs said as he indicated for Preston to open the case.

Preston unlocked it and flipped the lid up. Riggs grabbed a cable from the interior of the case that came out of the transmitter and plugged it into an outlet on the edge of the conference table. The dark screen flickered and then came alive with an electronic map of the wall. Overlaid in "nonessential areas" such as the South Pacific, Antarctica, most of Africa, Greenland, and other places were boxes filled with data. The data indicated the number of nuclear platforms available at this exact moment: missiles, submarines, aircraft.

At the very top, in the whiteness of the Arctic, was a red digital display. It currently read:

0:00:00

"Seal the room," Riggs ordered.

His sergeant major pulled a red lever just inside the door. Steel plates slid down with solid thuds.

Riggs sat down and pulled items out of the case: the black book, which he placed in front of him; the list of classified sites, which he tossed in the trash bin; and finally the three-by-five card with the authorization codes.

Riggs picked up the black book. Originally, when the first version was prepared, it was the size of a long screenplay, over 150 pages in very small type and so complicated even the team preparing it despaired of completely understanding all the options.

It was President Carter, the only president with a degree in nuclear engineering, who'd actually spent the time to try to read the black book one day. He'd thrown his hands up in disgust and ordered a simplified version, a "Denny's breakfast menu" summary so to speak. In keeping with that theme, the target listing was broken down into three main categories: rare, medium, or well done.

Riggs wanted well done.

He flipped through and it didn't take him long to find the meal he wanted—targeting all known nuclear launch sites in the world in nuclear powers considered "unfriendly" to the United States: Russia, China, and North Korea. Just for shits and grins, he also included Pakistan's and India's arsenals because those two prick countries were going to start World War III any day now and he might as well prevent that while he was at it.

At least that was Riggs's reasoning.

Riggs rattled off the option numbers and the PEOC staffers went to work, fingers clattering on keys. Red triangles began flashing on the world map.

"Oh, yeah," Riggs said, flipping through, searching. "Where the hell is Iran?"

Preston leaned over the general's shoulder, almost apologetically. Like a good waiter, he flipped two pages and lightly rested his finger on the page. "Here, sir."

"Let's take out the ragheads too," Riggs added. "Make a clean sweep of it once and for all."

███████████

A similar red display in the Pinnacle bunker began to flash and then numbers came alive.

0:10:00

The display clicked to 0:09:59 and the countdown had begun.

CHAPTER 14

"Yucca Flats." Neeley's voice was tinny, being relayed from the top of Raven Rock in Pennsylvania through various scramblers and frequency hoppers to the Nightstalkers seated in the rear of the Snake, which was still parked on the ramp at Area 51.

"That's close," Eagle said, without having to check a map. "Inside the same restricted space we're in." He looked to the southwest and pointed in the dark. "That way." There was just darkness hanging over the desert.

"That's the dead zone," Mac said. "The test area."

Nada was peering at the display of his iPad, Googling the location, the team looking over his shoulder.

Neeley continued with what she'd learned from Brennan. "They've got at least forty warheads, ranging from over sixty years old to current technology hidden in what he called Icecap, whatever the hell that is."

"Are they deployable by any means?" Mac asked. "Or just stored there?"

"That's the bad news," Neeley said. "He said there are three rail line spurs running right through this Icecap building. They've got three nuclear-tipped ICBMs loaded on three separate railcars as well as one in the building itself. The plan is if they are needed, they head out along the three spurs and launch at certain intervals. They stripped technology that had been used for Star Wars experiments for this setup."

"Targets?" Nada asked.

"He didn't know," Neeley said. "There's more."

Ms. Jones's voice cut in from the Ranch. "We must assume Area 51 is targeted at the very least since Pinnacle was started as a safeguard against Rifts."

"Not much flight time from there to here," Eagle observed. "Three minutes."

Nada stood. "Then we better get going."

"You just let him go!" It was more exclamation point than question mark as Moms learned about the military attaché breaking out to the PEOC with the nuclear football. And that the Keep had stood aside. They were in the pantry as the chief of staff and the Secret Service gathered everyone in the Entrance Hall at Moms's order.

The Keep sighed. "It wasn't my place to stop him. I thought the Secret Service would be able to, but I was unaware that General Riggs had taken over the PEOC and sent a breach team."

"Frak," Moms said. "He's got the launch codes."

"He won't launch," the Keep said.

Moms closed her eyes, a headache thrumming in her brain. She wondered if she'd missed something, if somehow she'd made contact with an infected person and this was the onset of Cherry Tree.

"What's going on in there?" the Keep asked, nodding toward the noise coming from the Entrance Hall.

"We're going to do a group hug," Moms said, leading the Keep out of the Pantry. "Everyone except you and me and the six agents we're sure aren't infected."

"Intriguing," was the Keep's only comment to that course of action.

They were intercepted by Chief of Staff McBride. A sheen of sweat glistened on his forehead. "I say we invite the president-elect here," he said. "Get her in, have her shake hands with the president, then put both of them in front of the cameras!" It was obvious he thought this was a most brilliant insight. "Then we'll see through all the bullshit she put out in the debates. I'd put my man against her telling the truth any day."

Moms halted a safe distance from him. "An intriguing idea."

One of the uninfected agents hovered behind him. He gave a thumbs-up. Moms and the Keep edged around the crowd. A fight briefly broke out between two staffers, but everyone around them ignored it. Several people were crying. One man was thumping his head, not overly hard, but repeatedly, against the wall.

"I never got that James Bond spy kit I asked for from Santa," a Secret Service agent was telling a secretary tearfully and she was patting him on the back, consoling him.

Several people stood isolated, making sure they weren't in contact with those who were obviously infected. Others seemed uncertain if they were infected or not.

Moms climbed up a few steps on the main staircase, the senior uninfected Secret Service agent next to her.

"Ladies and gentlemen!" She had to call out a couple of times to get everyone's attention. "I have good news!" *And bad*, she thought, but didn't say. That assured her she wasn't infected.

Everyone stared at her expectantly. "What you've been infected with, a truth bug, wears out four hours after contact. It has no bad side effects." A collective sigh of relief rose in the hall. "However," Moms continued, "we have to get this under control. There is no antidote. And we're in a circular pattern here, where even if you make it four hours, you've likely been reinfected. And on and on. So . . ." She paused and took a deep breath. "You're all going to do a group hug at the same time. So everyone's current infection starts at exactly the same time and will wear off at roughly the same time. We're going to burn this infection out in the next four hours. Once the hug is over, everyone infected is getting locked in the East Room."

"Fuck you!" someone in a suit yelled. "Why should—" And an infected Secret Service agent punched the guy in the face with a bit too much satisfaction, spraying blood from a broken nose.

"Anyone who does not participate," Moms said, "will be locked in the freezer."

"That's an order!"

Moms spun about. President Templeton stood at the top of the stairs, his wife on one side, his daughter on the other. "I've had enough of everyone whining and complaining." He looked to the side at his wife, who didn't meet his gaze. "We have a duty to this country and we need to get back on track." He strode down the steps, family behind him, and went by Moms and the Keep without even looking at them. He went to the center of the crowd, stretched his hands out and said: "Let's do this and get it over with."

And thus the entire White House, minus Moms, the Keep, and six Secret Service agents, were infected or reinfected at exactly the same time. The agents then began herding everyone into the East Room, the president leading the way.

Once everyone was in there, the doors were locked.

The Keep tapped Moms on the shoulder and indicated she should follow. They went up and up, to the very roof of the White House. Because of the restricted airspace, no television helicopters were flitting about, but for the first time in several decades, there weren't two Secret Service agents armed with surface-to-air missiles on duty here.

"I'm in contact with Hannah," the Keep said.

"And?" Moms asked.

The Keep pointed to the northwest. "We've got help coming."

A Black Hawk helicopter flared just above the top of the antennas on the roof. A thick Fast Rope tumbled out and a figure slid down, heavy rucksack tilting her almost sideways. The Fast Rope was disconnected, and just as quickly, the Black Hawk raced off into the night.

The Keep stepped between Moms and the newcomer. "Neeley, meet Moms."

They were at eye level to each other and both were a bit startled to be looking at their own doppelgänger.

"Moms," Neeley said, with a nod. "Heard of you."

"I haven't heard of you."

Neeley smiled. "That's good." The smile was gone. "I hear we've got General Riggs in the PEOC with the football. That's not good."

"So far he hasn't—" Moms began, but the Keep held up a hand for silence as she cocked her head to the side. Moms realized she had to have a transmitter/receiver surgically implanted behind her right ear.

The Keep delivered the bad news. "It's not good. He's prepared a target package and is getting ready to initiate a countdown using the authorization codes." She reached into a pocket and pulled out a watch and showed them a display: 05:50. "This is synched to the Department of Defense alert system. Someone is firing up the launch computer."

"Can we get into the PEOC?" Moms asked.

"We can try." The Keep was already moving, heading for the stairs.

In the PEOC, the red digital clock flashed, and then began its own countdown:

0:05:00

0:04:59

One of Riggs's staff, a colonel, jumped up. "Sir! You can't do this."

Riggs regarded him coldly. "I always knew you were chicken shit. You talked a good line, but the truth outs you after all."

And then Riggs shot him right through the heart.

Outside the sealed door to the PEOC, Neeley and Moms considered the steel. Neeley shrugged her backpack off, pulling out a shaped charge.

"That won't work," the Keep said. She glanced at the watch: 04:10.

"We've got to try." Neeley put the charge on the door.

"Do you have a better idea?" Moms asked. "Is there any way to stop the codes from going out?"

The Keep thought for a second, then sighed. "No. The system was built to prevent anyone from stopping it once the president initiated using the codes."

"But the president isn't in there," Moms said. "Can't he do something? Issue a command?"

The Keep shook her head. "No."

"I'm going to blow it," Neeley said. "Let's take cover."

They ran back down the hall and around the corner.

Neeley hit the remote and there was the sharp crack of an explosion.

Inside the PEOC, the detonation sounded distant, an echoing thud.

Riggs laughed. "It'll take them a year to get in here."

Then he shot a second officer who was sneaking toward the red lever. The man tumbled to the floor. "Sergeant Major!"

"Yes, sir."

"Take that lever off and bring it to me."

"Yes, sir."

Inside the Snake's cargo bay, Nada was going through another checklist. One he hadn't used in over twenty years.

Eagle had them flying fast and low, skirting around Groom Mountain, over the dry bed of Papoose Lake, and then banking hard into the Nevada Test Range, also known as Yucca Flats.

The terrain changed from desert to disaster. It looked like the surface of the moon. "Doc," Kirk asked, "how hot is it going to be?"

Doc had a meter out. "We're clean at altitude, but that dirt down there is guaranteed to be hot. I'll keep track."

████████████

A black smudge was the only result of the shaped charge. Neeley cursed and began digging through her pack, searching for more explosives.

The Keep checked her watch: 03:12.

Moms patched through to Ms. Jones. "The Acmes come up with anything? Any way to countermand the authorization?"

"Negative," Ms. Jones said. "They're still working on it."

"They need to work faster."

Neeley slapped another charge on the wall next to the steel door. "Might be weaker there. Maybe we can hit a power line or something."

The three ran back around the corner and Neeley fired once more.

████████████

"It's directly ahead," Eagle said. "A tower, probably one hundred and fifty feet high."

"Open the ramp," Nada ordered. He looped his arms through the straps on the package he'd drawn from the Vault. He tried to get to his feet, but it was too heavy. Mac and Kirk gave him a hand, and he staggered upright, every muscle in his body vibrating to remain that way with one hundred and fifty pounds on his back. The back ramp yawned open, revealing the pitted landscape fifty feet below.

Then Nada was promptly tumbled to the metal grating, hard, as Eagle jerked the Snake to the left.

"SAM!" he called out as a surface-to-air missile raced by the Snake, missing by scant feet. Eagle continued evasive maneuvers as the missile looped around and came back toward them, homing in on the Snake's hot engines.

Eagle hit a button and a spread of flares were fired from the side of Snake.

Now it was a matter of odds. What heat source would the missile take?

There wasn't time for Mac to even propose a wager as the missile took the bait and exploded 350 feet to the right of the Snake.

"Range?" Nada called out, getting to his knees.

"We're a klick out and I'm going in fast," Eagle said. "Who knows what other shit they're going to throw at us."

"Eagle, once you drop me, get the hell out of range with the rest of the team as fast as you can."

A hole in the wall was some progress. Except the hole exposed more steel plating.

"Ms. Jones?" Moms's voice had an edge to it as the Keep held up the watch: 01:15.

"Negative. We've got nothing."

"The team?" Moms asked.

"They're assaulting Pinnacle."

Neeley was rummaging in her pack, at a loss on what else to do. "Not on my watch," she was muttering. "Not on my watch."

"Ladies." The Keep's voice was calm. She showed them the time. 00:59. "We're inside a minute. The way the system works, once it gets inside a minute, there's no turning it off. Even if we were in there."

Inside the PEOC, everyone's eyes were riveted on the digital clock.

Except for General Riggs. He was looking at the blinking red triangles on the map of the world. The nuclear arsenals of all the other powers—soon to be vaporized, leaving the United States the sole world power.

Riggs stood. "Destiny, gentlemen. We are making history."

One of the officers pulled out his pistol and shot himself in the head.

Another opened a drawer and held up a bottle of champagne. "A toast!"

Eagle opened the compartment in the nose of the Snake and the 30mm chain gun extended. As he had feared, there was the muzzle flash of a radar-aimed antiaircraft gun letting loose on top of the tower.

As the first rounds hit the armor plating on the front of the Snake, Eagle let loose with his own gun. The depleted uranium rounds were right at home here in the Nevada Test Site. As his windshield splintered but held, Eagle kept his finger on the trigger and blew the gun off its platform.

"Ten seconds, Nada," Eagle said.

"Wish me luck," Nada told the rest of the team. Mac, Kirk, Roland, and Doc were holding him upright, near the edge of the ramp. Mac and Kirk each had one hand on Nada and the other on the steel static line cable that ran along the top of the cargo bay up into the tail. It was a good thing they did, as Eagle had to flare hard to stop the forward momentum of the Snake.

Roland was an anchor by himself without the benefit of the steel wire. He had both arms wrapped around Nada's waist.

Without their grip, Nada would have fallen out with the package.

As it was, the steel cable tore into skin, and blood flowed freely from both Mac and Kirk, but they held fast.

The Snake came to a shivering halt, wings half vertical, Eagle doing a magical juggling act with the controls to keep the edge of the back ramp less than a foot from the walkway that surrounded the top of the Icecap test tower.

"Got it!" Nada yelled and the other three let go of him.

Nada landed with a solid thud, grunting in pain as ribs cracked when the package slammed him down on the metal walkway. "Go, go, go," he yelled into his mike to Eagle.

Like that was going to work.

Roland was first, because in combat Roland was always first.

Mac and Kirk jumped in unison right behind him, Doc only a brief hesitation behind them. Doc did have four PhDs after all, and that did call for a momentary consideration about doing something stupid.

Still on his belly, ribs broken, the package pressing him down, Nada looked up and saw his four teammates at his side as the engine blast from the Snake washed over them as Eagle took the craft up to a tight hover in overwatch.

"Fuck me to tears," Nada said, and for the first time in his life, he really meant it.

00:10

"We tried," Moms said.

00:09

"We failed," Neeley replied.

00:08

The Keep said nothing, her book held close to her chest.

00:07

00:06

"Trying counts," Moms said.

00:05

Neeley slumped down, back against the wall.

00:04

"I'm tired of this shit," Neeley said.

00:03

"Ain't we all," Moms said, putting a hand on her shoulder.

00:02

00:01

00:00

━━━━━━━━━━━━━━━━━━━

Kirk and Mac helped Nada to his feet as Roland pulled the package off his back. Nada accepted the help, readying his MP5 for action. He went to the edge of the platform and peered down into the tower. An ICBM preparing to launch rested on top.

Looking out, they could see three diesel locomotives moving flatcars with ICBMs on them away, about four hundred yards out and the wheels slowly grinding away.

"Time?" Nada asked over the net.

"Four minutes, forty seconds," Eagle said.

Nada turned to the other three. "Here is as good as anywhere."

They put the package down and Nada ripped aside the protective covering on the control pad. He had the Standing Operating Procedures for the SADM out, even though he still remembered exactly how to arm it two decades after his last practice run with one.

━━━━━━━━━━━━━━━━━━━

Moms slid her back down the wall and sat next to Neeley. "It's easier when you have a team."

Neeley nodded. "Yeah. Hannah is a friend, but she's also my boss. Not that any of it matters now."

"It always matters," the Keep said. She still had the watch out.

"How long until the first nuke hits target?" Neeley asked.

The Keep shrugged. "It depends on what targeting protocol General Riggs used."

Inside the PEOC, everyone was watching the large screen. The tracks of missiles launched, both land-based and from boomer submarines at sea, were marked in red arcs. Clumps of yellow indicated strategic bombers heading toward targets.

It was the world war no one had ever really expected to happen.

That reality, along with the effects of Cherry Tree, had squashed the champagne toast within seconds of it being suggested. The military men stared at the screen as if seeing one of the deepest rings of hell.

Except for Riggs. He was still standing and he reached out and grabbed the unopened bottle. He popped the top and tilted it back, taking a big swig.

Then he slammed it down on the conference table.

"Finally," he muttered as his eyes tracked the weapons on the screen.

Nada had done everything exactly as laid out in the SOP. The W54 nuclear bomb was ready. All he had to do was push the button to arm it. He'd set the timer for the minimum: three minutes. Like that was going to happen.

"Three to one," Mac said, standing behind Nada and putting a hand on his right shoulder.

"Which way?" Kirk asked. He put a hand on Nada's left shoulder.

"Instant detonation," Mac said.

Doc was a spectator, perhaps regretting his decision to leave the Snake.

Perhaps not. "I think I will go with the one."

"Me too," Roland said.

"Kirk?" Mac asked.

"One."

"Well, shoot," Mac said. "You guys are ganging up on me and someone has to cover the bettor. I'll take the three then."

"It's been a pleasure, gentlemen," Nada said, then he pushed the button to arm.

CHAPTER 15

"Two minutes since launch," the Keep said.

Moms looked up. "And?"

"And time for a reckoning," the Keep said. "According to my book, this has the possibility of getting ugly, so I could use some, shall we say, team for backup."

Moms and Neeley looked at each other in confusion, but got to their feet. Neeley readied her HK416 and Moms her MK23 pistol.

The steel doors to the PEOC slid open. As if expecting that, the Keep walked in. Neeley and Moms flanked her, weapons extended.

The occupants of the room broke their mesmerized gaze from the screen tracking the nukes to the intruders.

"General Riggs," the Keep said. She held up the watch. "You've had two minutes to reflect on what you've just done. What if you had a do-over? Would you push the button again?"

Riggs blinked, confused. The rush of champagne on top of the Cherry Tree had muddied his brain. But the Cherry Tree prevailed.

"I damn well would."

"Kill him," the Keep said.

Neeley and Moms fired, both hitting him right between the eyes with a double-tap times two, which effectively blew his head off.

While General Riggs's body was still crumpling to the floor, the Keep walked over to the table. She stepped over his body and reached into the briefcase. She pulled the cord out and the screen flickered, then snapped into darkness.

"What the fuck?" someone muttered.

"There have been no launches," the Keep said. "The system is set up so that the person who has the code can enter it. They can think they launched. Then they get two minutes to reflect on what they've done. It's happened before. Kennedy during the Cuban Missile Crisis. Nixon while drunk one night. Reagan over a *Fail-Safe*–type scenario. And George Bush, the younger. They all launched. And two minutes later, when they got their chance to do over, they all thanked God on their knees they had that chance. And they never entered this room again."

The Keep held up the Book of Truths. "So it is written. So it is."

████████████████████████

"Only time I've ever been happy to lose a bet," Mac said.

"Bring it in!" Nada yelled into his transmitter.

"You owe," Roland said to Mac as the five members of the Nightstalkers gathered near the edge of the steel walkway. The W54 was armed and counting down next to them.

"Two minutes, thirty seconds," Doc said, staring at the old-fashioned analog clock on the instrument panel.

Eagle brought the Snake in fast, flaring to a hover.

"Hey," Roland said, looking down into the mine tower. "There's some guys down there. Running."

"Can't run fast enough," Nada said.

Eagle turned the Snake and the back ramp beckoned. They all jumped and even Doc made it without help.

"Go! Go! Go!" Nada yelled.

Eagle slammed the throttle and the Snake roared up and away from the tower.

Inside the abandoned Pinnacle bunker, the old system slowly counted down to launch.

It never made it as the W54 SADM went off, obliterating the tower and the four missiles as well as the stockpile of weapons.

What was more radiation on top of a landscape scarred with it?

CHAPTER 16

The 740th nuclear explosion in the Nevada Test Site lit up the sky behind the Snake. It was the first one that had not been a test.

"What about the outliers, wherever they are?" Doc asked. "Won't they go automatically to self-destruct?"

"We assume they will," Ms. Jones said over the net.

"I've been thinking about that," Kirk said.

"And?" Ms. Jones prompted.

"We got the alert for Nebraska from the old SAC headquarters, right?"

"Correct," Ms. Jones said.

"Well?" Kirk said.

"Very good," Ms. Jones replied.

"Kiss me. Kiss me as if it were the last time!"

Colonel Horace Egan, USAF Retired, was rounding third and ready to cross the plate with Mrs. Floyd as she cried out a line from *Casablanca*.

She was leaning against a console in the underground bunker, Egan pressed up against her. Her dress was in disarray and Egan planned on fixing that by taking it off her. She'd come back twice more since their first encounter, both times without her husband, and he'd advanced a base each time. Tonight he planned to bring it home.

She'd put up a good display, but Egan had always known that when he focused on an objective, he could achieve it. He leaned into her, kissing her once more, glad he still had all his teeth even if he were a bit short on the Samson hair.

"We'll always have—" he began as he parted lips with her, but his line was cut short as a board on the right side of the room lit up like a Christmas tree. Fourteen flashing orange lights.

"Oh crap," Egan said.

And then a red phone gave a shrill ring. Reluctantly, Egan separated his body from Mrs. Floyd, who pouted and pondered, not for the first time and not for the last time, why she was drawn back to this dark place and this randy old goat.

Men and their missiles.

"Yes?" Egan snapped as he picked up the phone.

"Colonel Egan, my name is Ms. Jones. We have a problem we were hoping you could help us with."

"All the self-destructs?" Egan asked, glancing up at the board.

"Yes. Is there a way to shut them down? They're all predigital."

"Need the arming code to disarm them," Egan said.

"We're trying to get it—" Ms. Jones began, but Egan suddenly laughed. His memory wasn't so bad after all.

"Lady, the last time this joint was active, everyone knew the code. Hold on." Egan walked over to the one working console in the control room. Eight circular pins were set in it, like a large bike lock. The numbers were set randomly.

Egan quickly dialed each one to zero.

He hit the red button above them and all the orange lights blinked out.

Peace once more reigned in the SAC control room.

Egan walked over to the phone. "Taken care of. Now, if you don't mind," he glanced over at Mrs. Floyd, "I've got an important matter to attend to."

CHAPTER 17

"Mister Nada."

Nada and the rest of the team paused in unloading the Snake at the Barn once they heard the omnipotent voice coming out of the cargo bay speaker. "Yes, Ms. Jones?"

"During the 'Clusterfuck in Nebraska,' you mentioned being on a SADM team. You were quite cynical about it all."

Mac couldn't help himself, bursting out laughing.

"Mister Eagle mentioned being expendable," Ms. Jones continued. "I want to assure you that you and your teammates are not considered expendable. I have done some research on the matter. The time delay you didn't think was built into the weapon? Do you still believe that?"

"Of course not," Nada said. "We got away."

"How do you know I didn't have the weapon modified with a delay?" Ms. Jones asked.

That stumped Nada for the moment.

"Aaaahh." Ms. Jones drew the sigh out so long, that once more, they thought she might just have given her last breath. "Cynicism has its place, Mister Nada. I am reminded constantly of my own."

Nada wondered who the hell told Ms. Jones she was cynical?

"We enmeshed ourselves deeply into a dark history on this operation. But we prevailed. In your previous time in the army, Mister Nada, you wore the Green Beret, did you not?"

"I did."

"And you know the history of it, correct?" She did not wait for an answer. "President Kennedy, in October 1961, instructed the Special Forces commander to have his men wear the then out-lawed headgear. He later called it a 'symbol of excellence, a badge of courage, a mark of distinction in the fight for freedom.' Do you think he meant those words?"

Nada shifted uneasily. "I imagine he meant them."

"In the summer of 1963, President Kennedy signed a presidential order that SADMs must be built with that time delay designed in the W54 system at the munitions plant. He was looking after those men who wore the Green Beret. He was looking after you."

"And then they killed him," Mac said bitterly.

"Ah," Ms. Jones said. "Let us not get into *that*."

Two weeks after the world had been saved from nuclear war, Neeley had been hanging in the climbing harness all night. One of the first things Gant had told her when they began training together was that patience was one of the most difficult traits for a covert operative to master, but one of the most essential. Neeley had honed that trait over the years. Twenty-four hours of surveillance on a target was considered an absolute minimum, yet most people couldn't sit still for five minutes.

Neeley had been in Peru for four days, crossing the border illegally from Brazil after a two-week journey west across the Amazon. The long journey, to keep anyone from backtracking her, was another form of patience.

After crossing the border, she'd spent one day making it to this remote part of the Andes. One day observing the climbers' base camp, which they broadcast on Facebook, which she found quite odd but very useful. And then one day climbing to get ahead of the team trying to ascend to the summit of Palcaraju Oeste, a peak northeast of Lima. At just under twenty thousand feet, it wasn't a world-record altitude, but it was a technically difficult climb. Not something for the faint and almost unheard of for someone to try solo.

Neeley didn't plan to go all the way to the top.

And she wasn't doing it solo.

It was a beautiful morning, the sun sending bright streaks of daylight over the peaks to the east.

"You know that saying?" Roland asked.

He was dangling four feet to the right, his bulk encased in Gore-Tex, his position triple anchored because he put a bit of strain on the rope.

Neeley waited for him to complete the question, having gotten used to his habit of thinking his way into the completion during their journey from the States, across Brazil, into Peru, and up the mountain. She'd insisted she could do the job alone.

Roland had insisted on coming along.

Hannah and Ms. Jones had conferred and thought this would be a good "cross-training" opportunity for the Cellar and the Nightstalkers.

As if what they'd just done wasn't enough.

"I think it was the Indians," Roland continued. "You know, Native Americans. They say, 'It's a good day to die'?"

"I've heard of it," Neeley said as she began the delicate operation of getting out of the sleeping bag without completely unhooking from the mountain.

It was a lot harder than it sounded.

"It's bullshit," Roland said. He hadn't used a sleeping bag. He'd claimed his Gore-Tex pants and jacket would be enough and he appeared to be correct, seeming none the worse for the night at altitude. "I prefer my own saying: It's a good day to help someone else die."

With one arm, he pulled himself up, unclipped from all three of his anchors, unsafe at any altitude, then put in a new piece of protection that would allow them to go up the fifteen feet they needed for the perch they had decided upon. Then he began to lift Neeley, hand over hand.

"Hey!" she protested. "I can climb."

"I know," Roland said, "but I need the workout."

Neeley settled in, shoulder to shoulder with Roland on a two-foot-wide ledge right next to a cornice of rock. One of the more difficult aspects of the route the two climbers below them would be taking this morning.

"Do you know why I told you about what happened in Pakistan?" Neeley asked Roland as she watched the two climbers struggling on their next pitch.

"You were bored?" Roland said.

Neeley smiled. "I usually operate alone. I don't get bored."

"To explain why we're here," Roland said.

"Yes." And Neeley waited. "And we're here."

Roland's forehead furrowed. If Mac had been there, he'd have told Roland not to hurt his brain by straining it too much. But by saying that, Mac would have stopped Roland from straining it and going to new heights, literally and figuratively.

"We're here," Roland finally said, "because you were on that Sanction."

"And?" Neeley prompted.

"The entire purpose of the Sanction in Pakistan was to find these two guys."

"Exactly," Neeley said. "You think anyone really gives a damn about some garbageman and his wife? Even if he gave up bin Laden? In fact, no one, not even the Cellar, wants those people around. In my job, I have to always suspect the reverse. Think strategically. You're great with tactics, Rollie."

Roland flushed red, impossible to see under the balaclava that protected him from the harsh wind and cold. The only other woman who had ever made him blush like that was Moms, but she was his team leader.

Neeley was different. He just hadn't figured out how yet.

Neeley continued. "But this is strategy. It's like . . ." Neeley searched for the right words. "It's like the difference between Patton and MacArthur. Patton was great in combat. Battle of the Bulge he turned Third Army on a dime and slashed apart the Panzers. But that was a reaction. MacArthur, in the entire Pacific Campaign with his island hopping, lost fewer troops than were lost in the single Battle of the Bulge. MacArthur thought ahead of his enemy."

"Why are you telling me this?" Roland asked.

And for once he had her stumped for a moment, and then she flushed. "Because I've only helped one other person and it's been a long time. I helped Hannah when she needed me. Because Gant helped me. And helping others, it's . . ." She fell silent.

"It's a good thing," Roland said. He nodded toward the two climbers. "Let's take care of business."

They fell silent as the two men continued up the mountain, reaching this difficult stretch. One took lead, putting in protection. He made half a pitch then halted. The other climbed up to him as he took belay. As expected, on their next pitch, they hit a protection point just eight feet underneath and on the other side of the rock wall from where Neeley and Roland waited. As soon as both were in place, protection put in and one beginning to climb, Roland swung wide on his rope around the shoulder of the mountain into the man on belay.

His move was so startling, the man in the lead teetered. Neeley swung around and gave him a gentle shove and he fell to the end of his rope.

Roland held on to his belay man, keeping both on the mountain. Roland looped their rope through a figure eight on the front of his harness, then cut their attachment to their own anchor point, in effect making himself their anchor.

As one man dangled over the abyss, the other stared wide-eyed at Roland. "Who the hell are you! What are you doing?"

Neeley climbed down and locked in on the mountain on the other side of him. "Hey!"

He turned his head toward her and she slapped his face with her gloved hand, drawing blood from the small needle in her hand.

The man blinked. "What did you do?"

"Cherry Tree, Mr. Nesbitt. You are Nesbitt, right?" She didn't expect an answer yet as she knew it would take a minute or so for the serum to work. "And our friend on the end of the rope is your partner, Mr. Porter."

"What the fuck?" Nesbitt sputtered. "Who the fuck are you?"

"I'm from the Cellar," Neeley said. "And you're going to tell me the truth."

At the word *Cellar*, what little blood was left in Nesbitt's face drained out. At the end of the rope, twenty feet below them, Porter was yelling something, twisting and turning in the wind, which blew his words away into the empty sky.

Neeley was watching his eyes. She saw his pupils dilate slightly and knew Cherry Tree had taken root.

"Did you compromise the mission?"

He blinked, shaking his head. "Mission?"

"The garbageman."

"Oh. Fuck." The next word was ripped from him. "Yes."

"Why?"

"We claimed the interrogation. My group. We had to maintain integrity on our story. Get the credit."

"Why?" Neeley asked in such a tone that Roland looked at her.

"Promotion."

"Did your supervisor know?" Neeley asked.

"No."

"Did he know?" Neeley pointed down.

Nesbitt followed her finger. "Yes."

"Anyone else?"

"No."

"Bye," Roland said as Neeley was getting ready to ask her next question. He cut the rope and the two men dropped out of sight into the abyss.

"I wasn't done!" Neeley yelled at him.

"Yes," Roland said, as he took her in his arms. "You are."

"Last day," the Keep said. "What have you learned?"

President Templeton glumly nodded. "I don't know if I'm relieved or just exhausted."

"Both," the Keep said.

They were seated, for the last time, in the same room on the top floor of the White House. Tomorrow there would be a new president. A new occupant of the position. A new person for the Keep to in-brief.

"Pretty amazing," Templeton said.

"What is, sir?" The Keep had her book open, quill poised, but so far, she'd written nothing, which didn't cheer the soon-to-be-ex-president very much.

"No one talked about it. What happened. Cherry Tree."

The Keep lifted the quill and tapped it against her cheek. "Yes. I have to admit I was surprised and so was Hannah. But the Nightstalkers called that right by having everyone get infected. Not only were they able to burn it out at the same time, the psychological dynamics were most intriguing. So many people baring their souls to each other. So many secrets exposed. No one wants that. No one wants to talk about that. Everyone is pretending it never happened."

The president laughed. "Nobody has looked anyone in the eye since then. I think everyone wants to get the hell out of here."

The Keep said nothing and the president sighed.

"Tell me something," he finally said. "The PEOC. Riggs had the code from the football. He had the targeting matrix. He launched. But he didn't launch. You haven't told me what happened. Why it didn't go off like he wanted?"

"Ah . . ." The Keep shook her head. "Surely you don't think it could be that simple. That a single man—or woman starting tomorrow—could simply open up a briefcase and begin Armageddon?"

She tapped the book. "It's in here, but so few see it. Kennedy ran on the missile gap, then suddenly shifted gears. Reagan called the Soviets the evil empire, but then came within a single treaty of getting rid of nuclear weapons entirely. Nixon was crumbling, under impeachment, but he walked out of here without destroying anything when he so desperately wanted to. Do you know what changed them? That room."

"It's fake!" Templeton sat bolt upright. "The whole war room thing is a fake. Like a movie set."

"No." The Keep shook her head. "It's real. The world could indeed be destroyed from that room. The Cellar or the Nightstalkers or any of us were never powerful enough to prevent that room being built for that possibility. What we could do was put in checks and balances. That's something the Founding Fathers were all for. We just moved it into the nuclear age.

"Everyone adapts. As General LeMay and the others started Pinnacle to keep civilians like you from reducing the power they felt they needed, others worked to make sure that ultimate power, the power to destroy the world several times over, was not so negligently placed in one person's hands."

The Keep put down the quill. "Really. Think about it. How amazing is it that since Hiroshima and Nagasaki we haven't used these weapons again? There have been studies on it, many studies, trust me, and the odds that we have never once used a nuclear weapon again are pretty astronomical. We've been in how many wars since the end of World War Two? The Berlin crisis, which we solved not with weapons but with food and coal. MacArthur wanted to use nukes when the Chinese crossed the Yalu. Nixon in Cambodia. Kennedy in Cuba. So many times we came so close, but it never happened.

"That was not chance, Mister President. Let me ask you something. May I, sir?"

Templeton seemed a bit surprised she was asking his permission. He nodded.

"What if you can only change when you truly, absolutely believe you have done the unthinkable? That you entered that code and pushed that button?" She tapped the book. "That's the biggest secret in the Book of Truths. That's the part you didn't get to read when you came into office. That she won't get to read when I brief her tomorrow night while she's still heady from the inauguration, when I will, as you say, destroy her dreams and promises."

"Who controls the nukes then? Or are they all a fake?"

"Oh, you know they're real. You received the After Action Report on Pinnacle and the Nevada Test Site."

Templeton snorted. "Hell yeah. Spent hours on the phone with the Russians and then the Chinese telling them we had an accident when they picked up the blast. But who controls them?"

The Keep tapped the book. "The Cellar, of course. The real launch codes are in here. And the only one who can authorize the release of that code is Hannah. Because this country needs people who don't push buttons.

"The PEOC is why some presidents have changed so dramatically while in office. Because they *did* push it. Then they sat there for those two minutes, watching that screen, realizing what they had unleashed, the true impact of what had happened hitting them so hard that when that door opened and the Keep walked in, they fell to their knees in relief. They'd truly realized that nuclear warfare is lose-lose. A zero-sum game. They changed.

"Truman started the Cellar because he actually did have the bomb dropped. Twice. It all comes down to a simple truth that dates back to this quill." She waved it. "Jefferson realized, after he had completed the Louisiana Purchase, that he had exceeded his constitutional powers. And he finally understood that one man can't have ultimate power because eventually he will use it."

The president got out of his chair and went over to a counter. He poured himself a stiff drink. He'd had the bottle and glass put there the previous day. He'd learned from his last meeting with the Keep to be prepared. He downed the glass, then poured another.

"I'm not buying it." He downed the second glass and poured a third. "We're not the only ones with nukes now. Truman had the power exclusive. But that changed."

"Oh," the Keep said. "There is a Russian version of Hannah. Sitting near the Kremlin."

"And a Keep there too?"

"I hope, but that's not within my need to know, sir. However, if you study history, you will see that many brave Russians have died keeping the world from destroying itself. One spy kept the Cold War balanced by keeping both sides up to date on the true balance of power. He was killed by the KGB as a traitor when they inserted him, still alive, into a crematorium inch by inch and filmed it to show to others as an object lesson. That man deserves a star on the wall at Langley. More so than the last two stars that went up on that wall."

The president walked to the window and gazed out at a wintry Washington, DC. He took a sip from his glass. "You should have told me."

"Then it wouldn't have mattered, sir," the Keep said. "You're a politician. That personality type is the complete opposite of the person we need to have their finger over that button. Reagan could have signed that treaty in Iceland and rid the world of nuclear weapons, but he put politics first. They all do. Then some go in that room and push the button and they learn. Why do you think their hair goes white?"

The president ran a hand through his hair without even realizing it. "I didn't go into that room. I never pushed that button."

The Keep stood. She shut the Book of Truths with a solid thud. "I know, sir."

He looked at her. "Is that why I wasn't reelected? Why you shut the book and don't want my last lessons learned?"

The Keep smiled sadly. She picked up the book and tucked it tight to her chest. "It's not a bad thing to be a good man, Mister President. It's just not enough."

"Like I said before, they shouldn't call that the Book of Truths," Templeton called to her as she headed for the door. "They should call it the Book of Secrets. And maybe, just maybe, all of this has taught us we shouldn't have secrets anymore."

The Keep paused at the door and looked over her shoulder. "That would be a very fine world indeed, Mister President."

For more on the Nightstalkers, read the first book, *Area 51: Nightstalkers*.

For more on how Hannah and Neeley, the housewife and the assassin, were recruited by Nero for the Cellar, read *Bodyguard of Lies*. And for how the Cellar operates, read *Lost Girls*.

AUTHOR'S NOTE

I write factual fiction. I gather real events and add in a fictional premise and characters.

Yes: There was a marine named Smedley Butler and he was awarded two Medals of Honor.

Yes: Churchill did say that truth must be attended by a bodyguard of lies.

Yes: The officially acknowledged first nuclear weapon ever "lost" by the US was in 1950 over Canada. Sorry, Canadians. Our bad.

Yes: When Secretary of Defense Robert McNamara instituted technical launch codes on nuclear weapons to prevent unauthorized deployment, the Strategic Air Command, on its own, decided to override that by setting all the codes to 00000000 and they stayed that way for a while before anyone caught on.

Yes: The Pentagon did secretly remove President Nixon's ability to launch nuclear weapons in his erratic, waning days before he resigned.

Yes: President Jimmy Carter did send the nuclear launch authorization codes out with his laundry.

Yes: President Ronald Reagan had the codes in his pocket when he was shot and they ended up on the emergency room floor, forgotten about.

Yes: General Curtis LeMay strongly believed in a preemptive first strike against the Soviet Union.

Yes: The Russians did open their nuclear "football" in reaction to a satellite launch by the Norwegians.

Yes: The scientists who worked on the Manhattan Project did have a betting pool as to the yield of the Trinity Test, with the low end being a dud and the high end igniting the sky on fire and incinerating Earth.

Which leads us to today where . . .

ABOUT THE AUTHOR

New York Times best-selling author, West Point graduate, and former Green Beret Bob Mayer weaves military, historical, and scientific fact through his gripping works of fiction. His books span numerous genres—suspense, science fiction, military, historical, and more—and Mayer holds the distinction of being the only male author listed on the Romance Writers of America Honor Roll. As one of today's top-performing independent authors, Mayer has drawn on his digital publishing expertise and military exploits to craft more than fifty novels that have sold more than 4 million copies worldwide. These include his best-selling Atlantis, Area 51, and Green Beret series. Alongside his writing, Mayer is an international keynote speaker, teacher, and CEO. He lives in Knoxville, Tennessee.

By Bob Mayer

Nightstalkers Series
Nightstalkers
Nightstalkers: The Book of Truths

The Area 51 series
Area 51
Area 51: The Reply
Area 51: The Mission
Area 51: The Sphinx
Area 51: The Grail
Area 51: Excalibur
Area 51: The Truth
Area 51: Nosferatu
Area 51: Legend

The Green Beret Series
Eyes of the Hammer
Dragon Sim-13
Cut Out
Synbat
Eternity Base
Z
Chasing the Ghost
Chasing the Lost

Books on Writing/Publishing
The Novel Writers Toolkit
Write It Forward: From Writer To Successful Author
How We Made Our First Million On Kindle: The Shelfless Book
The Guide to Writers Conferences
102 Solutions To Common Writing Mistakes